"A cantankerous parrot [...]
mined ghost vanquish a [...]
ing debut mystery."

—Carolyn Hart, national bestselling author of
Death Comes Silently

"A businesswoman, a parrot, and a ghost inhabit a souvenir store. That's not the set up for a joke, but for Christy Fifield's debut, *Murder Buys a T-shirt*, which packs a paranormal punch. Fifield expertly shifts the focus among the possible culprits and establishes Glory as a charming protagonist, sometimes impulsive, sometimes wary. And she invests the small-town setting with Southern spirit (and at least one spirit), as well as numerous recipes for traditional Southern food. A traditional mystery with an offbeat angle, *Murder Buys a T-shirt* will have readers, like Bluebeard, greedy for more."
—*Richmond Times-Dispatch*

"An entertaining and clever Florida whodunit."
—*Midwest Book Review*

"Fifield offers a nice blend of the cozy and contemporary with a hint of the paranormal. I look forward to getting to know Glory and her friends better. Good writing, an appealing ensemble cast, and a tightly woven mystery; definitely a series that's a promising addition to the 'cozy' genre."
—*Once Upon a Romance*

"A fun book that will make the dreariest of days a little brighter! Socrates' Great Book Alert."
—*Socrates' Cozy Café*

"Very enjoyable . . . [A] delightful cozy mystery, and I will definitely be reading more of the series. Yummy recipes of traditional Southern dishes are also included."
—*Novel Reflections*

Berkley Prime Crime titles by Christy Fifield

Murder Hooks a Mermaid

Christy Fifield

BERKLEY PRIME CRIME, NEW YORK

THE BERKLEY PUBLISHING GROUP
Published by the Penguin Group
Penguin Group (USA) Inc.
375 Hudson Street, New York, New York 10014, USA

Penguin Group (Canada), 90 Eglinton Avenue East, Suite 700, Toronto, Ontario M4P 2Y3, Canada
(a division of Pearson Penguin Canada Inc.) • Penguin Books Ltd., 80 Strand, London WC2R 0RL,
England • Penguin Ireland, 25 St. Stephen's Green, Dublin 2, Ireland (a division of Penguin
Books Ltd.) • Penguin Group (Australia), 707 Collins Street, Melbourne, Victoria 3008, Australia
(a division of Pearson Australia Group Pty. Ltd.) • Penguin Books India Pvt. Ltd., 11 Community
Centre, Panchsheel Park, New Delhi—110 017, India • Penguin Group (NZ), 67 Apollo Drive,
Rosedale, Auckland 0632, New Zealand (a division of Pearson New Zealand Ltd.) • Penguin Books
(South Africa), Rosebank Office Park, 181 Jan Smuts Avenue, Parktown North 2193, South Africa •
Penguin China, B7 Jiaming Center, 27 East Third Ring Road North, Chaoyang District, Beijing
100020, China

Penguin Books Ltd., Registered Offices: 80 Strand, London WC2R 0RL, England

This is a work of fiction. Names, characters, places, and incidents either are the product of the author's
imagination or are used fictitiously, and any resemblance to actual persons, living or dead, business
establishments, events, or locales is entirely coincidental. The publisher does not have any control
over and does not assume any responsibility for author or third-party websites or their content.

PUBLISHER'S NOTE: The recipes contained in this book are to be followed exactly as written.
The publisher is not responsible for your specific health or allergy needs that may require
medical supervision. The publisher is not responsible for any adverse reactions to the
recipes contained in this book.

MURDER HOOKS A MERMAID

A Berkley Prime Crime Book / published by arrangement with the author

PUBLISHING HISTORY
Berkley Prime Crime mass-market edition / January 2013

ISBN: 978-0-425-25184-3

BERKLEY® PRIME CRIME
Berkley Prime Crime Books are published by The Berkley Publishing Group,
a division of Penguin Group (USA) Inc.,
375 Hudson Street, New York, New York 10014.
BERKLEY® PRIME CRIME and the PRIME CRIME logo
are trademarks of Penguin Group (USA) Inc.

PRINTED IN THE UNITED STATES OF AMERICA

10   9   8   7   6   5   4   3   2   1

ALWAYS LEARNING   PEARSON

*With sincere appreciation to two marvelous
Southern women:*

*The "real" Linda Miller,
who willingly became a part of Glory's world, and*

*Martha York,
my incredible mother-in-law, for everything—
including her wonderful help with researching
authentic Southern recipes.*

Acknowledgments

A book starts with one person sitting alone in a room, making things up. However, if you're sitting there writing and life throws you a curveball—heck, life throws you a *beanball*—you appreciate the people around you that help you keep going.

I've had more than a few beanballs lately, and I want to thank the friends and family who stood beside me and behind me, and occasionally pushed.

My special thanks to:

Michelle Vega, editor, for your patience;

Susannah Taylor, agent, for your support and advice;

Colleen, first reader, and gym buddy, for the motivation;

Kris and Dean, for shoulders and a swift kick, and knowing which one was needed;

Jeanne, Jan, Jeri, Louis, Shane, and Lynette, for being a family not only of blood, but of the heart;

And most of all to Steve, who makes it all worthwhile.

Chapter 1

"COFFEE?"

The question greeted me when I came downstairs from my apartment over Southern Treasures, the eclectic gift shop I own in Keyhole Bay, Florida.

Maybe *own* is a slight exaggeration. I own 55 percent and my cousin Peter Beaumont owns 45 percent, but I was determined to change that in the near future.

The one thing I didn't share ownership of was Bluebeard, the foulmouthed parrot I had inherited with my share of the shop. Bluebeard begged for coffee every day, and every day I had to tell him no. Parrots can't have coffee.

Maybe saying Bluebeard begged wasn't quite truthful, either. He was just the spokesman—spokesbird?—for my great-uncle, Louis Georges, who had left me the shop and the parrot. Or at least for Uncle Louis's ghost.

Lately I had been forced to admit that Uncle Louis had

never completely left the shop. He was still hanging around, disrupting my life and talking to me through Bluebeard.

But since he was the closest thing I had to blood relations—if you didn't count the annoyance of Peter and his parents—I was growing rather fond of having him with me.

Except when he begged for coffee.

"No coffee, Bluebeard. I know you want it, but it's really bad for you."

I unlocked the front door and turned over the sign from "Closed" to "Open."

Across the street I spotted Jake Robinson doing the same at Beach Books. A newcomer to Keyhole Bay, he'd moved to town from the West Coast and bought the bookstore less than a year ago. In that time he'd turned the store into one of the best in the Panhandle, a spot that attracted tourists and locals alike.

Jake was a bit of an attraction himself—tall, with dark hair and gorgeous blue eyes—though I tried not to notice. He was helping me with my struggle to set up a website for Southern Treasures, and I was trading home-cooked meals for advice.

I stepped outside, waved to Jake, and called "Good morning" across the Monday-morning emptiness of the main drag.

"Coffee later?" he asked, waving back.

I nodded. Lately we had fallen into the habit of a mid-morning coffee break on slow days, though that would soon be a thing of the past. Spring break would start in a couple weeks, and we hoped not to see a slow day again until fall.

I went back inside, where Bluebeard greeted me with a

wolf whistle. "Pretty boy," he said. I was reasonably sure he wasn't referring to himself.

"I didn't ask your opinion," I answered as I got the shop, and Bluebeard, ready for the day. I changed the papers in the large cage where he slept and gave him fresh water and a shredded-wheat biscuit. It wasn't coffee, but it was one of his favorite treats.

With the radio tuned to WBBY, the local station, I settled down behind the counter to review my inventory. Southern Treasures' usual mix of vintage housewares, magazines and newspapers from the middle of the last century, and hand-made quilts didn't attract the spring break crowd much.

I worked through orders for garish T-shirts, postcards, seashell jewelry, and inexpensive snow globes. The snow globes still amazed me. I didn't understand the appeal, when Keyhole Bay only had snow a few times a decade, but they were popular with tourists of all kinds, so I kept them on the shelves.

With my notes ready, I pulled the computer keyboard toward me. I might not be able to program a web page yet, but online ordering had made my life much easier.

The bell over the front door jingled, and I looked up just as Bluebeard wolf-whistled.

"Bluebeard!" I admonished. He loved pretty girls—a trait from Uncle Louis, perhaps?—but not everyone considered his behavior a compliment.

Fortunately, it was Julie Nelson, my part-time clerk, and not a potentially offended customer.

Julie laughed at Bluebeard's whistle. It was good to hear her laugh, something she hadn't done much over the past few months. Not since her young husband had been arrested for murder, leaving her pregnant and alone.

Tougher than the pretty, blue-eyed, blonde cheerleader she had been only a couple years ago, Julie filed for divorce and took back her maiden name. Jimmy Parmenter would likely spend the rest of his life in a Florida penitentiary, but Julie wasn't going to wait for him.

"Bluebeard likes you, you know," I said as Julie walked across the store. Her eight-months-pregnant belly forced her into an ungainly waddle, and she slid cautiously into the narrow space behind the counter.

"I like him, too," Julie answered.

I wondered if she would like him quite as much if she knew about Uncle Louis. I had only shared *that* news with a few people, and Julie wasn't one of them. Not yet.

She settled into a tall director's chair with a sigh. It allowed her to watch the shop without having to stand all day, an advantage over her regular job as a checker at Frank's Foods.

"Man, I'll be glad to see my feet again," she said.

"How much longer?"

"Three weeks, give or take. I'll know more when I see the doctor on Wednesday."

I instinctively glanced at the calendar, checking her schedule. Off Tuesday and Wednesday, working Thursday and Saturday.

I was getting spoiled having Julie around three days a week, even if only for a few hours, and I hated to think I would lose her when her baby arrived. We had talked about her coming back in a general way, although I knew how completely things could change.

I went back to my ordering and was just finishing when the bell rang again, and Bluebeard whistled again.

"Bluebeard!"

In answer, Bluebeard chattered angrily, with an occasional clear profanity.

"Language," I cautioned, and his chatter quieted to a soft mutter. I could still catch an occasional curse, but his voice was so low I was the only one familiar enough with his antics to discern what he said.

"He'll never change." The new arrival, my best friend, Karen Freed, sounded upset. The "Voice of the Shores" for local radio station WBBY, Karen was usually calm and collected, but not this morning.

"He's just a parrot, and a spoiled one, but he isn't that bad, is he?" I asked, truly puzzled. Her anger seemed out of proportion, especially since she usually laughed at Bluebeard's flirting.

"Oh no!" Karen said, crossing to Bluebeard's perch and petting him on the head. "Not you, Bluebeard," she cooed. "Although you are pretty incorrigible."

"Pretty girl," he answered, rubbing against her hand.

Forgiven, Karen came back toward the counter. "Not Bluebeard," she repeated. "Riley." Annoyance made her ex-husband's name sound like one of Bluebeard's curses.

"Riley? Are you kidding me?" I struggled not to laugh. Karen and her ex were good friends, in spite of their brief, disastrous attempt at marriage. "There must be a statute of limitations on being mad at your ex, Freed."

Realizing what I'd just said, I stole a furtive glance at Julie, afraid I might offend her with my flippancy. Fortunately, she didn't seem to have related my comments to her own situation.

"It has nothing to do with being my ex," she said, a faint whine of defensiveness creeping into her tone. "It has to do with not living up to his commitments."

"And what would those be?" I asked.

"Fish! He promised me fish for Thursday."

Now it made sense. Housecleaning-induced stress, not anger.

And maybe a touch of panic. This week was Karen's turn to host our weekly dinner with Felipe and Ernie. Karen claimed her only domestic quality was that she lived in a house, and only by hosting dinner every four weeks could she make herself cook or clean. It was an exaggeration. I think.

"Did they open the fishing season early? I thought the commercial boats weren't going out until next week?" I asked. Riley made his living as a commercial fisherman, and owned his own boat, *Ocean Breeze*.

"No, they aren't. But he and Bobby planned to do a little sport fishing, and he promised he'd bring me something. Now he calls and says he's lending the boat to Bobby and he can't get me anything for dinner on Thursday. He always bails his little brother out, no matter what he promised anybody else."

Bobby, the little brother in question, worked for Riley as a deckhand. He attracted trouble like black trousers attract lint. Bobby always had some big deal that would make him rich and famous, if he could just borrow some money, drive your car, crash on your couch, or use your boat. And Riley helped him out every time.

I groaned. "I get it. No fish. But if I remember right, you always thought Riley looking out for his little brother was sweet."

Karen shook her head. "Sure, when he was sixteen and Bobby was twelve. But not when Bobby's thirty-three. He's old enough to take care of himself. Or at least he should be."

"Whatever. But the real problem is you need a main dish for Thursday." I held up one finger, signaling her to give me a moment. I quickly finalized my order and logged off the computer.

Pushing the keyboard away, I stood up and came around the counter. "I have an idea," I said.

I led the grumbling Karen to a shelf of old cookbooks against the back wall and pulled down several yellowing, spiral-bound volumes.

"Extension groups, women's clubs, lodge auxiliaries, they all made these cookbooks as fund-raisers," I explained. "I know we can find something in one of them. But I want the rest of the story about Bobby while we look."

We carried the books back, spread them across the counter, and started leafing through the pages. Julie slid her chair closer and took one of the books.

"The story?" I nudged Karen. "I deserve that much."

Karen shook her head. "The usual. Bobby's mouth wrote a check his body couldn't cash, and his brother came to the rescue. He met some guys in the Mermaid's Grotto." She named a tourist-trap restaurant and bar on the water-front. "They wanted to go diving, said they had gear and wanted to charter a boat, but nobody was available. You know Bobby. He can't resist a quick buck, or acting like a big shot. Told them he could get them a boat, for the right price."

"Eeeewww!" Julie's exclamation made us both turn and look. She pointed at a page of the book open in front of her. "There are a bunch of recipes for minced meat, and this one starts with 'meat of two hogs' heads.' Yuck!"

Karen laughed. "Okay, I can pass on that one."

"So, Bobby said he could get a boat," I prompted.

"Yeah. Of course, the boat in question belongs to his brother, not him, but that never stops him." She shook her head. "Why should it, when he knows Riley will bail him out?"

"They're taking *Ocean Breeze* on a dive trip? Have they looked at that boat? No way they're going to be happy with her."

Karen shrugged. "According to Riley, Bobby said they didn't care. Or course, that's Bobby's story. Who knows what the truth is."

I had to agree. Most sport divers didn't want the cluttered deck of a commercial fishing boat for their excursions into the Gulf.

"Here." I handed Karen a cookbook from 1950. "Chicken and dumplings."

She glanced at the recipe. "Cut up a chicken as for frying," she read. "Cut up a chicken?" She glared at me. "What do I know about cutting up a chicken?"

"Easy, Freed. Buy the chicken cut up. That's hardly a violation of the rules." Like we had any rules for our dinners. Sure, we were trying to experiment with traditional southern dishes, but nothing was set in stone. "It's not like the dinner police are going to come and get you."

She rolled her eyes. "Fine."

She took the book and headed to the corner of the warehouse I grandly called my office. A minute later I heard the whirring of my printer/copier/fax machine, and soon Karen returned with a thin stack of copies. She wordlessly handed back the cookbook, unwilling to give up her pout quite yet.

"I have to get back to the station," she announced, stuffing the copies into her oversize shoulder bag.

"Later," I called over my shoulder as I placed the cookbooks back on the shelf, but I didn't think she heard me. She was already on the sidewalk, hurrying to her SUV.

I looked at the vintage black-and-white cartoon-cat clock above the quilt display. Karen's next newscast was in ten minutes, and the station was a three-minute drive. She was cutting it close.

"He's waving," Julie said.

I didn't need to ask who. Julie had noticed my budding friendship with Jake, and had actively encouraged it, from her first week in the store.

"We said we'd have coffee if there was time," I said dismissively. "I suppose I could go, since you're here and my ordering's done."

A snort of decidedly unladylike laughter greeted my offhand manner. Julie still looked like a delicate southern belle, but she was more a steel magnolia with a bawdy sense of humor. "Yeah, you could probably tear yourself away for a few minutes. After all, he's only gorgeous and single. Why would you want to spend any time with him?"

Although she intended it as a joke, the question loomed a lot larger than she could know. My romantic history was beyond anemic: a boyfriend or two in high school and an occasional date during my short time in community college several years ago.

Orphaned before I finished high school, I had been too busy supporting myself and making Southern Treasures successful. It didn't leave a lot of time for a personal life.

Besides, dating in a small town was a dicey prospect. There were fewer eligible men each year, and I knew far too much about who cheated on his wife, who didn't pay his bills, or who gambled too much at the casinos over in Biloxi.

Or who, like Bobby, decided to "go with the flow" and let somebody else take care of him. No thank you. I was already taking care of myself—and Bluebeard.

Jake Robinson was smart, well educated, read a lot—he owned a bookstore, didn't he?—and he was definitely easy to look at. He defied the odds, though I had the nagging suspicion that one day I would find something that destroyed my fantasy of the perfect man.

In the meantime, though, a cup of coffee wouldn't hurt anything. At least that was my excuse, and I was going to hang on to it as long as I could.

It was safer that way.

Chapter 2

JAKE ALREADY HAD TWO LATTES ON THE TABLE BY the time I walked into The Lighthouse, on the west side of Southern Treasures.

"Thanks," I said, pulling out a chair at our regular table by the window. We always sat in the same place, where we could watch both our stores while we talked. "My treat next time."

Jake nodded, but I knew he'd manage to pick up the check the next time, too. He always did.

We talked for a few minutes about our plans for the coming spring break invasion. Jake bought Beach Books just before the summer season last year, and hadn't yet been through a spring break on the Redneck Riviera.

Keyhole Bay is on the edge of the madness. North of the intense crowds that clogged I-10, we fill with the overflow from the beachfront hotels and condos and the refugees from the inflated holiday prices.

The younger visitors flood out of town in the morning, heading for the white sands of the Gulf, straggling back when the sun goes down. Or when the bars close.

In between, families wander the streets and shops, visit the waterfront and local parks, and turn pink in the springtime sun.

"Sounds like the summer," Jake said, sipping his coffee. "And I survived that okay."

I shook my head. "I don't quite know how to describe it. There's a different energy. Sure, everyone is in a hurry to see the sun because they've been buried in snow for months, but they're almost *desperate* to have fun, no matter what. Whatever they want, they want it right now, not in five minutes or an hour."

Which might have explained Bobby's pals from Mermaid's Grotto.

"I'll keep that in mind."

I fiddled for a moment with my drink, stirring it with the straw, trying to get the nerve to ask for more of Jake's help.

"Uh, Jake, about the website? I was looking at what I've done so far, and it just seems really *plain*. It needs something."

He looked thoughtful for a moment, then pulled a smartphone from his pocket and tapped at it. After a few seconds, he laid it on the table where I could see the front page of my site.

We both stared at the tiny display for several minutes. Each time the screen dimmed, Jake reached out and tapped on the display. Although it was a far cry from the simple address and phone number listing I'd started with, something was still missing.

Jake reached out and touched one of the links from the front page. Photos of one-of-a-kind quilts filled the screen, and I knew detailed information about each of them was loaded onto the site, even if it couldn't be read on the tiny screen.

He tapped the back button and tried several of the other links. "I'm impressed," he said, sincerity clear in his voice. "You've done a lot with the site since you started."

"Thanks." I appreciated the compliment. "But what am I missing?"

Flipping back to the front page, Jake studied it again. "Where's your logo?" he asked. "Didn't we talk about having an image that was on every page?"

I slapped my forehead, and said, "Duh!" before I could stop myself. "Yes, we did. But I wasn't sure what to use, and then I got so caught up in doing the quilts, I completely forgot."

Jake looked puzzled, and I rushed ahead, trying to explain. "You have a bookstore, that's easy. One main product line. But I have this huge mix of things, and none of them really go together. Vintage cookbooks," I said, thinking of my morning recipe hunt with Julie and Karen, "don't have much in common with T-shirts and snow globes. And collectible magazines don't go with shot glasses and seashell jewelry."

Jake nodded while I babbled, then held up a hand to stop me. "You have the perfect logo," he said. "Bluebeard. He's the thread that ties everything together. And he attracts customers—I've seen it from across the street. They'll stroll along the sidewalk, catch sight of him, and turn around and go in your store."

He frowned. Something about the idea bothered him, and I waited patiently while he worked it out in his head. In the few months I'd known him, I'd learned that Jake's thoughts were worth waiting for.

"Just don't do the obvious pirate thing," he said at last. "Everybody and their dog does the pirate thing down here."

I knew exactly what he meant. Half the tacky souvenir shops on the Gulf Coast had *pirate-something* in their names. I was grateful Uncle Louis had avoided that trap when he named Southern Treasures.

"It gets worse with every movie," Jake continued. "Those guys out in Oregon even started Talk Like a Pirate Day."

"Aye," I said, unable to resist.

Jake groaned. "Not you, too!"

I shook my head. I wasn't going to join in the pirate parade. Still, I had an idea for spring break.

"You aren't going to like this," I teased Jake, "but you just gave me an idea." I laughed and continued. "Just for the next few weeks, I promise."

Jake groaned again and rolled his eyes. "You're going to rename the place Pirate's Treasure?"

I shook my head. "But what about a treasure chest display in the front window?" I spread my hands as though holding up a sign. "'Find the Treasure at Southern Treasures.' Think it'll work on the tourists?"

"Unfortunately, yes," he answered. He tried to look annoyed, but it didn't last long. "I have to admit, it does fit your shop." He paused. "But only for a few weeks, right?"

"Deal," I said, sticking out my hand. "And I'll throw in a home-cooked meal as compensation."

"With banana pudding?" he asked hopefully. Jake had become a big fan of my banana pudding.

"I'll even make the good stuff," I promised as we shook hands.

"I have one suggestion," he said.

"Yeah?"

"How about 'find *your* treasure' instead of 'find *the* treasure?' '*The* treasure' sounds like there's only one, but '*your* treasure' sounds more like there's a treasure for every customer."

I nodded. He had a point. "Good idea. Thanks."

Jake glanced across the street to the front of his shop. A middle-aged couple, sporting the standard tourist garb of straw hats and shorts in defiance of the temperature, had paused in front of his window.

"Gotta run," he said, stuffing his phone back in his pocket.

"Go." I waved him away as he started to pick up the debris from our table. "I'll take care of this."

"Thanks," he said with a quick grin.

I watched him dash across the highway that formed the main drag of Keyhole Bay and greet the couple. By the time I had gathered up our cups and napkins, he was ushering them into the store as though they were old friends.

Which, I supposed, they could have been. Jake's life before Keyhole Bay was still mostly a mystery; one I would like to solve.

Chapter 3

"BLUEBEARD, SIT STILL!"

With a baleful look, Bluebeard ruffled his feathers and posed on his perch *almost* long enough for me to take his picture. But when I looked at my camera image, all I could see was a vaguely bird-shaped blur of bright colors.

My patience with my avian companion had reached a critical level. I wanted a picture to use on my website, but in spite of two days of too many treats and massive amounts of coaxing, Bluebeard refused to cooperate.

His antics reminded me how few pictures I'd been able to find of my great-uncle Louis. A few grainy black-and-white shots in the local paper, all of them taken from a distance, and one battered photo-booth shot of a young man in an Army uniform, a cigar clenched defiantly in his teeth.

Was it Uncle Louis who didn't like the camera?

Frustrated, I left Bluebeard to his own devices and went back to assembling the merchandise for the window display.

I had a large collection of costume jewelry that wasn't acceptable for the sales case: single earrings, brooches with broken clasps, necklaces with missing strands, and decorative watches that didn't keep time. Spilling out of a worn travel trunk with a smattering of brass coins, they made the centerpiece of the display. I planned to put an ornate silver candelabra filled with dripping candles on one side, and a pair of silver-plated goblets on the other.

It would be enough to fill the larger of the two front windows. I went through the door to the back of the shop, hunting through the jumble of merchandise in my storage room for something for the other window.

The phone rang, and I hurried back into the shop and grabbed it, eager for a distraction.

"Glory?"

At the nasal sound of my cousin Peter's voice, I took a deep breath and started counting. Ten wasn't nearly enough.

"Hello, Peter." I didn't ask what he wanted; he always wanted me to do something, usually something utterly nonsensical, with Southern Treasures.

Peter owned 45 percent of Southern Treasures, though I had a secret plan to buy him out, just as soon as I figured out how. It really wasn't much of a plan, I guess, but I had to start somewhere.

Peter also had an engineering degree from the University of Alabama, and he thought his education made him an expert on everything. Including how to run Southern Treasures.

"Hi, Glory. How are you? Okay, I hope. Mother is

worried about you, you know. You missed your visit last month, and you know how she is."

I knew all too well. I visited my Uncle Andrew and Aunt Missy—it rhymes with *prissy* for a very good reason—a couple times a year. Andrew and Missy, and Peter and his family, were the only blood relatives I had in the world. Missing a visit was a direct violation of family responsibilities.

"I know," I answered. "But you know how it is when you own a business. You're working all the time."

Of course, Peter *didn't* know how it was. Uncle Andrew put him through college and grad school, and then Peter landed a good job. He couldn't imagine a career without paid vacations and sick days. But it did no good to tell him that. He thought he understood.

"I know, Glory," he said, as though he actually did. "But Mom and Dad are getting up there. Your visits mean a lot to them."

I counted to ten. Again. Uncle Andrew had retired a few years back, just before he'd turned sixty. They traveled several weeks a year and played golf every other day at their country club when they were home. Hardly the frail senior citizens Peter implied.

"They mean a lot to me too, Peter." They meant closing the store for several days, begging Karen to look in on Blue-beard, and driving a couple hours each way in my aging and not very reliable Civic.

In spite of it all, I still felt the tug of family. "Maybe after spring break," I told Peter. "There's usually a little lull before the summer crowds start."

"Good. Good. Mom and Dad would like that." Placated,

he moved on to the real purpose of his call. "I was thinking about the shop, Glory."

A bad sign. *One, two, three . . .*

"Have you considered putting up a website?"

Four, five, six, seven . . .

"You said most of your business is from out-of-state tourists."

Eight, nine . . .

"Why not give them a way to buy from you after they go home?"

Ten.

"I have a web page. It's not perfect yet, but I have one, and I've put a lot of work into it. Did you even *look* before you called me?"

"Of course I did. I found something about metal detectors." His whine intensified. "Why are you yelling at me? It's not my fault I couldn't find the page."

I bit my lip and took a deep breath. "That's because I couldn't get the exact name, so I used Southern Treasures Shop."

"I suppose that's okay then," he said, though he clearly didn't mean it. "I guess I'll have to go look it up and see what you have there."

"What I have," I said through clenched teeth, "is what I've learned to do so far. I'm still working on it, as time allows."

There was silence from the other end of the line. I could picture Peter pursing his lips in the way that said he was sure I had more time than I let on, and I was probably wasting it on things I shouldn't be.

I forced my jaws to unclench. "Thanks for thinking of

me, Peter. Please give my love to your folks, and tell them I'll be up to see them just as soon as I can. I have to go now. Give my love to Peggy and the kids. Bye-bye."

I hung up before he could say another word—and before I had to start counting again.

I *really* needed a plan to buy him out.

I also needed a break. It had been a quiet Wednesday, and the sun was sending long shadows across the street. Between Bluebeard and Peter, I'd been frustrated enough for one day.

I locked the door, flipped over the "Closed" sign, and turned out the lights. Bluebeard realized I was closing and let out a squawk of protest.

"Enough out of you," I answered. "You have been a huge pain all day."

With the shop—and Bluebeard—settled for the night, I debated what to do with my evening. For about thirty seconds. Then I picked up the phone and called Karen.

"I'll bring the pizza," I offered when she answered. "And I'll bet you still need help getting ready for tomorrow's dinner."

Her answering chuckle told me I was right.

"Meet you at your place in half an hour?" I asked.

"Sure," she said. "Extra onion and pepper?"

"You got it."

IT WAS CLOSER TO FORTY MINUTES BY THE TIME I pulled the Civic into Karen's driveway. Red-brick siding contrasted with bright white trim across the front of her small rambler. Karen and Riley bought the house when they got married, determined to be the perfect young newlyweds. When they divorced, Riley kept the boat and Karen kept the house. The style didn't fit with the driven newscaster Karen became, but in spite of the incongruity and the history, Karen loved her place.

I opened the front door, tapping on it as I walked in. "Pizza delivery," I called out. I carried the box into the kitchen, put it down, and started getting plates out of the cupboard.

Karen came down the hall from the bathroom, wrapped in a fluffy robe with a towel turbaned around her wet hair. She sniffed the air and nodded her approval.

"Pepperoni, onion, peppers, and tomatoes, right?"

Like she even needed to ask. Pepperoni had been our favorite since junior high, and we'd added the vegetables in an attempt to assuage our guilt as we got older.

Karen took a couple wineglasses from the shelf and poured us each a glass of our favorite cheap red. I know there are people that say life is too short for cheap wine, but we were eating pizza. Besides, it was pretty good cheap wine.

Not that we got to drink any of it.

We had barely settled into our chairs when someone knocked insistently on the front door.

Karen looked at me, puzzled. "I'm not expecting anyone . . ." Her voice trailed off as she rose from her seat and headed for the door.

My manners kicked in and I couldn't start eating without her, so I trailed along to see who was interrupting our dinner.

By the time I reached the door, Riley was already through it, standing in the living room and cursing like, well, like Bluebeard.

And like Bluebeard, I could only make out every second or third word, many of them profanities. Among the other words were *police*, *Bobby*, and *Coast Guard*.

It didn't sound good.

Karen had Riley by the shoulders, gently propelling him toward the kitchen. He walked without protest, too caught up in whatever was going on to notice her guiding him to the chair she had just vacated and pushing him down into it.

He was seated at the table before he even realized he had an escort. He blinked at me a couple times, muttered "Hi, Glory," and went back to his rant.

Karen clamped a hand over his mouth, interrupting the flow of words. "Slow down!" she commanded. "I can't understand a thing you're saying."

A slight exaggeration, I suspected, but it worked.

Riley drew a long, shuddering breath, then another. It took him a full minute of deep breathing, while Karen and I stared impatiently, before he could talk again.

My mind raced with imagined disasters as I willed Riley to regain the ability for coherent speech.

In all the time I had known him, I had never seen him this rattled. Riley Freed was the calm one in any group, the guy who knew how to take care of things. It served him well as the captain of his own fishing boat, dealing with one of the most dangerous jobs on a daily basis. Nothing got to Riley.

Until now. Now his face was pasty beneath his tan and was covered with a sheen of sweat. His hands shook and a vein at his temple throbbed with his racing heartbeat.

"Bobby," he said at last. "They took Bobby, and the boat. *My* boat. They took it."

"They? Who, Riley? Who took Bobby?"

"Chief Hardy," Riley answered. His voice came out in a strangled whisper. He swallowed hard and tried again. "Chief Hardy took Bobby, and the Coast Guard impounded *Ocean Breeze*."

Karen rolled her eyes. "What the hell has he got himself into this time?" She glared at Riley. "And you let him take your boat to do it!"

Riley hung his head, unwilling to meet Karen's eyes. "He's my brother," he said quietly. "He's family."

And there was the core of the argument. Every time, in every way, the commitment to family trumped all other considerations. Bobby was family, and Riley was there for him.

Karen sighed and unwound the towel from her hair. She ran her hands through her hair, finger-combing the damp chestnut strands into a messy ponytail.

She looked longingly toward the rapidly cooling pizza on the table, and the untouched wine, before trudging down the hall toward her bedroom.

Taking my cue from her look, I closed up the pizza box and stuck it in the refrigerator. We could heat it up later. I set the wineglasses on the back of the counter and covered each one with a piece of plastic wrap, although I wasn't optimistic about our chances of getting back in time to drink them.

Riley hadn't moved. It was scary, seeing the vulnerability in someone who never let anything rattle him.

Riley looked up at me, doubt clouding his weathered face. "What if I can't get *Ocean Breeze* back in time?" he asked. "The season opens in a few days. Without a boat . . ." He left the rest of the thought unspoken, as though he couldn't bear to say it out loud.

I knew the rest of it anyway. Without a boat, there was no season for Riley and his hands. He'd lose his crew as they scrambled to find berths on other boats, berths he'd have to compete with them for if he wanted to pay his own rent.

"We'll get her back," I said with more conviction than I felt. "You've got Karen on your side. When has she ever let you down?"

"She divorced me," he replied with a shrug.

I shook my head. "Don't go there. From where I sit, there was enough blame to go around. And maybe you couldn't live together, but she's been on your side as long as I've known her." I paused, trying to lighten the mood. "And that's a lot longer than I care to admit."

Riley's mouth twitched in the imitation of a grin, but the expression didn't reach his eyes.

"Ready?" Karen called as she came back down the hall. Wearing worn jeans, an oatmeal-colored waffle-weave pullover, and sneakers, she stuffed her wallet into her back pocket and dangled her keys from her finger.

"You riding with me?" she asked Riley, "or taking your own truck?"

"I can drive."

Karen nodded and turned to me. "Coming?"

Like she even had to ask. We'd all been best friends since junior high. I was as much a part of this rescue mission as she was.

Karen locked the door behind us, and Riley headed across the scrubby lawn toward his pickup.

"Meet you at the police station," he called over his shoulder as he heaved himself up into the cab.

Chapter 4

KAREN DROVE SILENTLY, HER LIPS DRAWN INTO A tight line. On the console between us, the police scanner crackled with static, but no radio conversation broke the silence.

A strong sense of déjà vu filled me. How many nights when she was with Riley had I ridden with her on rescue missions? Back then most of them had involved fender benders, unpaid parking tickets, or a conveniently forgotten wallet, not handcuffs and impounded boats.

But the feeling was the same.

By the time Karen slipped her SUV into a parking space at the police station, I could see Riley running through the front door. Considering Karen's driving, he must have broken several speed limits to beat us there.

Inside, we located Riley by following the sound of raised voices down the corridor. He stood at a low counter, leaning over and talking loudly to the duty officer.

"I told you," he said, "you have my brother back there, and I want to know what's going on!"

"Have a seat, Mr. Freed," the officer said, forced patience clear in his tone. "Chief Hardy will speak to you as soon as he has time. But for now you will just have to take a seat and relax."

His voice hardened with authority on the last sentence. Clearly, Riley would be wise to follow his instructions.

Wisdom wasn't part of Riley's plan. He opened his mouth to protest, but Karen beat him to it. "Thank you, officer," she said, grabbing Riley's elbow and dragging him away from the counter before he could react.

Taking advantage of Riley's surprise, Karen pulled him to one side and pushed him down into one of the colorless molded plastic chairs against the wall. "Sit down," she hissed.

"And shut up!" she added when he opened his mouth.

Riley stared at her, his mouth hanging open with no sound coming out. It was the second time tonight I'd seen Karen take charge of Riley. Riley was usually the take-charge guy—a trait he and Karen had in common, and one I suspected was at the heart of many of their troubles. Letting Karen push him around was a measure of just how distressed he felt.

Karen dropped into the chair on his right and signaled me into the chair on the left. She took Riley's chin in her hand, pushing his mouth shut and turning his face to hers.

"Whatever Bobby did this time is serious, Riley. Do you know anything about what happened?"

Riley shook his head. He'd bounded from manic to silent and back several times already, and he was dropping into silence again.

Karen shook his shoulders. "Tell me what you know. I need to know everything if I'm going to help you. And Bobby."

Riley winced at the mention of his brother's name. Apparently he knew something, something he didn't want to know.

"Bobby needed the boat for a dive charter. I told you that, right?"

Karen nodded, tight-lipped. I remembered her angry response when Riley told her he couldn't get her any fish. Oh yeah, he'd told her.

"Well, he called me and said the guys wanted to go out into the Gulf, and they were leaving before dawn today." He shrugged. "It was supposed to be a half-day trip, so I figured I might be able to do some fishing this afternoon after they got back."

A wry smile twisted his lips for a split second. "Figured if I could get you some fish, you might get over being pissed at me a little quicker."

That surprised Karen, and she had the good grace to look sheepish. "Sorry," she muttered.

"No," Riley said. "You were right. I put Bobby's problem ahead of a promise I made. You had a right to be mad."

The conversation felt a little too personal for an audience, and I started to stand up. One glare from Karen changed my mind.

I sat back down.

"Anyway," Riley went on, "I went down to the dock about one, thinking Bobby should be back pretty quick, and he was already there. He had *Ocean Breeze* tied up to the dock, and he was helping carry the divers' gear back to the rental car."

Karen nodded impatiently.

"I waited until they had everything stowed, and the divers were ready to leave." He looked away, as though ashamed of what he were saying. "I didn't want Bobby's guys to know he didn't own the boat."

I saw Karen literally bite her lip to keep from pointing out the absurdity of letting Bobby masquerade as the owner of *Ocean Breeze*. Bobby couldn't be responsible for a used bicycle, much less a boat, but Karen kept her comments to herself.

"Next thing I know, there are uniforms all over the place. Boomer Hardy grabs Bobby and stuffs him in a squad car, Coasties are all over the boat, and there's a bunch of guys with crew cuts putting cuffs on the divers."

"Who were they?"

"The divers?" Riley shook his head. "I have no idea."

"No, not the divers." There was an edge in Karen's voice. "The crew cuts. Any idea who they were?"

"State bulls, or Feds of some sort, would be my guess," Riley said. "But I didn't exactly go over and introduce myself. Didn't seem like a bright idea."

"But if they took the other guys, why didn't they take Bobby?" I asked. It seemed like the logical next question.

Riley turned and looked at me, as though he'd forgotten I were there, which he probably had. "I don't know, truth be told. Seemed like maybe they wanted to, but Boomer sent the car back here right off. It wasn't till later that the crew cuts started asking about Bobby."

"And by then he was already in Boomer's jail," Karen said slowly. It was no secret that the local police, and especially Chief Barclay "Boomer" Hardy, had a bad attitude toward outside authorities.

The way I heard it, several years back the Feds ran a drug sting operation without bringing in the local authorities. Later they would claim they didn't know who they could trust, but relations had been real chilly since. Boomer was just as likely to keep Bobby in his jurisdiction as long as he could.

"Yep," Riley answered. "Boomer told them real nice-like that they could come down and get Bobby when they had an arrest warrant, and Boomer would hold him for them in the meantime."

"So it's only a matter of time before they show up," Karen said.

Riley nodded.

It was actually a matter of several hours, hours that we spent sitting in the uncomfortable, cold plastic chairs, drinking vending-machine coffee and trying unsuccessfully to carry on a conversation.

We also tried to talk to Boomer. The duty officer reminded us, forcefully, that he was too busy.

But it never occurred to any of us to leave. Bobby was family.

It was nearly midnight when a couple of guys in crew cuts paraded three stone-faced men in cuffs through the front door.

The crew cuts paused at the counter, and I strained to hear the conversation. After they were waved through, I turned to Riley.

"Are those the guys?"

He nodded. "Did you hear what they said?" he asked.

"Sounded to me like they're going to keep the divers here," I said. "That what you heard?"

"It is," Karen said. She smiled one of those cat-with-acanary smiles, and I realized her digital recorder was in her hand. She never went anywhere without it. She glanced at the recorder, then back at me, and stuck it back in her shoulder bag. "I'll check it later, but I think the officer said something about their accommodations being ready." She tilted her head to one side, as though listening to the conversation replay in her head. "He didn't sound too happy about it, either."

Riley stood up and took a step toward the counter. "Maybe now they'll tell me something about Bobby," he said.

"Damn you!"

Bobby's shout carried to the front of the station, stopping Riley in his tracks. His hands curled into fists, and his broad shoulders knotted with anger at the sound of his brother's voice. Karen and I jumped up, and the three of us took another step toward the counter.

"What did you do?" Bobby shouted again.

Riley made a move toward the counter and the disturbance beyond, but Karen and I each grabbed an arm and held him back. Whatever was going on, this was the wrong time and place to try to interfere.

Riley struggled, and I tightened my grip. If we let him go, there would be two Freed brothers in Boomer's jail, along with the divers who'd hired their boat.

A real recipe for disaster.

As though we didn't already have a disaster on our hands. Out of our sight, Bobby continued his tirade.

"You son of a bitch!" he yelled. "This is all your fault! I swear I'll kill you for this!"

Chapter 5

SILENCE FILLED THE STATION FOR THE SPACE OF A
heartbeat, immediately replaced by sounds of a scuffle.
Chairs scraped across the floor, and running feet pounded
down the hallway.

At the desk, the duty officer hesitated, glancing toward
the fracas, then back at us. He stayed at his post, though it
was clear he wanted to investigate the commotion.

We stood in the middle of the reception area, unwilling
to return to our seats.

After several seconds, Boomer's voice carried over the
jumble of noise. He didn't raise his voice so much as simply
project a tone of command.

"Now just settle down, all y'all."

The noise paused, and Boomer continued. "Bobby
Freed, you put your skinny ol' behind in that chair and stay

there. You two, take your prisoners on back. We have three of our best cells ready for them."

Faint sounds of shuffling feet and muttered conversation carried to our ears, but there were no more shouts or threats.

I could imagine Bobby sitting on a hard chair, his head hanging down, much as his brother's had earlier. But Bobby's hangdog expression would be far different from Riley's. Riley was scared, sure, but he was still ready to fight. Bobby, in spite of his threats, would be terrified and looking to be rescued.

Just like always.

Karen and I managed to drag Riley back to our spot along the wall, though none of us sat down. Instead, we stood in front of the chairs, debating in whispers what to do about this latest development.

Riley was ready to storm the desk and demand to know what was happening to his brother, and it took all of Karen's persuasive powers to hold him back. I kept a tight grip on his arm, in case Karen lost the argument.

Fortunately for us, Boomer appeared at the desk in a few minutes.

The three of us approached the desk together, Riley dragging Karen and me along with him. Boomer waited for us, a resigned expression on his face.

"We gotta hold him, Riley," Boomer said before anyone else could speak.

"They nabbed the other three, and it was all I could do to hold on to Bobby. Now they have us holding their suspects—say they don't have a facility available," he went on, his tone implying that he didn't believe them.

"Can't we get him out on bail?" Riley asked.

Boomer shook his head. "No way we can get him in front of a judge before tomorrow afternoon at the soonest. Especially not after he made threats against those guys."

Riley winced. "You know that don't mean a thing, Boo—Chief Hardy. Bobby wouldn't hurt anybody, not really."

"What I know doesn't matter, Riley. They want him held on a smuggling charge, they have a valid warrant, and that's that.

"What I can do is let you talk to him and get him calmed down. Five minutes. That's it, and it's a gift, because I told the Feds you'd get him settled down.

"Beyond that, I'd advise you to find a lawyer. He's going to need a good one."

As Riley followed Boomer down the hall, Karen and I exchanged a glance. There was no question of leaving until Riley returned with a report on Bobby.

True to his word, Boomer escorted Riley back into the reception area in five minutes. The two men shook hands, a sign of the respect the police chief had for our friend.

None of us said anything until we were outside the station and standing next to Riley's pickup.

"I don't really understand the charges," Riley said with a shake of his head. "Something about the divers trying to rendezvous with smugglers."

"Drugs?" Shock made Karen shout. She stopped and stared at Riley. A drug charge would definitely mean the forfeit of *Ocean Breeze* and the end of Riley's business.

But Riley shook his head. "Bobby didn't know exactly what they were supposed to be smuggling, but he was adamant that they weren't running drugs. I guess I believe him." He laughed harshly. "If he's wrong, I am so screwed . . ." His voice trailed off as he turned to unlock his truck.

Before he climbed into the cab, Riley turned around and hugged me, then Karen. "Thanks for waiting with me." He looked at Karen, his expression somber. "But you've always been there for me, haven't you? And for Bobby."

"You're still family, Riley," she said softly. "You always will be."

She pulled away abruptly. "It's late, and I have an early call. Better get going."

"Keep us posted," I called to Riley as I trailed along in the wake of Karen's sudden retreat. "And let us know if there's anything else we can do."

The interior lights of Karen's SUV faded as I belted myself in, but not before I saw a suspicious damp shimmer in Karen's eyes. I knew she still had a soft spot where Riley was concerned, but she refused to discuss it.

Whatever had happened between the two of them remained between the two of them. I'd always been grateful that they had avoided pulling me into their disputes; as a friend to both, I never wanted to know the gory details. But now, watching Karen struggling to keep her emotions in check, I wished I knew a little more.

Though she wouldn't admit it, I was pretty sure Riley was unfinished business.

When we pulled into Karen's driveway, she offered to reheat our pizza, but exhaustion slowed her step and lowered her voice as we climbed out of the SUV.

"You're beat," I said. "How about we have it for lunch tomorrow? You just have the early broadcast, right? So you're off the rest of the day, and Julie's working for me. I think I can leave her alone in the store for the day. Then I can come and help you get ready for dinner, since tonight's plans got scuttled."

She didn't argue.

Driving home along the deserted main drag of Keyhole Bay came automatically. It left my mind free to turn over the events of the night, and to ponder the complex relationship between Karen and her ex-husband. And her ex-brother-in-law.

She said they were still family. Not many people truly felt that way about a former spouse. Although I believed Karen, I had to question just what that might mean down the road, because I didn't believe it was over between them.

Not after what I had just seen.

I parked the Civic behind my store and let myself in the back door.

Dim night-lights turned the storage shelves into shadowy giants, looming overhead. I recalled with a shudder the day I'd come home to find the place in a shambles and the door hanging off its hinges. It had been several weeks before I could leave the main lights off, and tonight I wished I'd left them on.

I made a quick tour of the first floor, checking the locks and tugging the door of the ancient safe, reassuring myself the place was secure.

Spending the evening in the police station brought back all my paranoia, and I tried unsuccessfully to shrug off the feeling of dread that had settled over me during the slow hours in those cold plastic chairs.

It didn't help when Bluebeard stuck his head out of his cage and gave me a bleary-eyed stare. "Stop borrowing trouble," he said in the clear voice I had finally accepted was my great-uncle's.

Then he squawked, ruffled his feathers, and spat a string of profanities before retreating back into the darkened cage.

"Trying to sleep here!"

I took the hint and headed upstairs.

EXHAUSTED, I SLEPT SOUNDLY, UNTIL ABOUT FIVE
A.M. But the instant I woke up, the events of the previous
night came flooding back, and more sleep was impossible.

I crawled out of bed, wrapped myself in a thick robe,
and made coffee. The rich aroma of the freshly ground
beans filled my small apartment, and I sipped my first cup
while watching the early morning fog lift from the tiny bay
that gave my hometown its name.

The apartment over my shop was small, but it was all
mine, and the view was my own little treasure. Looking
over the houses on the side streets, I could see the bay beyond and the boats at anchor.

The docks were quiet, empty of the predawn bustle and
purpose they held during the fishing season. A purpose
Riley Freed wouldn't have if he didn't get *Ocean Breeze*
back from impound.

Shaking off the melancholy that settled over me, I carried a fresh cup of coffee into the bathroom and started the
shower. It was time to face the day.

Bluebeard hadn't come out of his cage by the time I
brought the rest of the coffee downstairs, but he soon poked
his head out.

"Coffee?" he said hopefully.

"Not for you," I answered, following our morning ritual.
"Parrots don't drink coffee."

Instead I gave him a couple pieces of banana, another of
his favorite treats, and some fresh water. It didn't really

satisfy his craving for coffee, but it was as good a substitute as he was going to get.

The early morning passed quickly as I tended to the mundane details that made a business run. No matter how much I did, there were always checks to write, shelves to stock and dust, or merchandise to price and catalog.

When Julie arrived at ten, I gave her an abbreviated version of the previous night's events and left her in charge of the shop. "Just lock up at five," I told her. "And call if you need anything in the meantime. I'm just over at Karen's, and I can come back if you need me."

She flashed me her perfect-teeth cheerleader smile. "We'll be fine," she said, her arm draped protectively over her protruding stomach. "Now the doctor says two weeks, maybe a bit more. Mama says she'll come when she's ready, just like me." She grinned, and I remembered her telling me she had been two weeks early, much to her mother's surprise.

I hoped her daughter was a bit more cooperative.

KAREN, HER HAIR PULLED BACK INTO A DISHEV-eled ponytail, met me at the door. A streak of flour dusted one cheek, and her flustered expression told me she was already deep into dinner preparations.

"I got cut-up chicken," she said without preamble. "But from there . . ." Her voice trailed off, and she turned and led me back into the kitchen.

"Hello to you, too," I said, following in her wake. I took in the living room as we passed through, noting that the majority of the clutter had been removed.

I made a mental note not to open the door to the spare bedroom that served as Karen's office. I had a strong suspicion I would find the missing piles of paper and half-finished projects stashed alongside the hyper-organized file cabinets that held her work life. The dichotomy was just one of the contradictions that characterized my best friend.

The kitchen, predictably, was in a state of chaos. Somehow the organizational skill that allowed Karen-the-reporter to instantly locate contact information for a source she quoted once five years ago didn't translate to cooking. Or any other domestic chore—some months she couldn't be sure she'd paid her electric bill.

The source of the flour smudge was obvious. A bowl of dry ingredients sat on the counter, a can of cocoa powder next to it. Taped to the cupboard door over the bowl was a copy of a recipe for red velvet cake.

A handwritten note was taped next to the cake recipe. I read over the list for tonight's dinner: chicken and dumplings, glazed carrots, green beans, biscuits, sweet tea, and red velvet cake.

Ingredients lined the counter on the opposite side of the sink, and a pot of water waited on the stove for the chicken. Beneath the seeming chaos lay a hint of organization after all.

"Looks like you have it under control," I said, nodding at the array of canisters and spices. "You don't need me. I can just go home and get back to work."

"Not a chance." Karen shot out a hand and grabbed the sleeve of my jacket, leaving a line of floury fingerprints. "I need all the help I can get! Have you *seen* this place?"

Panic pushed her voice into an upper register. I imagined dogs all over the neighborhood perking up their ears.

"Joking, Freed! Just joking." I slipped out of my jacket and slung it over the padded vinyl back of a kitchen chair.

The vintage dinette set, decades older than we were and complete with faux marble plastic surface and curved chrome legs, was Karen's pride and joy. Although the style was at odds with her 1970s ranch house, she didn't care.

I watched while Karen added the cocoa powder to the bowl and set it aside. While she went to the refrigerator for buttermilk and eggs, I put the cocoa away. The fewer things left on the counter, the less chance of a disaster.

Mindful of her need to concentrate, I maintained a respectful silence while she measured the buttermilk, oil, food color, vinegar, and vanilla into a bowl with the eggs.

"Have you heard from Riley?" I shouted over the roar of her superpowered mixer as she added the dry mixture to the bowl of liquids.

She shook her head. "Not yet," she said through tight lips. "I expect he'll call when he knows something."

She didn't say it, but I could see in her expression the rest of her thought: *Or when he needs something.*

I mentally corrected myself: *When* Bobby *needs something.*

I let the subject drop, moving to the safer topic of the evening's menu. "Carrots and green beans?"

"Yep." She stopped the mixer, checked the cake batter, and nodded in satisfaction. "I looked at a bunch of recipes for chicken and dumplings. Some of them had vegetables and some didn't." She thought for a minute. "I've had it both ways, and I kind of prefer it without. I mean, if you put vegetables in it, it's just chicken pot pie without the crust."

"What's wrong with that? Sound good to me."

She shrugged. "I don't know. It's just one of those choices.

I didn't even know I had a preference until I started looking for a recipe."

The oven beeped, alerting us it had reached the proper temperature for the cake, and Karen poured the batter into the pans, then carefully slid them onto the center rack. She set the timer for fifteen minutes. "It says to rotate the pans halfway through," she explained, double-checking the baking time on the recipe.

With the cake safely in the oven and time to spare, we turned our attention to the living room. Karen had already moved most of the clutter, and it didn't take long to have the room ready for company. Not that we spent a lot of time in there. Mostly we hung out in the kitchen, and we ate at the dinette, rather than in the actual dining area.

The buzzer sounded in the kitchen. Karen bustled back in to turn the cake just as someone knocked at the front door.

"Would you get that?" she called from the kitchen.

"Sure."

I opened the front door to find Riley on Karen's porch. And, if anything, he looked worse than he had the night before.

Chapter 6

RILEY WAS HALFWAY ACROSS THE ROOM BY THE time Karen emerged from the kitchen, her face flushed from the heat of the oven. When she caught sight of Riley's face, though, she went white.

Judging by Riley's demeanor, however bad we thought Bobby's situation was, we were wrong. It was much, much worse.

"They charged him with smuggling, drug trafficking, and operating a commercial vessel without a license," he blurted out. "He's got a public defender who talked to him for about five minutes, and bail is set at two hundred thousand dollars." He stopped, as though in awe of the number. "Two hundred thousand! Where am I going to come up with that kind of money? *Ocean Breeze* and her gear are worth twice that, but the public defender says I can't pledge her because she's impounded. He's in a meeting with the judge and the prosecutor now, trying to get that changed. But what if he can't? What then?"

"Then we figure out another way," Karen answered. I could see her sizing up the situation. "But first we wait and see if the lawyer can get the bail reduced. If he can, we raise the money and bail him out."

I already knew where the money would come from.

Bobby was family after all.

"In the meantime," she continued, "do you have anything you need to do? You can't spend your day stewing about something you can't control."

"You're right," he muttered. "I can't. But this thing has me tied up in knots." He stopped and looked from Karen to me. "You don't think they could be right, do you?"

The room was silent as we each sat awhile with our thoughts—as my memaw used to say—but it was clear that none of us believed what they were saying about Bobby was true.

"No way," I said, as Karen and Riley nodded in agreement.

Bobby Freed might be a lot of things, but he was what you might call "risk averse." He didn't take big chances. Never had, never will.

Sure, Riley had to bail him out plenty of times, and he couldn't be trusted not to do some damned fool thing. But it was always relatively petty stuff. The risks of getting involved with a drug ring in Florida were huge. Get into a disagreement with your associates, and you could end up dead, or wishing you were.

Bobby didn't take those kinds of risks.

"They're wrong," Karen said with finality. "He wouldn't go near anything that dangerous."

Riley relaxed, as though reassured that someone else had said exactly what he were thinking.

By the time Riley left ten minutes later, he was back to his usual, in-charge self. He had places to go and things to do. He promised to call Karen as soon as he heard anything.

The oven buzzer sounded, reminding us that there was still a meal to prepare. I followed Karen to the kitchen. She checked the cake layers and pronounced them done. With a deftness that belied the chaos in her kitchen, she loosened the layers and turned each one out onto a plate and then onto the waiting cooling racks.

When she was finished, she looked up at me. "Not a word, Martine. Not. One. Word. I know what you're thinking; it's written all over your face."

Karen took last night's pizza out of the refrigerator, turned up the oven heat, and slid her pizza stone into the oven.

"Bobby is still family, and this was Riley's house, too."

"But—"

"No buts. I'll help them out if I can." Her expression dared me to argue.

I didn't.

But I did have a serious question for her. "Just what's the deal with you and Riley? He comes to you before he goes to his folks, or his other friends?"

"It's . . ." She drew the word out, as though searching for the right way to describe what she didn't want to tell me. "Complicated," she said at last.

"Complicated how?" I asked, suspicious. Karen had been acting strangely lately, and now I thought I knew why.

She shook her head. "Just, uh, complicated."

"As in . . . ?"

She didn't answer, but she didn't need to. There was something brewing again between Karen and her ex. I knew it, and she knew I knew, but she wasn't going to admit it.

I let it drop. I'd get the details when she was ready, and not before, but at least I had an explanation.

While we ate, Karen made notes about dinner. "The chicken takes two to three hours to stew," she said, "so I have to start it about three thirty if we're eating at seven."

She continued down her menu, scheduling tasks so as to bring everything to the table at the same time. It was a process I'd seen her do hundreds of times—from homework lists in junior high to multipart news features at WBBY—but she didn't often apply it to her personal life.

And it kept me from asking any more awkward questions.

When we finished lunch, Karen checked her list and announced it was time for cream cheese frosting. Of course, the cream cheese and butter were still in the refrigerator. That was more like the Karen I knew and loved.

In a few minutes—with the help of the still-warm oven—the cheese and butter were ready, and Karen began mixing them with powdered sugar. The whirring of the mixer kept conversation to a minimum.

She was just adding the vanilla when the phone rang.

Her conversation was swift and her reaction swifter. Setting aside the frosting, she ran down the hall to her bedroom, returning with her purse over her shoulder and a sweater tossed over her arm.

"I hate to ask, Glory," she said, her voice hesitant, "but

I have to go. Can you stick around, in case I don't get back in time to start the chicken?"

She glanced at the watch on her wrist. "It's only one, so I have a couple hours. I should be home in plenty of time. Can you, please?"

I nodded. I always have a book in my bag, and there was a brand-new big-screen TV in the den, though I had no idea what I might find on at one o'clock on a Thursday.

"How much?" I asked.

"Forty grand. His lawyer convinced the judge Bobby has 'ties to the community.' All three divers already made bail this morning, but it's cash or bond, and Riley just paid for the supplies for next week's fishing.

"I'll put up the house if I have to, Glory. It's the right thing to do. We both know Bobby didn't do anything wrong, just something stupid, and we need to get him out of there before his mouth gets him in any deeper."

That argument made sense. Bobby would run his mouth without thinking and say something that would get him in even more trouble. I'm sure his lawyer told him to keep quiet, but I'd never known Bobby Freed to be able to do that for very long.

The sooner he was out of jail and away from the ears of the officers—and from fellow inmates looking for information they could trade—the better.

I could have gone back to the store, but Julie would call if she needed me. Instead, I took advantage of the rare treat of an unscheduled afternoon off. Two hours of peace and quiet stretched in front of me, and I intended to make the most of them.

When Karen came home just after three, she looked as

though a huge weight had been lifted. "Much better," she said, dropping her purse and sweater into a chair. "Oops!" She picked them back up. "Company coming, I better put these away."

I heard her go in the bedroom and then in the bathroom. She came back and shot me a look of sheer gratitude.

"The bathroom is spotless! You didn't have to, really. I would have done it when I got home."

Okay, guilt got the better of me, and I didn't relax the *whole* time she was gone. But it was just the guest bath, which didn't get used much.

"It took about ten minutes," I replied. "No big deal."

"It is to me. I was not looking forward to having to do that when I got home."

I got up from my spot on the couch and stowed my paperback in my purse. I never had enough reading time, and yet I seemed to be buying more books lately. It couldn't have anything to do with the bookstore owner.

I helped Karen get the chicken started in a simple chicken broth with salt and pepper. We took the chilled frosting out and started assembling the red velvet cake: three deep red layers trimmed to stack neatly atop one another, cushioned with rich cream cheese frosting. When she had the cake covered to her satisfaction, Karen brought out the final touch: a ring of toasted pecan halves.

Steam rising off the bubbling pot wafted the aroma of chicken through the kitchen. Karen turned down the heat and covered the pot.

The rest of the afternoon passed peacefully as we chopped carrots and laid out the ingredients for the dumplings and biscuits that would accompany the meal. Although dumplings and biscuits were the same basic dough, southern cooks always serve some kind of bread for sopping up the gravy or sauce from the main dish.

The topic of Riley Freed remained closed. I'd found out as much as I was going to. I'd learned long ago that when Karen made up her mind, there was no argument that would change it. Besides, if their history was any indication, she and Riley would soon find a way to blow it all to hell without any outside intervention.

Chapter 7

FELIPE AND ERNIE ARRIVED AT SIX THIRTY. I AN-
swered the door and led them back to the kitchen, where
Karen was dropping dumplings into the bubbling chicken
broth.

She replaced the lid on the pot and turned to greet the
new arrivals. "Stylin'," she said with an approving nod at
Ernie. Tall and slender, he somehow made chinos and a
1950s bowling shirt look elegant.

His partner, Felipe, grinned proudly. "He does look
good, doesn't he?"

We exchanged hugs all around. Felipe set a six-pack of
perfectly chilled longnecks on the table and extracted a pair
of bottles. He twisted the caps off and offered them to
Karen and me. "Ladies first."

He took out another pair, gave one to Ernie, and stashed
the last two in the refrigerator. We'd established the pattern

early on—a round of beer while we finished cooking and settled down, then sweet tea with the meal and more tea, or coffee for Felipe, with dessert.

I took a long pull on my bottle, feeling the cold beer slide down my throat. Outside the weather was still cool, but in a kitchen warm from several hours of cooking, the cold liquid was refreshing.

The table was set, and Felipe and Ernie took their usual places while I helped Karen with the last-minute tasks: glazing carrots, heating green beans, and putting biscuits in the oven.

Karen began ladling chicken and dumplings into bowls, and everyone pitched in to ferry food to the table. Empty beer bottles were stowed in the recycling bin, replaced by a pitcher of sweet tea and tall glasses of ice.

For the first several minutes, the conversation revolved around the food. "I was going to have fish," Karen explained, "but then I couldn't get anything fresh because Riley didn't go out like he'd planned."

Ernie and Felipe exchanged a look. Clearly they had heard about Bobby. There was no such thing as a secret in a town as small as Keyhole Bay. It was only a question of how long it took for news to travel.

And bad news traveled fast.

"How is Bobby doing?" Ernie asked. His usual wide smile was gone, replaced by a concerned frown.

"Bobby?" Felipe snorted. "How about Riley? His idiot brother takes *Ocean Breeze* out for a joyride with some shady guys and ends up getting arrested and costing Riley his boat. He's the one should be asking about."

"Is that what you heard?" Karen sounded incredulous. "Is that really what people are saying?"

Felipe leaned back in the face of Karen's onslaught. "Down, girl! Yeah, that's what we heard. But we've been here long enough to know all about Bobby."

"What do you mean, you know 'all about' Bobby?"

Ernie intervened, laying a hand on Felipe's arm to stop his response. "What we've heard," he said, "is that Bobby is impulsive and undisciplined. That he's always looking for shortcuts to big money. That you can't believe his promises, and you shouldn't invest in his schemes. I've also heard," he continued with a warning glance at Felipe, "that he's a nice guy, fun to be around, and he'd give you the shirt off his back—even if it isn't his shirt to give."

By the time he finished, Karen had relaxed slightly, but her expression was still troubled. "I don't suppose I need to ask where you heard all this," she grumbled. "The Merchants' Association gossips more than the little old ladies of the church auxiliary quilting circle."

"Don't insult the quilting circle," I chimed in. "At least they try to do something for the community."

"So does the Merchants' Association," Felipe shot back. "Just because *some* people"—he shot me a pointed look— "choose not to participate, doesn't mean they aren't a good organization."

"I've told you a thousand times," I answered, "I'm not old or a boy, so I'm really not qualified."

Ernie shook his head at Felipe. "We will never change her mind, *cher*. But someday she will see the error of her ways." He shrugged his shoulders in an elegant gesture. "In the meantime, we can only share our wisdom with her."

I giggled at his pious pronouncement. Couldn't help it.

We'd been having this same argument for years. Even

though I understood the importance of sharing business information locally, facing a room of backslapping good ol' boys was too much to ask. I settled for getting reports from Ernie and Felipe and supporting the other local merchants whenever I could.

"Back to the question of Bobby and Riley," I said, once again serious. "What you've heard is wrong. Or at least greatly exaggerated."

I looked at Karen, giving her the chance to step in.

"I was with Riley last night," she said, "and again this afternoon. Yes, Bobby got arrested, and *Ocean Breeze* was seized.

"But that doesn't mean Riley's lost his boat," she continued. "And it doesn't mean Bobby's guilty of anything, either."

She sighed. "Yeah, my brother-in-law can be an idiot, and he does some pretty stupid stuff because he can't see past his next beer. He can trust the wrong people—especially if they act like they're buying his big-shot act—but he's not cut out for a life of crime. Too risky, and Bobby is kind of opposed to taking risks when it comes to his own safety and comfort."

I bit my tongue to keep from commenting on the fact she had referred to Bobby as her brother-in-law, without her usual qualifier of *former. Interesting.*

"And yet he works on a commercial fishing boat?" Felipe asked. "That doesn't sound safe or comfortable."

"Fishing's what he knows," Karen said. "He grew up on the water—his dad fished, his uncles fished—and now his big brother owns a boat and can give him a job. To him, fishing is just what his family does. He isn't much of a long-term kind of guy. Probably doesn't think about what might happen in the next month, so if there isn't a storm right now, he doesn't see the danger."

"I have to agree with Karen," I said. "I've known Bobby almost as long as I've known her and Riley, though mostly just as Riley's little brother. But he's way too laid-back and go-with-the-flow to get involved with smugglers."

I mentally added, *Except maybe as a customer.* But even then, he wouldn't know anything of value to the investigators, and the most he could be busted for was simple possession.

"It sounds like you're convinced he's innocent," Felipe said.

"I am," Karen replied. "Enough to put my money where my mouth is. I posted Bobby's bail."

Ernie's eyes widened in shock. "Girl, you must have *way* more money than I thought! I heard a bunch of numbers thrown around, some as high as half a million. Where'd you get that kind of money?"

He stopped suddenly. "I'm sorry, that is absolutely none of my business. My mama would be washin' my mouth out with soap for saying that, and then lecturing me about respect. My apologies, Miss Karen."

It was difficult to tell with his cocoa-colored skin, but it looked like he was actually blushing.

Karen just laughed at his distress. "Don't I wish! It was nowhere near that much. I paid a few thousand for the bond and put up the house as collateral."

She saw the stricken look on the two men's faces and hurried ahead. "It was Riley's house, too. And he couldn't pledge *Ocean Breeze* while it was impounded. It's really okay," she reassured them. "Riley will get the boat back, and he'll pay me back. He always does."

Always does? Apparently there were a few more things my best friend wasn't telling me.

"Don't look at me like that," she warned me. "It's like any other business: sometimes he needs money before he gets paid. I've made a couple loans, is all. And I make better interest than I do letting the money sit in the bank."

Somehow I didn't think she was getting interest on the money she paid for Bobby's bail.

And why wasn't I reassured? Probably because we always underestimated Bobby's ability to get himself in trouble.

It didn't take long to get an answer to my question.

Karen was cutting the cake when the phone rang. I jumped up to answer it, since her fingers were sticky with frosting.

I listened to Riley's voice for a minute after I answered, my heart sinking into my shoes. Finally I stopped him.

"I think you better talk directly to Karen, Riley."

Karen wiped her hands on a dish towel, her face twisting into a scowl at my words. "What?" she said to me.

I just shook my head and held out the phone. I didn't want to be involved in this conversation, although I knew I would be.

I served dessert and poured Felipe's coffee. I paused a moment, then poured a cup for myself.

It was going to be a long night.

Chapter 8

WE PICKED AT OUR CAKE, TRYING NOT TO LISTEN TO Karen's end of what was clearly a distressing conversation. I knew what Riley was telling her, but I couldn't share it with Felipe and Ernie. That was Karen's choice, although the news would be all over town by morning.

When she finally came back to the table, her scowl had deepened, twisting her face into a mask of anger. And fear.

Ernie reached out and wrapped his long fingers around her arm. "What is it, darlin'? You look like you been hit with some powerful bad news."

"Yeah. It just"—she pulled herself together with an effort—"just doesn't get much worse."

Ernie loosened his grip and rubbed her arm. "It's all friends here, girl. You can tell us."

"I can't believe it," she said, but the fear in her eyes told us she maybe could believe, though she didn't want to.

"That was Riley," she said unnecessarily; they'd all heard me call him by name. "Bobby's back in jail. Bail revoked."

"But that really isn't your problem, is it?" Ernie was genuinely puzzled. "It means you're off the hook for the bond. And you said Riley would pay you back for the fee."

"He will, for all the good it did him. But that was never the issue."

"Then what *is* the issue?" Felipe blurted out.

"There's no bail this time because he's charged with murder. One of Bobby's diver clients was just found behind The Tank with a gaff hook in his chest."

Felipe turned a sickly green at her description.

I looked down and found myself staring at the dark brown-red of the red velvet cake. My stomach roiled, the dark black coffee suddenly turning to burning acid, and I pushed the cake away. I couldn't bear to look at it.

"Oh man! You didn't need to know that," she moaned. "I shouldn't have told you."

"No, no," Ernie murmured, still stroking her arm. "You can't keep something like that bottled up inside."

I got up and moved around to stand beside Karen's chair. I put my arm around her shoulders and she leaned against me, as if she couldn't hold herself upright.

"So what do we do now?" I asked her.

She hesitated, and I knew what her answer was. Riley needed her, and she needed to go.

"I'll clean up," I said. "You go do whatever you need to."

She looked up, clearly relieved. "You sure?"

"Sure I'm sure," I answered. "It's family. You need to go."

It took another few minutes for Karen to gather her

shoulder bag, which bulged suspiciously, like someone had
stuffed in a change of clothes. The ruse wasn't lost on Felipe and Ernie, and as soon as she was out the door they
were on me like ticks on a hound, wanting to know what
exactly was going on.

"I don't know *exactly*," I said. It was the truth. I had
some suspicions, but no real confirmation. "It's clear that
she and Riley are still close, maybe closer than I thought.
But this is about family. Karen has her own family, true,
but the Freeds made her part of their family long before she
married Riley.

"I always figured that was a big part of why she and
Riley stayed so cordial after the divorce: his folks would
have lost their only daughter.

"Now I'm not so sure there weren't other reasons."

I cleared the table while I talked. Ernie came over
and started loading the dishwasher, and Felipe stowed left-
overs in the fridge.

Our cake sat on the table, still untouched.

"You should take that home." I dug out some plastic con-
tainers from the bottom cupboard and rooted around to find
the matching lids. But this was Karen's kitchen, and I finally settled for stretching pieces of plastic wrap over the
tops.

Karen did have a cover for the cake plate, a diner-style
pedestal that echoed the mid-century design of her dinette. I slid her untouched piece back onto the plate and put
the dome over the stand. It looked right at home in the
middle of her chrome-and-Formica table.

It was still early by our Thursday-night standards when
I got home and unlocked the back door. Julie had set the

alarms I'd installed after the break-in last fall, and I disarmed and then reset them.

I walked up front, intending to make a quick tour of the shop and then head upstairs. To my surprise, Bluebeard was awake, as if he'd been waiting for me to come home.

I crossed the dimly lit shop, pale shadows thrown across the displays by the faint light filtered through the front windows.

Only a few months earlier, I'd found the shop trashed and Bluebeard waiting for me. Tonight, even with nothing out of place and everything locked and secured as it should be, I had a strange sense of foreboding.

But instead of speaking up, Bluebeard hopped off his perch onto my arm and nestled his head under my chin, a sure sign he was upset and needed comforting.

"What is it, Bluebeard? What's wrong?"

In spite of several minutes of cajoling, he refused to speak. He ate a biscuit, then hopped back into his cage and tucked his head into his chest. He was going to sleep, and he had nothing to say.

Somehow, his silence was spookier than anything he could have said.

I think.

I needed some comforting myself, and there was one person I could call any time, day or night. Linda Miller. A friend of my mother's and my foster mom after my parents were killed, she was like the older sister I never had, and she was always there when I needed her. Like right now.

Linda picked up on the second ring. I could feel her concern through the phone the instant she recognized my voice. "You don't sound so good," she said.

How did she get that from *Hello*?

Before I answered, she went on. "I heard about Bobby getting himself in hot water last night. How's Riley holding up?"

I didn't have to ask how she'd heard. Gossip was a time-honored tradition in small towns, and Keyhole Bay did its part. In fact, I'd have been surprised if she *hadn't* heard.

"He's been better," I answered. "You have a minute? It's been a bad night, and I could use someone to talk to."

"I'll be right over." She hung up before I could stop her. I could have called her back, told her we could talk on the phone, but the truth was I would be happier with her there.

A couple minutes later, she tapped at the back door.

We went upstairs, and Linda immediately put a pot on the stove. It was her universal cure for every ailment: a cup of hot cocoa. Even if the cocoa didn't do any actual good, there was something incredibly comforting about her fixing it for me.

I could feel her watching me as she stirred the cocoa. She had questions, but she was willing to wait until she could sit down and give me her full attention.

"Now," she said when she handed me a steaming mug and joined me on the sofa, "tell me what's bothering you."

"It's Bobby. They revoked his bail, and he's back in jail."

"That doesn't make sense," she said.

"Unfortunately, it does." I tried a sip of the cocoa. Still too hot to drink. "Riley called about the time we finished dinner. One of Bobby's customers was killed. They found him behind The Tank, and the cops think Bobby did it." I left out any mention of the gaff hook. It was just too gruesome to think about.

Linda stared at me in shock.

"That's really all I know. But I can't imagine Bobby doing anything like that. He wasn't a fighter; he'd try to talk his way out of whatever trouble he got into."

"And if that didn't work," Linda said, "he'd get his big brothers to help him out."

She shivered. "Chilly in here." She dragged a quilt off the back of the sofa and draped it over my shoulders. She was cold, so I needed a blanket.

"I suppose," she continued after she had the quilt arranged to her satisfaction, "Riley put up the boat to get him bailed out. At least he'll get it back now."

So she hadn't heard everything after all. "Not quite. The boat was impounded, and the bondsman wouldn't accept it as collateral. The boat's forfeit if it was used for smuggling."

I nearly used some of Bluebeard's saltier vocabulary, biting my lip to keep the frustrated curses from streaming out. "Which is ridiculous! I really, really can't believe Bobby did that. Not knowingly."

"Then how did he make bail?"

"Karen pledged her house." The cocoa had cooled slightly, and I took a sip, letting the hot, sugary liquid slide down my throat. As the warmth spread through me, exhaustion dragged me down.

Concern drew Linda's eyebrows together. "You think that was a good idea?"

I shook my head. "I honestly don't know. She still thinks of the Freeds as family, and what I think really doesn't matter."

She took the cup from my hands and set it on the table. "Go put on your pajamas," she instructed.

Too tired to argue, I walked into the bedroom and did as

I was told. Linda had been telling me what to do since I was four, and obeying her came naturally.

When I opened the bedroom door, she was waiting. She shooed me toward the bed. "Crawl in," she said. "I'll let myself out once you're asleep."

I didn't argue. There are times, even when you're thirty-something, that you just need someone to watch over you.

Chapter 9

FRIDAY MORNING WAS DREARY, FOG CREEPING IN off the bay and shrouding the entire town in a soft, gray cloud. Sound didn't carry, and without the sun I couldn't tell if it was morning or afternoon.

The day dragged on, my normal activities a mechanical ritual of routine chores and occasional customers. I listened to WBBY. The substitute newscaster had taken Karen's place for the day. She wasn't usually off on Fridays, but I think this qualified as a family emergency. Question was, whose family?

I shoved the question of Karen and Riley to the back of my brain and tried to concentrate on work.

Late in the morning—the only way I knew was by looking at the clock—Linda came over from her shop next door. Linda and her husband, Guy, owned The Grog Shop, the liquor store on the east side of Southern Treasures.

"I just came to see how you're doing, honey," she said, wrapping me in a big hug. I hugged her back and assured her I was okay.

"Are you sure? You had enough trouble with that Parmenter boy to last a lifetime. I don't want to see you mixed up all this."

"I'm not. Riley is, and Karen, and they're my friends. That's all." I hoped it was the truth.

"Have you heard from Karen? That other guy was doing the news this morning."

"Haven't heard. I'll give her a call later today, find out what the latest is."

"Well, you let me know if you need anything, y'hear?"

I assured her I would.

Karen called shortly after noon. She was at the Freeds, and it was clear she hadn't been home all night.

"We cleaned up and put the leftovers away," I assured her, "and Ernie left the dishwasher running. All you have to do is put the clean dishes away."

"Thanks," she said, sounding distracted. "I really appreciate it. Did one of you take the cake? It shouldn't sit there and get stale."

"I covered it." I had an idea. "How about I go get it and bring it over there after I close up?"

"It's a good idea, but you don't have to do that, Glory. You've already done so much."

I really hadn't, but it was sweet of her to say so.

"Anyway, I have to go home in a little while. I'll just bring the rest of the cake back here with me."

Despite her initial distraction, she seemed inclined to chat, and I settled down in the tall chair behind the counter. "How are the Freeds holding up?"

"About as good as could be expected, I guess. Riley's mom is tore up pretty good. His dad isn't saying much—you know how the men around here are—but he looks about a million years older than when I saw him last week."

She'd seen Riley's dad last week? I filed that information to examine later.

"Tell them I'm praying for them." It was a polite fiction. I wasn't much given to praying—not since my parents were killed by a hit-and-run driver—but it was our way of saying we cared.

"I do have a question, though, Karen. You said Bobby hooked up with these guys at Mermaid's Grotto. I can't figure out what he was doing there. I thought The Tank was more his style."

I could almost hear her shrug over the phone. "Beats me," she said. "He usually hangs out at The Tank with the rest of the crew, but Riley said he's been stopping in at the Mermaid every couple nights. Riley didn't know exactly why, either."

"Just seems odd," I said. "I can almost understand the tourists going to a tourist bar and thinking they can find a charter—they don't know any better—but the locals almost never go in there."

She agreed, but she didn't have any explanation to offer. We talked another couple minutes, but soon she had to go.

"We're trying to find a lawyer for Bobby," she explained. "You don't happen to have a good criminal attorney up your sleeve, do you?"

I chuckled, then felt guilty. Finding Bobby a good defense lawyer was serious business, and I shouldn't be laughing.

"Sorry, but no. The only lawyer I know is Mr. Clifford Wilson. He's my family attorney, but I think he mainly does wills and estates and stuff, not criminal law. And he's about a million years old."

It was only a slight exaggeration. Mr. Wilson—I couldn't imagine calling him by his first name—had been Uncle Louis's attorney when he was still alive, and he'd taken care of my family's legal affairs for three generations.

Karen sighed. "We're going to have to go down to Pensacola to find somebody," she told me. "And we're looking for any recommendations we can get."

"I'll let you know if I think of anything," I promised before hanging up.

By closing time, I had a serious case of cabin fever. I'd been out two nights in a row, but restlessness didn't respond to logic, and I found myself pacing the floor the last hour before I turned out the lights.

I'd finished the display windows, and I stepped out onto the sidewalk to admire my handiwork. While I stood there, cocking my head from side to side trying to decide if I was happy with the final product, Jake loped across the street.

"Looks good from my vantage point," he said. "It should definitely draw some customers."

"Thanks for the vote of confidence."

"Well, I am impressed with your eye for display. It's like you see what should be there, and then you do it. I'm in awe."

I stood silently, not knowing quite what to say.

After a moment, Jake looked down at me, his blue eyes clouded. "What has you so worried?"

"Is it that obvious?"

"It is to anyone who's watching," he answered, softly.

"It's clear you have something on your mind, and it isn't anything good."

Jake hadn't been in town long enough to be well connected to the local gossip mill, and it seemed he hadn't heard the latest about Bobby and Riley. And Karen.

"It's a long story," I said. "But if you have some time, I'll fill you in." He'd hear it all eventually anyway. Might as well get the truth the first time.

"I don't close for another hour," he said. "Have you got plans for dinner?"

I didn't, and we agreed he'd come over when he closed up. In the meantime, he said it was my responsibility to choose a place to eat. And I wasn't allowed to cook.

It took me about two minutes to realize where I wanted to go: Mermaid's Grotto. Maybe I could find the reason Bobby had been hanging out in a tourist trap.

I told Jake I wanted to show him a piece of Keyhole Bay history, and I made him promise to split the check. Mermaid's Grotto was a tourist place, with prices to match.

LIKE MANY TOURIST RESTAURANTS IN RESORT towns, the Grotto didn't have much of a dress code. Jeans were fine, and chinos were considered dressed up, and the Friday-night crowd in the restaurant wasn't exactly fashion forward. Which meant I fit right in.

Mermaid's Grotto was a throwback to another era, and I watched Jake's eyes widen when we walked in. I had to admit, if I hadn't seen it before, the giant fish tank would have been overwhelming. Even knowing it was there, it was still pretty amazing.

"There really were mermaids here, once upon a time," I told Jake, after we were seated in the dining room. "There was an underwater show with mermaids swimming in the tank."

Jake stared at the giant tank that formed a wall between the bar and the dining room. "They swam in there?" he asked.

I nodded. "They used a system of air hoses that let them breathe underwater. That way they could stay down through the whole show, without having to use respirators or tanks or anything."

"How long ago was that?"

"Well, I remember coming here a couple times when I was a little kid. Really little, like three or four. I thought the mermaids were the most beautiful things I had ever seen, and I remember telling my dad he was a liar when he told me they were real people."

I reddened a little at the memory. My parents usually didn't allow such back talk, but that one time my dad had just laughed and let it pass—which was probably why I remembered it so clearly.

Jake chuckled. "So you've always had strong opinions, eh?"

"I guess so. I also told him I was going to grow a tail so I could be a mermaid." I glanced at the tank, then back at Jake. "Which wasn't such a great idea, since at the time I couldn't even swim."

"But you lived here, right by the beach. You must have learned."

"I did, once I had some incentive. I spent that entire summer and the year after that practicing holding my breath underwater. Got pretty good at it, too. But by then they'd closed the show, and I couldn't see much future as a mermaid.

"I understand there is still a show somewhere down south, Weeki Wachee Springs, maybe. But I think I'm over my dreams of being a mermaid."

The waitress arrived to take our orders, and I stopped to take a quick look at the menu. The prices were even higher than I remembered, but I managed to find a salad I could shoehorn into my budget without too much pain.

After she left, Jake gave me an appraising look, a grin playing around the corners of his mouth. "And that was when you were three or four? So the mermaid show's been gone, what? Maybe twenty years?"

"Oh, please!" I took a sip from my water and laughed. "More like thirty years. Sometimes I'm amazed that they've kept this place going that long!"

"They look pretty busy." Jake glanced around with the shrewd assessment all local businesspeople seemed to make on a daily basis, judging the number of paying customers and how much they appeared to be spending.

I followed his gaze. There were several families in the dining room. Judging by the frazzled looks on the adults' faces, I would guess most of them had driven down that afternoon and were looking forward to getting the kids fed and in bed for the night.

On the other side of the giant tank, a decent crowd was starting to fill the bar. Most of them were clearly tourists, their brightly colored Hawaiian shirts and deck shoes without socks advertising how cool they thought they were.

Jake caught my eye and winked slowly. "Yes, I do think we're the only locals in here," he said. "But you can blame it on me; you had to show me the historical sights."

"It really is a piece of Keyhole Bay history. The restaurant's been here since the forties, at least. Maybe longer. You know, you have a section of local histories in your store," I reminded him. "You probably have some books with pictures from when the mermaids were here."

"I probably do," he said.

Jake angled his chair slightly so that he could look at the fish tank. "I'm trying to imagine you in one of those mermaid tails, swimming around and flirting with all the guys at the bar. Probably have to cut your hair, though."

I raised one hand and smoothed it over my long, dark-blonde hair. I'd clipped it back and let it hang loose down my back. "Oh no! The girls all kept their hair long. That way it swirled around in the water."

Our dinners arrived and we ate quietly for a few minutes, watching the fish schooling in the tank and the tourist singles schooling in the bar. It was a reminder of all the reasons I didn't much like the dating pool.

I was sure I hadn't spoken out loud, but Jake broke into a few bars of a Jimmy Buffett song, and I nearly fell off my chair.

"How did you know *exactly* what I was thinking?" I asked.

"It's obvious, isn't it?" he answered. "The sharks are circling."

"Which is why the locals pretty much avoid the place."

"Then where do the locals go?" he asked. "I need to know the best places to see and be seen."

I rolled my eyes. "Yeah, there's such an amazing nightlife in Keyhole Bay," I said drily. "But we can't let just anybody find out about our special locals-only *in* spots."

Jake did his best to look lost and brokenhearted.

"Okay," I said. "But just this once. You can't go telling people I let you in on the secrets."

"Cross my heart." He made a broad gesture, looking serious. But the effect was spoiled by the breadstick in his hand. It looked more like he was waving a magic wand.

"I suppose we should start with this place," I said. "It's always been a tourist attraction, but it was also the place where you took a date for special occasions. A lot of marriages in my parents' generation started with a proposal in front of the mermaids. I remember hearing about a couple of guys who even got a mermaid to 'find' an engagement ring buried in the sand."

I didn't mention that one of those guys was my father. I'd been embarrassed by how corny it seemed when my mother first told me about it. After their deaths, I couldn't bear to think about it, the tragic romance story resonating with my inner teenage drama queen. Now it was something I tucked in a back corner of my memory.

Jake nodded, and I went on. "By the time I was in high school, though, it became very uncool to come here. It was that place your parents went when they had a birthday or anniversary with a zero in it. No one under thirty would be caught dead in here."

I took a long look around. The restaurant had changed very little since then. Most of the decor would look right at home in my store, or in Carousel Antique Mall, Felipe and Ernie's high-end shop.

The dark paneling and tall leather booths represented the height of sophistication at the time they were installed, and the ironic hipster everything-old-is-new-again vibe had made it popular with the young crowd once more.

"But the high-rise condos and big hotels were going

in on the beach, and there were new restaurants for all the people who stayed in them. If you really wanted to celebrate—and you could afford it—you'd go to the beach and spend a night or two."

Jake poured me another glass of wine from our shared carafe. "So, I better take it off my list if I want to hang around." A smile lifted the corners of his mouth. "I hope you won't tell anyone I was here."

I grinned at him. He'd been here almost a year, but he had quickly recognized that many of us came from families who measured their lives in Keyhole Bay in generations rather than years.

"I won't tell, if you don't," I said.

"Deal."

Jake reached across the table to shake my hand. After we shook he didn't let go, letting our clasped hands rest on the table.

I looked at the remains of my salad and decided it wasn't worth retrieving my hand in order to finish. I slid my plate to the side and took another sip of wine.

"So where else shouldn't I go?"

"The other famous place is the Sea Witch Fish and Chowder. Do you know it?"

"I've seen it. I've never been in, never had the time to stand in the lines."

"Like I said, it's famous. At least with people who don't know better. Then it's more like infamous. The chowder is mostly potatoes and flour, and the fish is . . ." I shrugged. "It's okay, but it isn't anything special. Especially not when you have to stand in line forty minutes for lousy service."

Before I could continue my diatribe, the waitress came

and cleared the table. "Did you save room for dessert?" she asked.

I shook my head.

She pulled a check presenter from her pocket and set it in front of Jake. I didn't give him a chance, quickly letting go of his hand to snatch the bill. If I hadn't, he would have found some way not to let me pay my share.

I glanced at the total, mentally figured a tip, and rounded up a couple bucks. I pulled bills from my wallet and slid the folder across the table.

Jake opened it, and I could see the rapid mental math run through his head. "This is way too much," he said. "I ordered the wine, and my meal was a lot more expensive than yours."

I shook my head. "We shared the wine, and we agreed to split the bill." When he opened his mouth to protest, I held up my hand. "Besides, you're always buying my coffee, and you bought dinner the last time we went out. This time it's my turn."

He tossed some bills into the folder and closed it, sliding it to the side of the table. "We probably should let them have the table," he said, gesturing toward the hostess stand. "They have people waiting."

As we stood up, he took my arm. "How about we go over to the bar and you let me buy you an after-dinner drink?" he said. "Strictly research into the local nightlife."

"Yeah, right." But I followed him through the lobby and around to the bar side of the fish tank.

The light was dimmer in the bar, the blue of the tank more intense in the low light. I'd never been on this side when the mermaids still performed; the bar had always been off-limits to kids. But as I watched the brilliant colors of the fish gliding past, I could imagine the mermaids in their glittering tails and flowing hair swimming gracefully by, turning slow loops, and throwing kisses to the men at the bar.

Jake led me to a small table in the back of the bar, as far as possible from the wooden postage stamp that passed for a dance floor. The small square was packed with young bodies in a wide variety of shapes, colors, and sizes. But no matter the size or shape, the girls wore a standard uniform of short dresses, strappy high-heeled sandals, and dangling earrings.

I felt impossibly old and underdressed. The jeans that were just fine on the restaurant side branded me as out of touch with the hip crowd in the bar.

The band was surprisingly good, and I found myself smiling as Jake threaded his way through the crowd to snag Mexican coffee from the bar. He came back with a single coffee, and a tall glass of clear liquid with a slice of lime. "Club soda. I'm driving," he said, putting the footed glass mug in front of me.

"So now I know one place not to go," he said as he sat down, leaning close to be heard over the music. "Are there any places you recommend?"

"There are a few good places," I said, scooting my chair closer. "Curly's makes the best burgers in town."

Jake nodded in agreement. "I've had theirs a time or two. Glad to know they're on the approved list."

"For barbecue, York's is the best, and Neil's has the best pizza."

"Outside of your kitchen, of course," Jake amended, raising his glass in a mock toast. He liked my homemade versions, and I was secretly delighted when I found out we were pizza compatible.

"Nice of you to say so." I returned the salute and took a cautious drink of the hot spiked coffee.

"And then there's The Shark Tank. But nobody calls it that; it's just The Tank if you're a local."

"Haven't been in there," he said. "It's good?"

"It's basically a tavern, and they serve tavern food," I answered. "Fried fish, chicken strips, fries, the best onion rings around, and the best chowder in the state. No, really," I added at his skeptical look. "They've won competitions. It's down next to the dock, and it's where the guys go after they unload a boat full of fish. It's not fancy—some people would call it a dive—but it's good, and the prices are reasonable."

The band finished their number, and the dance floor thinned. A few couples remained on the floor, as though not wanting to break the tenuous connection they had formed while shouting at each other over the pounding beat.

As I watched the crowd filter back to their tables, I was reminded of the reason I'd wanted to come here in the first place. This was where Bobby hooked up with the divers who had hired him, and while I could understand clueless tourists looking for a charter—or a hookup—in a tourist bar, I couldn't understand what Bobby was doing there in the first place.

Or maybe I could. Because when the crowd thinned and I got a good look at the bar, I was pretty sure I knew what brought Bobby into Mermaid's Grotto on a regular basis: Megan Moretti.

When Megan and Bobby were in high school, she'd dated him for a while, mostly as a way to get closer to his big brother. But Riley and Karen were inseparable, and Megan had finally given up and dumped Bobby.

I'd heard she'd married a guy from Jacksonville and moved over there a few years back. But now she was back, standing behind the bar in a tight leather vest that displayed two of her greatest assets. She had bottles in both hands, and there was no ring on her left hand.

I wondered if she would remember me.

Megan's gaze swept the room, a practiced look that missed nothing. She'd been doing this for a while. She turned her head, looking past me, then snapped her head back. He eyes widened in recognition, and she handed the bottles to the other bartender. She said something over her shoulder, coming from behind the bar and heading directly for our table.

"Glory! Glory, is it true? They really arrested Bobby?" Her voice was thick with emotion, her full lips trembling. Tears pooled in her dark eyes, threatening to spill over.

She was still a beauty. Dark curls framed a face that could stop a man in his tracks, her olive complexion still as flawless as when she was voted Most Photogenic her senior year.

I bit back the impulse to ask her if she really cared. She'd treated Bobby badly, broke his teenage heart, and left him convinced he would never be as good as his older brother.

He'd spent the years since living down to that expectation. Not that it excused his behavior; lots of people managed to get over their teenage selves and become adults. Bobby wasn't one of them, and Megan bore part of the blame.

"It's true," I said, keeping my voice low.

"What happened?" she asked. Concern creased her brow, a preview of what she would look like at fifty if a surgeon didn't intervene. "Is there anything I can do? Can I see him?"

I noticed she hadn't asked about the rest of the family, including Riley. Maybe she had grown up in the last decade, even if Bobby hadn't.

"I can't tell you much. Not here." I glanced around at the nearby tables. A couple guys were watching us. Correction: they were watching Megan. And it was clear they weren't interested in what she was *saying*.

Megan nodded. "I get a break in about half an hour." She looked down at our table. "I'll send another round. If you'll wait?"

"Sure." Jake spoke up, to my relief. "But make mine a plain black coffee. I'm the designated driver."

She flashed him her million-watt smile. "Got it. But I'll make you something tastier than plain coffee."

She went back to work. A few minutes later a waitress brought a tray to our table. She put another Mexican coffee in front of me, and a steaming mug in front of Jake. "These are from Megan," she said. "Her cappuccino is to die for." She gestured at Jake's mug and sighed dramatically.

I tried not to flinch at her choice of words. She had no way to know Megan wanted to talk about murder.

Chapter 10

THE BAND STARTED THEIR NEXT SET. JAKE AND I
sat in our corner listening and watching, comfortable with
our own silence as we sipped our drinks.

Jake offered me a taste of his cappuccino. I hesitated at
the familiarity of drinking from the same cup, finally com-
promising by using the straws from my coffee. It felt safer,
less intimate somehow.

It only took Megan about twenty minutes to escape from
behind the bar. She waved to us to follow her and slipped
through a door at the end of the bar.

I led Jake through the door, expecting a storeroom re-
sembling the one at The Grog Shop. Instead we found a
cramped room, little more than a closet, stacked with cases
of beer and booze. In one corner a tank and regulator stood
next to a rack of soda syrup boxes, the tank making a little
hiss each time it charged the soda gun at the bar.

There wasn't really enough room for three people in the center of the room. Jake was so close I could feel the warmth of his body through the back of my T-shirt.

"Come on up here," Megan said, starting up a narrow flight of stairs. As we climbed the stairs, I realized we must be right next to the giant fish tank.

At the top of the stairs, we found a large room with tables and chairs, obviously retired from the restaurant, their scratched and pitted tops relegating them to the employee lounge.

Several benches, bolted to the floor, ran through the space. Next to the benches, discolored patches showed where something had been removed.

"That's where the mermaids changed," Megan said, waving at the benches. "There used to be lockers in front of each bench, where they kept their stuff."

I stared at the benches. This was the place I had dreamed about all those years ago. Of course, in my four-year-old brain it had been an underwater castle, not a utilitarian concrete locker room. Still, I was here.

I didn't have time to explore, though. Megan was only on a break, and Jake was waiting to drive me home.

We dragged chairs around one of the tables, and Megan looked at me expectantly. "What's happened to Bobby?"

"He was arrested on smuggling charges on Wednesday."

"I heard about that. But I thought he got out on bail. Besides, it was a bogus charge. Bobby didn't do anything wrong. He only came in here to see me, and those three guys just kept bugging him until he said he could take them."

I sat up, the fuzziness of the alcohol from the Mexican coffees chased from my brain by her assertion. "You saw them?"

"Of course I saw them. Bobby and I were trying to have a private conversation, and one of these big blond guys comes over and says Bobby looks like a boat captain, and could he talk to him? Bobby says, in a minute—cause he never says no to anyone, 'less he can't help it—and the guy just stands there like he was listening to our conversation.

"Finally Bobby stops talking to me and asks the guy what he wants. He says they need a boat to take them diving and they can't find one of them that'll take them the next day."

She stopped and I waited, afraid to ask the wrong question and derail her story. She stood up and grabbed a bottle of water from a case on the floor behind her, holding two more out to me and Jake.

"Anyway, Bobby told him no, that he was going fishing with his brother the next day. But that didn't stop the guy. He says Bobby can go fishing any day, that they really want to dive. Bobby shook his head, and then the guy started flashing a wad of cash. Said this was the last day of some special dive trip, and basically he gave Bobby a big sob story about how they didn't want to waste their last day, and blah, blah, blah."

She sucked down about half the bottle of water and sighed. "Bobby was just trying to be a nice guy, to help these guys have one last day of diving. Instead they got him arrested."

She balled up her fist and smacked it on the scarred tabletop. Away from her customers, her accent thickened. "It ain't fair! Bobby's sweet. He don't deserve this."

Her story changed everything, and it changed nothing. It meant Bobby was telling the truth, he hadn't been involved in whatever the divers were up to.

It also meant he had a helluva motive for murder.

"Didn't he get out on bail, Glory?" she asked.

"Yeah, I thought he got bailed out yesterday," Jake said. "That's what Linda said when I stopped in the store last night."

Obviously Jake was at least starting to tap into the local gossip circuit.

I propped my elbows on the table and buried my head in my hands. "He did," I said, not looking up. "But they arrested him again, and this time he can't get bail."

Megan jumped up, fists at her sides, ready for a fight. "What did those guys tell the cops? What lies did they tell?" She grabbed a jacket off the row of hooks near the door. "I told the cops Bobby didn't know those guys! I'm going down there right now and make Boomer let him out!"

"Sit down, Megan," I said softly. "There isn't anything we can do right now."

She didn't budge, and I looked up at her. "Please, sit down."

Jake looked at me warily, then up at Megan. Although we never got around to my story over dinner, he could tell I had more to say, and he could guess it wasn't going to be good.

"I think you better sit down, Megan." He got up and took her jacket, putting it back on the hook. "I'm pretty sure Glory knows more than she's told us so far."

Megan perched on the edge of the chair, ready to bounce back up at any moment.

I drew a deep breath, dreading the reaction my next words would bring.

"They found one of the divers behind The Tank last night. He'd been killed with a gaff hook from *Ocean*

Breeze. Bobby can't get bail because they've charged him
with murder."

Jake stared at me in shock, and the fight drained out of
Megan. "No," she whispered. The tears that had been
threatening spilled over and ran down her face. "He would
never . . ." Her voice trailed off into a sob.

I went to her and put an arm around her shoulders. She
turned her head and buried her face in my side.

Below us a door opened, and the noise of the bar blasted
up the stairs. "Megan?" a voice called over the din. "Band's
about to take a break. We're gonna get slammed. We need
you down here."

The door slammed again. Megan pulled away from me,
her eyes red. "I better get back to work." She dragged a tis-
sue from her pocket and wiped her eyes.

She walked over to a small sink, splashed water on her
face, and added a quick dash of dark coral lipstick from a
tube in her pocket. When she turned around, her eyes were
clear and there was no sign of the emotional storm that had
passed through her.

"Better go," she said, leading us toward the stairs. The
calm mask slipped for an instant, and she gave me a quick
hug. "Thanks for talking to me. I'm glad I didn't have to
hear that from the radio or something."

I nodded my agreement, though I wasn't quite sure of
her meaning, and we followed her back downstairs to the
bar. As she'd been warned, the band was putting down their
instruments, and the crowd was headed for the bar.

Megan turned around long enough to wave, then was
swallowed up in the crush of bodies clamoring for fresh
drinks.

"Ready to leave?" Jake leaned down, so close I could feel his breath against my neck as he spoke.

I nodded, and he reached for my hand, pulling me along as he snaked through the crowd. He seemed to anticipate which way the crowd would move, as he found a narrow path to the door.

As we walked out and the doors closed behind us, I felt as though a physical load had been lifted from my shoulders. I realized it was the noise and heat of the crowd, now trapped inside the building. I let the relative silence fill me as I drew a deep breath of the cool night air, and relaxed for the first time since I'd spotted Megan behind the bar.

Jake continued holding my hand as we walked to his car.

Adrenaline had chased the effects of the alcohol from my system, but I was still relieved Jake was driving.

When we were in the car with the doors locked, safely away from prying eyes, I turned to Jake. "Why would somebody pressure Bobby like that? What were they doing?"

Jake shook his head. "Beats me," he said, putting the car in gear and pulling out of the lot. "It doesn't make any sense."

"I wonder if Karen has heard Megan's story. Or Riley."

"Why don't you call her?" Jake asked. "They need to know what she said, if they don't already."

I took out my cell phone and hit speed dial. Karen was at the top of the list.

"Hi, Glory. What's up?"

"Just wondered how you guys were holding up."

"Hanging in there, I guess. Still trying to find a lawyer and figure out just what is going on. Nothing we have heard makes any sense."

"Actually, that was kind of one of the reasons I called. Are you still at the Freeds?"

"Yeah. I went and got the cake and a clean shirt, but I came right back here, in case there was anything I could do."

Jake pulled up in front of Southern Treasures, but he left the engine running and gestured to me to get my attention. I told Karen to hang on a sec and put my hand over the phone.

"Do you want me to take you to the Freeds?" he asked.

I shook my head. The last thing I wanted to do was intrude on the family. They needed each other, but they didn't need outsiders.

"How about we meet her somewhere, then?"

I noticed he said *we*.

"Karen? How about we meet you somewhere? I don't want to barge in there, but I've heard a couple things you might want to know."

I could hear her talking to someone in the background for a minute, then she came back on the line. "Actually, I think it would do us some good to get out of here for a while." She named a chain restaurant near the Pensacola airport. "Meet us there in twenty?"

I glanced over at Jake, who had overheard her, and he nodded.

"See you there," I answered, without mentioning my companion. I was pretty sure the *us* she referred to was she and Riley, which was going to be awkward enough.

"I can take my car," I said to Jake as I gathered up my purse and jacket. "No sense running you all over the county in the middle of the night."

"First off, that isn't all over the county, and second, I haven't been drinking. Third, I heard what Megan said, too.

I might actually be of some help." He stopped and grinned at me. "Oh, and fourth, you don't get rid of me that easy."

He put the car back in gear and pulled away from the curb before I could argue. Not that I really wanted to.

We arrived first, which wasn't surprising. I could imagine how long it would take Riley and Karen to break free from the family gathering.

I just hoped they wouldn't be too much longer. Megan's story was like found money burning a hole in my pocket, and I could hardly wait to see what it was worth.

Chapter 11

JAKE AND I GOT A BOOTH. HE ORDERED COFFEE, FOR which he seemed to have an infinite capacity, and I ordered an herbal tea.

"Another cup of coffee," I told him, "and I won't sleep until Tuesday." It was an exaggeration, but the mix of alcohol, coffee, and adrenaline already in my system was enough to keep me wired for quite a while. No need to add anything more.

A few minutes later, Karen and Riley arrived. I spotted them as they pulled in, but I was surprised to see Riley climb out from behind the wheel of Karen's SUV.

If she let him drive her prized vehicle, this was getting *serious*. And, as they crossed the parking lot to the front door, their body language reinforced my suspicions. If they weren't a couple again, they would be soon.

And disaster would follow.

When they entered the restaurant they made sure to keep a little distance between them, like they were trying to pretend they weren't together.

Karen spotted us and raised an eyebrow. I shot a glance at Riley and back at her, a warning that whatever questions she might have for me, I would have a few of my own in return.

Sometime in the next few days we were going to have a very interesting conversation. But it would likely have to wait until Bobby was free again.

Karen slipped into the booth across from me, and Riley slid in next to her, careful not to sit too close. She looked back and forth from me to Jake, waiting for one of us to say something.

The waitress arrived in the middle of our awkward silence.

"What can I get you?"

Riley looked at her and blinked, like he was just waking up. "I'd like a burger," he said. Then he turned to Karen. "Do you want something? I don't think we ate dinner, did we?"

She shook her head slowly, as though she had to think about her answer. "No, I don't think so." She looked up at the waitress. "Can I get bacon and eggs, over easy?"

The waitress scribbled the order on her pad and promised to come back with the coffee in a minute.

When she left, Karen turned to me. "Things have been so insane, we literally forgot to eat. There's a mountain of food—everybody and their grandma brought us a covered dish—but we didn't eat any of it."

I'd seen her do this before, get so wrapped up in a project that she forgot meals. But it was a new thing for Riley.

His work was physically demanding, and he usually had a healthy appetite, which was to say he ate enough for a small army and then burned it right back off. Until today.

With coffee at hand and food on the way, Karen started to ask a question, but Riley beat her to it. "What did you want to tell us?"

"I think I figured out why Bobby was hanging out at Mermaid's Grotto," I said.

Riley furrowed his brow. "Huh?"

"We were talking," I explained hastily, "Karen and I, about how it didn't make any sense why Bobby was hanging out at a tourist trap so much, instead of at The Tank."

"But he was at The Tank," Riley countered. "We all were."

"Yes, but you told Karen he was going by the Grotto, too. Every day or two. That was where he hooked up with those divers, and nobody could figure out why he was there. Well"—I straightened my shoulders proudly—"I know why."

"So tell us already!" Karen never was very patient.

"Two words: Megan Moretti."

"Megan?" Riley said. "What's she got to do with this?"

"She's the reason Bobby was at the Grotto." Hadn't I just said that? I thought I'd been pretty clear. Maybe Riley was more confused than I thought. "He went there to see her."

"So she's back, I presume." Karen stated the obvious.

"I just talked to her an hour ago," I said. "So I guess the answer would be yes."

"And Bobby's been hanging around her again?" It was Riley's turn to ask a question.

The tag-team approach was disconcerting. Usually these two talked over each other, each one trying to run the show.

Now they were taking turns, and the change was very unsettling.

"I just said that. But that's not really what's important."

"So if that isn't important," Karen said in a tone that implied she thought it was, "then what is?"

The waitress returned with plates, and put them in front of my friends. Now if they would just keep their mouths busy with food, I could tell my story.

"We went to the Grotto for dinner." That was as far as I got before Karen gave me another look. "Jake was asking about local restaurants—what was good, what was overrated—and I suggested the Grotto. I told him it was a piece of local history." I snuck an apologetic glance at Jake. "I kind of had an ulterior motive in choosing it."

"It was good," Jake said with a smile. "And we got some useful information. A good choice for lots of reasons."

"Anyway, we stopped at the bar after we ate, and there was Megan serving drinks behind the bar. Last I heard, she got married and moved to Jacksonville, but there she was, with her, um, assets on display, and no wedding ring."

They both had their mouths full, and I filled them in on our conversation with Megan. Jake spoke up a couple times, adding bits and pieces I forgot.

By the time we'd told them what we knew, Riley looked like he wanted to punch somebody. "So whoever these guys are, they harassed Bobby into taking them out, then when they get busted they give the cops some song and dance and get Bobby arrested?"

"I don't know about that," Jake said evenly. "As I understand it—and correct me if I'm wrong—Bobby was arrested right along with everybody else. And they did let him make bail. The real problem is the dead diver."

Karen made a sour face. "Yeah, and we all—well, ex-cept Jake—we all heard him threaten to kill them."

I shook my head. "He was just mad. He didn't mean it."

Riley nodded vigorously in agreement. "He was just blowing off steam."

"But to anyone like me who doesn't know Bobby," Jake said, "it sounds like a serious threat. Especially when one of the guys is murdered the next day."

"What's that supposed to mean?" Riley's voice held a challenge. "You think he did it?" His voice rose, and heads turned at nearby tables. "Well, he didn't. I know he didn't."

"But I don't," Jake said, an edge creeping into his tone. "And that was my point. I *don't* know him, or have any reason to believe or not believe. Except"—he pointed at me, then at Karen—"that two people I *do* know and trust tell me he didn't do it."

No one said anything for a few minutes. Karen stirred her coffee, even though she hadn't added anything to it, and Jake fiddled with his napkin, wadding it into a tiny ball.

Finally, Jake broke the silence. "Has anyone heard who the divers were? What they were doing here?"

The three of us shook our heads.

"That's actually one of the weirdest things," Karen said. "Usually there's gossip or rumors or an unofficial leak. *Something.* But I checked in with my station manager, and he said nobody's heard a thing. Not a peep. It's like the lo-cals aren't being told what's going on."

"Maybe this is just a little part of something bigger," Jake suggested.

"But what?" Riley asked. "And I still don't know why my brother got mixed up in this."

"From what Megan told us, those guys were pretty persistent," I said. "What if they were afraid the cops were getting close? They wanted to finish their business and split. That would explain why they were so pushy."

"And if the cops—or whoever they were—thought the divers were spooked, they would have grabbed everybody before they could get away," Karen said.

She looked at Riley. "Your brother got mixed up in this because he wanted to impress a girl, I'm betting. He was acting like a big shot in front of Megan and promised to get the guys a boat."

I had a hunch it might have been more than simply acting like a big shot; the more I thought about it, the more I suspected Bobby was trying to make Megan stop thinking of him as Riley's little brother.

"A man can purely mess himself up trying to impress a girl," he said, looking across to Jake for support.

"So true," Jake said.

"But if Bobby didn't kill that guy," I asked, ignoring the moment of male bonding, "who did? Because the cops clearly think they have their guy, or they wouldn't have arrested Bobby.

"That's the most important question right now. Until we find the person who killed that diver, Bobby won't get out."

"Isn't that the cops' job?" Riley said.

"Yeah, like that worked so well for Kevin Stanley," Karen replied, drily. "The police tried to call that an accident and make it go away."

The previous fall, Kevin, star quarterback for the Keyhole Bay Buccaneers, had been killed in what looked like a tragic accident. But there was nothing accidental about his death, as I'd discovered.

"And if it hadn't been for Sly and Bobo," she continued,

looking at me, "you would have been the next one to have an 'accident.'"

I shivered at the memory of my close call. Jimmy Parmenter, raging on steroids and fueled by jealousy and anger, had come close to making me seriously dead in the junkyard behind Fowler's Auto Sales. Only the intervention of junkyard owner Sly and his dog, Bobo, kept me from joining Uncle Louis as a ghost.

"Be fair," I said. "It wasn't just Boomer. Everybody thought that was an accident."

"Everybody except Uncle Louis," Riley shot back.

"What? How did you know?" I stopped and glared at Karen. "You *told* him, didn't you? What the—?" I clamped my mouth shut before I used several of Bluebeard's—or should I say Uncle Louis's?—favorite words.

Jake's forehead wrinkled in confusion. "Am I missing something here? I thought Uncle Louis died when you were a little girl. How could he have anything to do with that Stanley kid?"

I buried my face in my hands. I didn't want to tell Jake about Uncle Louis, not yet. I didn't want him to think I was a crazy person, just as we were getting to be, well, whatever it was we were getting to be.

But it looked like, thanks to Karen's loose lips and Riley's big mouth, I might have to.

"Long story," I muttered. "I'll explain it later." I didn't mention how much later. Three or four years ought to be enough.

We talked a few minutes more, but none of us had any bright ideas about who might have wanted to kill Bobby's customer. The best anyone could come up with was Karen's suggestion of "a falling out among thieves."

In the car on the way home, Jake brought up the subject of Uncle Louis again. "What did Riley mean when he said Uncle Louis didn't believe Kevin's wreck was an accident? It was pretty obvious there was something I didn't know."

I turned my head and looked out the window on my side, watching the dark waters of the bay slide past. The glow of a nearly full moon reflected on the water, broken by the light chop from the night wind. It looked as confused and chaotic as I felt, trying to come up with an answer.

"I'm sorry," Jake said when I didn't say anything. "Obviously, whatever it is, it's none of my business. Forget I asked."

The silence stretched uncomfortably between us. The car was suddenly cold in spite of the warm air flowing from the heater vents, and I wrapped my jacket around me.

We pulled up in front of Southern Treasures, and I grabbed my purse. "Thanks, Jake."

That seemed inadequate, and I struggled to find the right words to dispel the chilly atmosphere. "I'd ask if you want to come in for a cup of coffee, but I'm willing to bet you've had enough for one night."

That got a brief chuckle. "I think I've actually had enough coffee," he said. "But I'd be glad to stay if you want company."

"Okay."

I wasn't entirely sure what I had just said yes to, but I'd decided I had to trust Jake. He was still a mystery, but somebody had to make the first move.

That first move would be telling him about Bluebeard. Or, more accurately, about Uncle Louis.

I unlocked the front door and Jake followed me in. I

hesitated before I switched on a light, wondering what fresh chaos might greet us.

Bluebeard, still awake, stuck his head out of his cage, and I realized with a start that it was not yet midnight. With all that had happened, it felt like it should be much later.

Everything was in order, though that wasn't always the case. Sometimes Bluebeard, or Uncle Louis, would move things in order to get my attention.

Tonight Bluebeard settled for simply staring directly at me, and saying clearly, "People don't just come back for no reason."

Chapter 12

I SNUCK A GLANCE AT JAKE.

His eyes grew wide, and he turned to me. "Does he talk like that often?"

"That," I said drily, "is what I have to tell you about. Come on upstairs." I gestured toward the staircase at the back of the shop.

It was going to be another long night.

"You're going to think I'm nuts," I said once we were settled on the sofa. I'd made cocoa, just as Linda had the night before, looking for something to hang on to while I destroyed my budding friendship/romance/whatever-it-was with Jake.

"I doubt it," he said. "Besides, I like people who color a little outside the lines." He grinned, trying to lighten the mood, but I wasn't reassured. He didn't know just how far outside the lines I went.

"Downstairs," I continued, "you asked if Bluebeard talked 'like that' often. Well, he does and he doesn't. He does say things that seem a bit, um, *unusual* from time to time. But I am pretty sure it isn't really Bluebeard who comes up with them."

I looked away, afraid to face Jake. "I think it's Uncle Louis." I hesitated, then the words tumbled out, like water spilling over the banks of a flooded stream.

"I didn't want to believe it, I wanted to think it was Bluebeard. But stuff was always out of place in the shop, and sometimes it was things Bluebeard couldn't have moved. Then he started saying things that didn't make any sense coming from a bird. Things Bluebeard couldn't ever have heard.

"Parrots are smart," I said, distracting myself from what came next. "But they only repeat things they've heard. They don't learn words any other way."

"Okay," Jake said slowly. He kept his voice low. "But how do you go from the parrot saying something you don't think he's heard to you thinking it's Uncle Louis? The guy taught Bluebeard to talk, didn't he? How do you know he didn't learn that from him thirty years ago?"

"It's not just that," I said, still not looking at him. "It's *when* he says stuff, and *what* he moves."

I turned around. It was suddenly important that Jake understand and believe what I was telling him. "Like the time last fall when I brought home this incredible antique quilt. I didn't have a display place that was quite right, so I put it in the back until I was ready to put it out. Then a woman came in with a wad of dough she'd won over in Biloxi. She wanted to buy a quilt, and there was that antique sitting on the counter behind the register.

"I didn't leave it there, I swear," I said, watching his expression. "It was just there, in plain sight, when she walked through the door with cash in her hand. It was folded just as pretty as you please, and it was way too heavy for Bluebeard."

"You still haven't told me what Riley meant," Jake said. Judging from his expression, he wasn't dismissing my story, but he wasn't ready to accept it, either.

If I was really going to trust Jake, I had to tell him about Kevin. He knew most of the story, as I quickly reminded him: how Karen and I had seen the aftermath of the single-car crash, how I didn't believe it was an accident, and how, as Karen had pointed out earlier, I had nearly become Jimmy's next victim.

"What started all of that was something Bluebeard said," I confessed. "The night of the accident I came home and found the shop in a mess. Karen was with me. She saw it, too."

"No wonder the break-in—" He paused to think. "—which was what, a couple days later? No wonder it upset you so much."

I nodded, and continued with my story. "When we came in and found the shop trashed, Bluebeard said very clearly, 'It wasn't an accident.' At first I thought he meant he'd trashed the shop on purpose, but I eventually had to admit he was talking about Kevin. And once I accepted that, I couldn't let it go until I found out what really happened.

"There was something else. While the investigation was going on, Bluebeard kept yelling about a 'bad man.' At first I thought he meant Matt Fowler, but I finally figured out he meant Jimmy."

"So, you're telling me you have a ghost in your shop," Jake said.

I nodded, and looked away.

"But he just says obscure things? And he moves stuff around? He doesn't actually *tell* you what things mean, or answer questions?"

I shrugged. "I don't know how it works. Maybe there are rules or something. Or maybe I would understand more if I knew more about Uncle Louis." I sighed. "I've been trying to find out what I can about him, but there just isn't much to find. He died almost twenty-five years ago, and there aren't a lot of people around who still remember him. But you heard what he said this time: 'People don't just come back for no reason.' There's a reason he's here; I just don't know what it is."

"I have to say," Jake said, "that wasn't quite what I expected. But I don't know what I did expect."

"It's actually kind of sweet, him hanging around."

He put his hand on my shoulder, and I turned back to look at him. Judging by his expression, I hadn't destroyed our friendship after all.

"So, who all knows about this ghost?" he asked. "Obviously Karen does, and she told Riley."

"Linda," I said. "Felipe and Ernie. They all found out when Kevin was killed. And now you."

"I guess I'm in good company, then. And I'm flattered you trusted me enough to tell me."

"And you don't think I'm crazy?"

Jake tilted his head a little to one side, as though he were thinking hard. "Maybe a little, but I've learned to keep an open mind. I admit, I might be a lot more skeptical if I hadn't heard what he said tonight."

Just why had Bluebeard spoken up when we came in? The only other time he'd done something like that was with

Karen, and it had forced me into admitting my suspicions to her.

I was being played. By a bird. Okay, a bird and a ghost, working together, but I was being played.

"I think maybe he did that on purpose."

"Would you have told me if he didn't?" Jake asked.

"Probably." I thought for a few seconds. "Yes. That's why I asked you in, and I hope I wouldn't have chickened out, even if Bluebeard hadn't said anything."

Jake tilted his head a bit more and moved closer.

Apparently he didn't mind kissing a woman who might be just a little bit crazy.

Chapter 13

I KISSED JAKE GOOD NIGHT WHEN I WALKED HIM downstairs, drawing a sleepy wolf whistle from Bluebeard, but no complaint that we were disturbing his night-time rest.

Jake just chuckled.

We had talked for a long time. Just talked. With my limited romantic history, I was wary, and Jake quickly recognized my reticence and respected it.

I locked the door behind Jake, trying not to think too hard about the change in our relationship. It was too soon to know where we were going.

Besides, I had another mystery to contemplate. Bluebeard had said people don't come back for no reason, and I had no idea what Uncle Louis's reason was. There must be something he wanted, or needed. I fell asleep wondering what that something was that brought him back to Southern Treasures.

By morning I still had no idea, and I once again pushed the question of Uncle Louis to the back of my mind. I had a business to run, and the problems of Bobby, Riley, and Karen were a more immediate concern.

Julie worked behind the counter, but she didn't seem able to settle down for very long. Her restlessness proved contagious, and I found myself rummaging through the shelves. I didn't know what I was looking for and wasn't sure I would recognize it when I found it. But I couldn't sit still, either.

WBBY played in the background all day. Late in the day, the backup announcer was still on the air, and Julie asked about Karen.

"She's dealing with this family business," I told her. "I doubt she'll be back until it's settled."

"But can she do that without getting fired? Will her boss *let* her do that?"

I laughed at her question. "The station manager doesn't really have a choice, not with Karen. Short of firing the best on-air talent in the Panhandle, he doesn't have much way of making her do anything. They've had a couple run-ins before," I explained. "And Karen comes out on top every time. She's just stubborn enough to get away with it."

Julie looked uneasy. It was clear she was relating Karen's family situation to her own. Julie, after all, was facing several weeks away from her jobs. She had every reason to worry whether they would still be there for her when she returned.

"Don't look so worried," I said. "Your job will be here

when you get back, whenever that is. You're doing well here—I've seen you charming the customers—and I'll be glad to have you back. And I know Frank feels the same way."

Frank Beauford owned Frank's Foods, where Julie had worked until she couldn't stay on her feet any longer. He'd told me just a week ago that he was anxious to have her back.

"Thank you, Miss Glory," Julie said.

It always made me feel ancient when she called me that, but it was the way polite southern youngsters were taught to address their elders. I didn't feel that much older than Julie—except when she called me "Miss Glory." Still, it could have been worse. At least she didn't call me "ma'am."

Julie rested her arm across her swollen belly. "But who'll take care of her while I'm working?"

I laughed again. "I've seen your mama," I told her. "She can't hardly wait to get her hands on that grandbaby. She's planning to spend a lot of time with her."

I had an idea I'd been thinking about for several weeks. I'd talked it over with Julie's mom, Anita, and we'd planned a surprise. "I've been thinking," I said, "that there might be a way we could fix up a little nursery for her here at the shop. That way she could come to work with you, at least for a little while."

I didn't know much about babies, and I really wasn't sure what all a nursery might involve, but I was willing to try if it would keep Julie working.

"At least through the summer," I added. "That's when I really need the help."

"You'd do that for me?" Tears welled in her blue eyes. "Really?"

I shrugged. "Sure, if we can make it work. That way I

keep a good employee, and you have a little more flexibility with your babysitting. I mean, your mama wants to have her grandbaby around, but she can't have her all the time, no matter how much she wants to."

Anita had promised to babysit, but she still had her own responsibilities. She and Stan, Julie's dad, owned a small motel, and there would be times she wouldn't be able to keep the baby.

Julie waddled out from behind the counter and hugged me. "That is so sweet." She pulled back and swiped her fingers under her eyes, flicking away the tears. "Can we"—she hesitated—"can we look at how we can do this?"

"Sure." Now that I'd told her about it, I should show her what I'd done. "I thought we might take the office space out back"—I nodded toward the storage area—"since it's already kind of a separate space."

We walked through the door to the back. There wasn't a lot of room, but I had cleared out the corner where my desk and filing cabinet had been.

"I got some office dividers," I told Julie, "to wall off this area a little more."

The office space wasn't much more than an alcove, but with the dividers in place it was big enough for a crib, changing table, and a chair for Julie. Her mom said she'd need someplace to sit with the baby.

The bell over the front door tinkled, and I went out front, leaving Julie staring at the empty space.

My timing had been excellent. Coming through the front door was Felipe, a giant grin on his face. "Ernie's pulling the van around the back," he said. "Are you ready?"

"I guess," I said. I was as ready as I was going to get.

"I'll go unlock the back door," Felipe said as he walked

past me. "Just wait here. I think there are a couple more people on the way."

Sure enough, within a few minutes the rest of the renovation crew arrived. Jake closed his shop and crossed the street about the same time Linda walked over from next door. And right behind them came Anita Nelson.

Anita hurried through to go see her daughter as I greeted the new arrivals. Another car pulled to the curb. Shiloh, Fowler's Auto Sales' office manager, got out from behind the wheel, and my friend Sly got out on the passenger side.

Sly was a surprise, but a welcome one. I'd met him when I was investigating Kevin Stanley's murder, and he was one of the few people I knew who remembered Uncle Louis. But it was the first time he'd been to the shop.

I'd only told a couple people what I was going to do for Julie, but it seemed like everyone I told invited someone else. It was a pleasant side effect of the gossip mill that ran Keyhole Bay.

Sly came through the front door, a wide smile creasing his dark face and exposing gaps where he was missing teeth. The crinkles around his eyes and the laugh lines that bracketed his mouth told of a long life spent outdoors.

Before Sly could speak, Bluebeard hopped across the shop—there wasn't really room for him to fly—and looked quizzically at our visitor. He cocked his head one way, then another, then dipped it as though nodding.

"Sylvester."

Sly's eyes widened, and he looked at me. I shrugged. "He never forgets a face," I said by way of explanation. I knew I would have to explain about Bluebeard and Uncle Louis—the circle of people who knew was growing quickly—but not in front of Shiloh. Not if I could avoid it.

Sly must have seen something in my expression, because he just nodded at me. "Quite a talent. I ain't been in here in pro'ly thirty years."

I smiled at him, sure he could see the relief on my face. As the group headed to find Julie, I held back a minute, and Sly waited with me.

"I can explain," I said. "But I don't want to tell everyone."

"Thought so," Sly answered. "How about you bring me some more doughnuts next week? 'Sides, Bobo's been missing you."

"Deal."

"Thanks. We better be getting back there, see how Julie's doing."

Predictably, Julie was in tears, leaning on her mother's shoulder. Ernie and Felipe had already rolled out a pale pink area rug, and Jake was helping them lug in the crib parts from their van.

Linda and Shiloh disappeared out the back door and reappeared a minute later with packages that had been stashed in the warehouse area at The Grog Shop.

While Julie struggled to regain control, the crew set to work. Ernie and Felipe brought in so many pieces of furniture and so many decorations, I could hardly believe their van had held it all.

Jake and Sly set to work assembling the crib as soon as the pieces were inside. Next came a small dresser. Linda and Shiloh enlisted my help to unpack all the tiny clothes and blankets they'd brought over and stack them carefully in the drawers.

A changing table appeared, along with an enormous supply of diapers. "That should take care of the first week," Anita said to the stunned Julie. I tried not to stare. How could one tiny infant need that many diapers in just a week? Obviously, I had a lot to learn.

We filled the drawers of the changing table with diapers and put sheets on the mattress of the now-assembled crib.

As we worked, I stole occasional glances at Julie. She had stopped weeping, although she still looked like she was in shock. At one point she seemed a bit uneasy, but she leaned against her mother and seemed to relax again.

The room came together more quickly than I had imagined possible. In just a few minutes we had transformed the tiny alcove into a miniature nursery, ready for the arrival of its part-time resident.

We stepped back to admire our work, and Felipe furrowed his brow. "Of course," he said, "there's something missing."

He ran out the back door as though he had just thought of what he needed, but I don't think any of us believed that for a second.

Especially when he came back with Frank and Cheryl Beauford right behind him, carrying a rocking chair with a big pink bow. "I know your mama made sure you had a proper rocker at home," Frank said, "but we all wanted to make sure you had one here, too. This is from me and Cheryl, and from all the crew at the store."

He stopped for a minute as Julie burst into a new bout of tears. She quickly regained her composure, and he continued: "You just be sure you don't get too comfy over here. We want you back at the store, just as soon as you're ready."

Chapter 14

ELEVEN PEOPLE MADE A HUGE CROWD FOR THE small nursery, but we were almost as big a crowd upstairs, as Julie's party moved to my apartment. Frank and Cheryl begged off, saying they had plans, but the rest of us trooped up to my place.

We hadn't planned it that way, but it just seemed natural to invite everyone to come up. Ernie immediately started rummaging through my cupboards. He stacked ingredients on the counter and dug into the refrigerator. Within minutes he had a package of ground beef browning in a soup kettle with garlic and onions.

Julie sat on the sofa with her mother next to her, smiling but still looking a little shell-shocked.

I was kind of stunned myself. I had to admit, I was amazed at how quickly the nursery had come together.

A happy buzz of conversation filled the living room as I joined Ernie in the kitchen. "What're you up to?"

"Vegetable soup. Want to give me a hand with biscuits?"

"Sure." I pushed up the long sleeves of my T-shirt and pulled my hair up into a knot. I washed my hands and started measuring dry ingredients.

Ernie poured a can of vegetable juice into the pot with the beef, then added water and seasonings from my spice rack.

The doorbell at the back door rang. Felipe glanced at Ernie and me, busy with the cooking. "I'll go," Felipe said, heading downstairs.

He returned a minute later with Karen. She caught my eye from across the room. It was clear she had more news, but she shook her head, an almost invisible gesture that told me whatever it was would have to wait.

I finished mixing the biscuits, then rolled and cut them.

Ernie turned to me. "I'll put them in the oven when it's time. Go play hostess."

I nodded, leaving dinner to Ernie for the moment. Julie was still sitting on the couch with Anita, but she looked tired and uneasy.

"I think we're going to go," Anita said. "Julie needs to get home and get some rest."

"Are you sure?" I said. "Ernie's cooking."

Julie nodded without speaking. Her mother stood and offered her a hand to help her up from the sofa. Julie wrapped her arms around me, her stomach pushed against mine, her head on my shoulder.

"Thank you," she whispered. "For everything."

"You're welcome," I answered. I walked her downstairs to let her and her mom out the front door. When we came in the shop, Bluebeard whistled softly. "Pretty girl," he said.

Julie chuckled, but she cut the laughter short. Her face tightened, and both her mother and I reacted immediately.

"Are you okay?" we asked, nearly in unison.

"Yeah," she answered, her voice shaky. "A cramp is all. I just need to get home and lie down."

I shooed her out the door with her mom, who wrapped an arm around her daughter and led her to the car. Assured she was in good hands, I returned to my guests.

The impromptu party showed no signs of slowing down, even though the guest of honor had departed. Felipe was helping Ernie in the kitchen, adding frozen vegetables and potatoes to the boiling broth. The oven beeped when it reached the proper temperature, and Ernie slid the tray of biscuits in.

Within a couple minutes, the aromas of baking biscuits and simmering soup filled the small apartment. My stomach growled, reminding me I hadn't eaten since midmorning.

I would be quite happy when dinner was ready.

Karen and I stood to one side watching the activity in the single room that composed most of my apartment. Shiloh, Linda, Jake, and Sly sat around the low chest I used as a coffee table, deep in conversation. I wondered what they were talking about.

"Betting on when the baby's coming," Karen said in answer to the question I hadn't asked. "Sly insists it'll be Tuesday morning, but Linda says he's wrong, that she won't last that long. They've been arguing for ten minutes, with Jake just sitting back and watching."

She turned to look at me. "Speaking of Jake," she said,

lowering her voice, "was that the most awkward double date in the history of the world, or what?"

"Since it wasn't a date, I don't think it can be a double date, can it?" I countered, dodging her question. On an awkward scale of one to ten, I'd call it about a twelve, but that wasn't what she was really getting at. "Unless *you* were on a date?"

She shook her head. "I don't think any interaction with an ex-spouse can be described as a date. Period. But we were talking about you, not me. And if that wasn't a date, what was it?"

I felt my face turning red at the memory of the previous night. "I need to turn on the fan," I said as I turned toward the kitchen. "This many people and all the cooking is making it way too warm."

Karen followed me. "This conversation isn't over," she said. "We'll talk after dinner."

I switched on the exhaust fan, as though that had been my entire goal. "Whatever." I hoped I sounded a lot calmer than I felt.

I took soup bowls out of the cupboard and handed them to Karen. Over the years, I had accumulated a collection of unmatched pottery that went with my mismatched kitchen chairs and farmhouse table. One of the perks of running Southern Treasures was choosing pieces from the store to use myself. I had to resist a lot of temptation, since I needed to sell the things I bought, and the limited cupboard space in my apartment helped. Every time I brought in something new, I had to take a piece downstairs and sell it. It made me very choosy.

When the biscuits came out of the oven, Felipe piled

them on a platter and put them on the table with butter and honey.

"It's soup," he called over the hum of conversation.

Shiloh hesitated, and Sly nodded at her. "My mama told me to respect my elders," she said with a shy smile. Sly was probably old enough to be her grandfather.

"And my mama always said 'Ladies first.' So you and Miz Miller go on ahead. Me and Jake will be along in a minute."

Linda stood up and grinned at Sly. "If Ernie's cooking," she said, "you don't have to ask me twice. Come on, Shiloh."

They each grabbed a bowl. Ernie ladled the steaming soup directly from the pot on the stove, and the two women took seats at the table. Sly followed them with Jake right behind.

Ernie and I were the last two to get our food, and the table was already full. Jake jumped up, offering me his seat, but I gestured at him to sit back down.

"You're a guest," I said. "And no proper hostess would ever have a guest eat standing up while she sits. It's just not done."

"And letting a lady eat standing up is?" Sly said, sliding his chair away from the table.

"Sit!" I said, imitating the command Sly used with Bobo when the junkyard dog got too rambunctious.

Sly's face split into a grin as he recognized the tone. "Yes, ma'am," he said, planting himself back in the chair.

I pulled out the old wooden breadboard above the silverware drawer, creating a makeshift table. Ernie dragged a couple folding chairs in off the tiny deck, and we sat down.

The surface was too tall, and the chairs too short, but it really didn't matter. The joy was in the company and the food, not the furniture, and I was glad of the respite from the worry over Bobby. I let myself relax, savoring the warmth and friendship that filled my small home.

Linda finished eating and cleared her dishes, stacking them on the counter next to the sink. "I hate to eat and run, but I have to get back," she said. "I left Guy alone in the shop on a Saturday night, and I've already been gone longer than I should."

I insisted she take a bowl of soup and a couple biscuits for her husband. If Linda was like a sister, then Guy was an adored older brother. I tried not to imagine how my life might have turned out if it hadn't been for them taking me in when my folks died. It was a frightening prospect, and I owed them more than I could ever hope to repay.

A few minutes later, Shiloh carried her bowl to the counter. "I came straight from work," she said. As the office manager for a car dealership, she worked on the weekend like the rest of us. "I should be getting home, too."

She nodded to Sly. "If you're ready to go?"

"Yep." He picked up his bowl and added it to the stack on the counter. "I best be getting, seeing as how Miss Shiloh is my ride. Besides, Bobo will be anxious for his dinner."

I managed to convince Sly to take some of the soup for lunch the next day. Telling him I would have to come pick up the container clinched the argument.

"Bring that fella of yours with you," he said, nodding toward Jake. "I like talking to him."

I felt myself blush when Sly called Jake my "fella," but I nodded. "If we can find a time that works," I promised.

I walked Sly and Shiloh downstairs. Bluebeard peered out to check on who was coming through the shop. "Night, Sylvester," he called.

"Goodnight, Bluebeard," Sly said. He turned to me, with a look that reminded me I owed him an explanation. "And to you, too. I'll talk to you real soon, y'hear?"

"I promise, Sly." I gave him a quick hug and managed to get the two of them outside before Bluebeard said anything more.

Once the door was closed, I walked across the shop to where Bluebeard had emerged from his cage.

"What are you up to?" I asked, not really expecting an answer. Uncle Louis decided exactly what, when, and to whom Bluebeard spoke. And he didn't answer my questions.

"People don't come back for no reason," he said, as though that made some kind of sense.

I remembered Sly telling me he came back to town after his stint in the army. Just like Uncle Louis, except about twenty years later. I wondered if there was some connection between the two men.

That was all I got out of him. I offered a biscuit, which he took, but he didn't give me anything in return. After a few minutes, Karen called down the stairs to make sure I was okay.

"Just taking care of Bluebeard," I called back. "I'm coming back up right now."

Following my promise, I headed back up the stairs. Bluebeard—well, Uncle Louis—would tell me what he wanted me to hear when he was ready.

And not a minute sooner.

Chapter 15

BACK UPSTAIRS, THE KITCHEN WAS ALREADY SET TO rights. Felipe was up to his elbows in soapy water, and Karen was wiping up the table. Jake was dragging the deck chairs back outside while Ernie was putting away the left-overs.

I moved over to the sink and started drying dishes. Normally I'd just leave them in my miniature dish drainer, but there wasn't room for the dishes from that many people. When Ernie finished putting away the food, he and Jake disappeared downstairs while Karen, Felipe, and I finished the cleanup.

By the time we drained the sink and put away the last of the clean dishes, Jake and Ernie returned with a six-pack of microbrew from The Grog Shop.

"Guy says thanks for the soup," Jake said as he opened

bottles for everyone. "Said it was keeping Linda out of trouble for being gone so long."

We all chuckled, not for one minute believing it. Guy adored his wife, and whatever she did was just fine with him. It helped that she felt the same way. The two of them were like poster children for marriage, and I hoped someday I would find the same kind of devotion and contentment.

I glanced across the room to where Felipe and Ernie had their heads close together in a quiet moment of conversation. Like Guy and Linda, they made good role models.

I accepted a cold bottle from Jake and sank into the corner of the sofa. He sat next to me, close but not too close. Karen sat across from me, her expression saying clearly that Jake was plenty close, and I still owed her an explanation.

After a minute, Ernie and Felipe drifted over and sat down.

It struck me that our regular foursome—Felipe, Ernie, Karen, and me—had become five somewhere in the past few weeks. The ease with which Jake had become part of the group surprised me, since we had been a tight-knit bunch for several years. I was happy and relieved that my friends had taken to Jake so quickly, and he to them.

"Okay, Karen," Felipe said. "You said you had news, and from the look of you it isn't good. So let's hear it and see what we can do about it."

I glanced at Karen. "What have you heard?"

"I asked the guys to stay while you were downstairs. I don't want to have to tell this twice." She slapped her hand on the arm of the chair. "Hell! I don't want to have to tell it once. In fact, I don't know if I'm even supposed to know, much less tell anyone else."

She balled her hands into fists. Now that we were alone, she could set her emotions free. Her face reddened, and her voice rose. "Not that I care what I am, or am not, supposed to know."

Nothing new there. The best reporter at WBBY never put limits on what she wanted to know.

What was new was how visibly angry she was. I couldn't remember the last time I'd seen her like this. Several years ago at least, that was for sure.

She took a long pull on her bottle of beer and drew a couple deep breaths. "Okay. I was late because I was waiting for Riley to get home from visiting Bobby. He got to talk with Bobby about the new charges, and he found out something that changes everything: the diver that was killed was an undercover federal agent. Bobby wasn't sure exactly what they were investigating, or even which agency he was with." She buried her face in her hands.

"There isn't even a word for how bad this is," she said, her voice fading away.

Stunned silence filled the room for several long seconds.

Jake broke the silence. "If we knew what they were looking for," he said, "we might be able to tell which agency. Or vice versa." He looked from me to Karen and back again. "Did Riley tell you anything that might help?"

Karen shook her head. "We did talk about it, though. Bobby wouldn't have been involved with drugs, but he wouldn't have been involved with anything else illegal, either."

"Like we told Ernie and Felipe"—I pointed at the two men—"Bobby was what you could call *risk averse*. Smuggling of any kind was too big a chance for him to take."

"He was really hard-nosed about most drugs," Karen said. "And especially about anyone selling them. Last year one of Riley's hands got in trouble with some local dealers. Got himself beat up. Riley helped him make bail, and kept him on *Ocean Breeze* when the judge agreed to work-release."

"I don't remember hearing anything about this," I said.

"He managed to keep it pretty low-key," Karen replied. "The *News and Times* runs the police log on the back page in tiny type, so the arrest didn't get a lot of attention, and most plea bargains never even get reported."

"But what's that got to do with Bobby?" Jake asked.

"Bobby was against giving the guy another chance, especially if it meant letting him back on the boat. He was afraid the guy might get them all in trouble."

"Which really wasn't his business," Felipe grumbled. "It's his brother's boat, not his."

It was the second time Felipe had made reference to Bobby's pseudo-ownership of Riley's boat. I wondered why that particular fact was stuck in Felipe's craw.

"But Bobby was family," Karen continued, "and Riley listened to him, even if he didn't agree. He compromised by keeping the guy on, but only until he could find another job."

"Was Bobby's attitude common knowledge?" Jake asked. "Seems to me that if it was, he wouldn't have been a likely target for a drug sting."

"I think it was," Karen answered. "But does it even matter? We all know Bobby wasn't involved with smugglers, and we know he didn't kill the guy, whatever agency he was with. The question is: What can we do about it?"

"Is there any chance the police or Feds are still investigating?" I asked. "That they are still looking for suspects and might find the right guy?"

"I doubt it," Ernie said. "Once they decide they have the right person, the investigation shifts from finding out who did it to finding evidence to support their charges. If Bobby's been charged, they think they have the right guy, and they aren't looking for anyone else."

"Just like when they think it's an accident, even when it isn't," Felipe said, referring to Kevin Stanley.

"Unless they believe he had accomplices," Jake added. "How about the other two guys who were arrested with him? Are they Feds too?"

"Nobody knows who they are," Karen answered. She set her empty beer bottle on the table. "They all made bail, but nobody seems to think they're involved with the death of the agent."

I shook my head. "That makes no sense. The three of them recruited Bobby to take them diving. Unless all three were agents, wouldn't it be just as likely that one of the other two did it?"

"It does seem that way," Jake agreed. "But who knows what's in the heads of the investigators?"

The conversation continued in the same circles for a while, with none of us able to come up with an answer we liked.

Felipe and Ernie left, saying they had to be at the shop early in the morning. One of their best customers was in town, and she was coming by to pick up several pricey antiques before heading back home.

That left me with Karen and Jake. Karen kept looking

back and forth between me and Jake, as though she could conjure up answers to her questions just by staring.

Jake levered himself out of the couch and stretched. "I better be getting home, too. Thanks for letting me help. It was nice to be part of something good."

He turned to Karen. "I really hope things turn out all right for your brother-in-law. If there's anything I can do, please don't hesitate to ask."

I started to get up, but he waved me back down. It was clear he'd had another vision for the end of the evening, but it could wait. "Stay here. I'll let myself out and lock the door behind me. Just don't forget to set the alarm."

I nodded. "I'll talk to you tomorrow," I said as he headed down the stairs.

I heard the bell sound over the front door as Jake let himself out. Bluebeard's squawk of annoyance—his standard response whenever his sleep was disturbed—followed.

Karen looked beat. Fatigue and stress had taken the color out of her face, and she seemed smaller and more fragile than just a few days before. She looked defeated.

I picked up a blanket and draped it around her shoulders. "You need to sleep," I told her.

"I need to get home," she replied.

I shook my head. "First, I know you won't *go* home. Second, you look too beat to drive anywhere, even just from here to your house. And third, I still want to know what's up with you and Riley and, in your weakened condition, I might even get an answer."

Karen took a deep breath that turned into a jaw-cracking yawn. "That couch is starting to look pretty enticing," she admitted. "But they're expecting me . . ." Her voice trailed off as another yawn seized her.

"By *they* I assume you mean Riley." Her wordless glare told me I was right. "I'll call him and tell him you're staying here." I picked up the empty beer bottles and carried them into the kitchen.

I opened the refrigerator and fished out the last bottle, twisting the cap off as I walked back into the living room, and handed it to Karen. "I'll go get you some clean pajamas," I said. "Then we'll talk."

I came back in a couple minutes with a clean T-shirt and pajama pants. Setting them on the couch, I went downstairs to check the locks and the alarm.

For once, Bluebeard didn't squawk at me for interrupting his sleep.

Chapter 16

AFTER I CALLED RILEY, KAREN FINALLY RELENTED and changed her clothes. In spite of her protests, there was a faint hint of relief in her acceptance of the situation. Unfortunately, it didn't stop her from grilling me about Jake once she was settled on the other end of the sofa.

I finally had to admit there was something between us. "I really don't know what it is yet," I explained. "But we are maybe a little more than friends. Maybe. A little." I shrugged. "But what about you and Riley? It seems like this is more than just you helping him out with Bobby's problem."

Karen sighed. "I don't know. Honestly, I really haven't a clue. Don't look at me like that! Some days I think maybe we should be together, then I think not. And sometimes I change my mind three or four times in a day. It's like being in junior high all over again."

"Well, if you decide not," I kidded her, "Megan Moretti's back in town. Maybe she'll make another play for him, just like we really were back in junior high."

Karen picked up the pillow from the sofa and feigned throwing it at me. "You don't really think so, do you? From what you and Jake said, it sounds like she was actually pretty upset over Bobby."

"She was. She wanted to go yell at Boomer, and she kept insisting that Bobby didn't know the guys, that he hadn't done anything wrong."

Karen circled back to our previous discussion. "I sure wish I knew who the other two guys were." She sat up, her reporter's instincts boosting her energy. "They've been arraigned, so their names should be on the record." She tapped her forehead as she realized what she had said. "Where did you put my bag? I need to look this up."

I signaled her to stay where she was and went into the bedroom to retrieve her shoulder bag. She never went anywhere without that bag, which always seemed to contain whatever she needed. It was like a magic purse from a fantasy story, except many times larger, since, unlike a magic purse, this one had to follow the laws of physics.

It also weighed about a million pounds. Or at least that's what it felt like when I lifted it.

"Are you lugging around anvils?" I asked her when I carried the bag in and set it on the floor next to her.

"No. Just stuff I might need. My phone, my tablet, a change of shoes, my digital recorder. You know, just the necessities."

Karen's definition of *necessity* was far different from mine. On the other hand, she carried her job around with her all the time. I left mine in the shop.

Karen pulled her tablet computer out of her bag and connected to my wireless. The password was already saved to
the machine, and within a few seconds she was busily tapping in commands and sifting through data, looking for the
information we needed.

As I watched, Karen seemed to get a burst of energy
from doing the work she loved. To most people, Karen's
talent was her ability on the air, but most people didn't know
how hard she worked to research and develop her stories.
She was very good, and it helped that she'd spent several
years developing contacts all over the state.

Within minutes she was copying information into a file
and cross-referencing the names.

"Charles 'Chuck' Irving and Frederick 'Freddy'
Davis," she said a couple minutes later. "Same local address for both. Bail was set at forty K, just like Bobby's bail
after it was reduced, and all three divers were released
just before Bobby was." She shrugged. "Maybe the Feds
wanted them out, hoping they'd lead them to the rest of the
gang."

"What about the third guy?" I asked. "Did you find the
name of the agent? Or anything about him?"

"I'm working on it."

She frowned at the screen and tapped on the display,
swiping her fingers across the screen and muttering to
herself. It was a process I was used to when Karen started
getting into a story. She turned a hundred percent of her
considerable smarts and tenacity to the problem and shut
out the rest of the world.

I got up and put on the kettle for tea. It could be *another*
long night.

"I don't know why I didn't think to do this sooner,"

Karen said as she continued going from one resource to another. "I know how to find this stuff."

"You had other things on your mind. You were so wrapped up in the family drama, you didn't have any brain-power left for anything else." I thought about it for a min-ute. "You put all your effort into finding a lawyer and helping raise the bail money. Is it any wonder you didn't do this sooner?"

"But you'd think I'd do the one thing I'm really good at," she said. "Instead I was doing a bunch of stuff that anybody could have done."

"But they really couldn't," I pointed out. "Nobody was thinking straight. I mean, I saw Riley let you push him around and tell him what to do. Not just once, either. He wouldn't even let you do that when you were married."

The kettle whistled, and I escaped before Karen could argue the point. I fiddled with the teapot, heating it with the boiling water while I measured the loose tea.

I drained the pot and set it next to the bubbling kettle, bringing the pot to the water. I added the loose tea and then slowly poured boiling water over the leaves.

Memaw had insisted a good southern lady had to know how to brew a proper pot of tea. She wouldn't approve of my using tea bags when I made sweet tea, but at least I knew the right way to do things when I wanted to.

I was bracing myself for Karen's argument when some-thing she had said finally sank in. I turned and looked at her.

"Those two guys had the same *local* address?"

"Yeah," she said without looking up, clearly immersed in whatever she was doing. "So what?"

"*Local* address?" I repeated. "Megan said they wanted

to dive because it was the last day of their vacation. So why would they have a local address if they were on vacation?"

"A seasonal rental," Karen suggested. "Or the address of their hotel." But she stopped what she was doing and looked at her notes. With a few keystrokes she brought up another web page. And immediately started to sound like Bluebeard.

I went to look over her shoulder at what was on her tablet, and immediately saw what had made her swear. The local address was a massive apartment complex just outside of Pensacola.

"So," I said, "not a seasonal rental."

"Not by a long shot. Dammit! I should have looked sooner."

I patted Karen's shoulder and went to get her a cup of tea. She was on the trail now, and there was no way I was going to get her to rest anytime soon.

She kept up the search for another half hour as I sat and sipped my tea and wondered about Irving and Davis. They had an apartment near Pensacola, which meant they had been around the area for a while. If they were smugglers, it didn't seem likely that Bobby was the first person they'd approached.

In fact, the longer I thought about it, the less sense that made. And why make the approach in Mermaid's Grotto? They should have known the local crews hung out at The Tank.

"I wonder who else they tried to recruit."

Karen jerked her head up. "What?"

I didn't realize I'd even said it out loud until she reacted. "I wonder who else they tried to recruit," I repeated. "If they were here long enough to have a local address, they must have tried to get some of the other local captains or crews, don't you think?"

"Probably," Karen said. "And I know how to find out. What time do you open the store in the morning?"

"This time of year? Ten o'clock on a Sunday. But what does that have to do with this?"

"Because you and I are going to do some digging before you open tomorrow. If these guys did try to get another captain or crew in on their scheme, somebody will know about it. And we went to school with half the Keyhole Bay fleet."

She set aside her tablet, and pulled the blanket up to her chin. "You better get to bed, Glory. We need to get down to the docks early in the morning."

I thought about pointing out that she had been the one keeping us up with her research. Instead I just nodded and went to bed. Morning would come far too early.

WHICH IT DID. THE SKY WAS STILL GRAY WHEN I woke to the smell of strong coffee. With a groan I rolled out of bed and wrapped a heavy robe around me before I staggered to the kitchen.

I found Karen up, showered and dressed, ready to face the day. Me? Not so much.

After a shower and an actual sunrise, I was about ready. As I drank a third cup of coffee, I checked the bay from my windows. The boats were all still at the dock, but there was a good deal of activity as the captains and crews readied for the opening of the season in another couple days.

With a sigh I drained my cup and put it next to the sink.

"I suppose we better get going, since I still have to come back and work all day."

Karen ignored my whining and slung her bag over her shoulder. "Can you drive?" she asked. "Riley has my car."

"Really? Then how did you get here?"

"He dropped me off. I was going to call him to pick me up, but then you insisted I stay over."

I didn't quite remember it that way, but she also hadn't mentioned she wasn't driving when I suggested she stay.

"You say you don't know what your thing with Riley is, and then you let him take your car? Seems pretty serious to me."

Karen didn't answer; she just started down the stairs as though there were nothing to say.

I did a quick check of the apartment, then followed her down. She was in the shop tending to Bluebeard when I reached the bottom of the stairs. She knew his routine almost as well as I did. His water was fresh, and she was giving him a shredded-wheat biscuit treat from the can under his perch.

"Pretty girl," Bluebeard cooed at her.

I shook my head and went to disable the alarm. I followed Karen out the back door into my tiny parking area and reset the alarm.

The Civic started on the first try. It didn't always, but Roy, my mechanic at Fowler's Auto Sales, kept it running as cheaply as he could. It still needed work, but as long as I didn't go too far it was okay. Still, I was going to have to replace it one of these days, and I dreaded the expense.

It felt as though everyone else in Keyhole Bay was still in bed until we reached the bay. I parked the car in the fisherman's gravel lot a couple blocks up the hill, and we walked back past the empty blacktop lots that would fill with tourists in a couple hours.

The sharp tang of ocean tickled my nose. I could smell it from my apartment when the windows were open, but this close to the bay the smell grew stronger with each step.

As we passed the empty lots, Karen shot me a puzzled look. "Really, Martine? You couldn't have parked a little closer?"

It took me a second to realize what I had done. I laughed. "Force of habit. I'm never down here this early, so I always park in the locals' lot with the crews. Never even thought about the lots down here being empty."

We reached the bay front and passed the empty departure points for the local excursion boats. Canopies shaded simple benches where tour guides conducted safety lectures and youngsters sold sunscreen and bottled water from pushcarts to forgetful tourists.

There were only a few slips—most of the tour business was in Pensacola—and they were deserted at this hour. Later, as the sun climbed into the morning sky, the visitors would come looking for a little adventure, out into the bay or up the river that fed into Keyhole Bay from the north.

We walked down the docks, past the public fishing pier where a couple early morning anglers, their poles resting on the rail alongside steaming coffee cups, stared out across the bay.

Their languid poses reminded me of what Memaw used to say when my grandfather would return empty-handed after a morning visit to the docks. "They call it fishin', Glory, not catchin'. It's the fishin' that counts."

It took a long time—years after they had both passed

away—before I understood what she meant, but looking at the two silent men staring at the calm water of the bay and drinking their coffee explained it better than I ever could with words.

I followed behind Karen, wondering if she had a plan. If she did, she hadn't told me.

We passed *Eastwind*, and Cliff Noble waved from the deck. We waved back. He'd been a year ahead of us in school, in the same class as Riley. He'd taken over as captain last year when his father retired, but I'd heard the old man had had trouble letting go. Which I guess was true, since just then his dad popped up out of the hold and issued a string of orders. So much for Cliff taking command.

Next to *Eastwind* was *Terry's Treasure*, and just past her was an empty slip. It was where *Ocean Breeze* would be docked under normal circumstances. But now the slip sat vacant, the coils of mooring ropes and piles of fenders a haunting reminder of the boat that belonged in that slip.

At the next berth, Karen stopped and waved at Barton Grover, the captain of *Excelsior*. Barton—no one ever called him Bart—hopped down and met us on the dock. A year behind us at Keyhole Bay High (Go, Buccaneers!), Barton still had a soft spot for Karen, his high school crush, even though there was now a Mrs. Barton and three little Grovers.

Karen gave Barton a friendly hug, just as though she had never known how crazy he was over her. Believe me, she knew. I mean, there was a reason we stopped at *Excelsior* and not one of the other boats that lined the docks.

"How's Darcie?" Karen asked. "And the little ones?"

"Darcie's great." Barton grinned. "Still putting up with me, which probably qualifies her for sainthood. But who are these 'little ones' you mention? Nobody in my house is little anymore." He chuckled. "Don't give me that look. Ellen's a teenager, and the boys are almost there, Freed."

The mention of her last name seemed to bring him up short, and he instinctively glanced toward the empty slip beside his boat. "Damn shame, that," he said with a nod of his head. "We tried to warn him when he renamed her, but even so, he don't deserve this much bad luck."

"Is that all it is?" Karen asked quietly. "Bad luck and superstition? Sure seems like a lot worse than that."

"Bad luck and an idiot brother, maybe."

"But what about the other guys? That's what I don't understand. You'd think they'd look for the dive boats, maybe even some of the little excursions." She shook her head. "Doesn't make sense for them to hire a fishing boat. Especially *Ocean Breeze*. No way they could set her up for a decent dive trip."

Barton glanced over at the deck of *Excelsior*. Several hands were cleaning and stowing gear. At the rail, two older men sat, repairing nets and trying to pretend they weren't listening to our conversation.

"Let's walk," Barton suggested, leading us back up the dock. "I could use a cup of good coffee—I'll be drinking plenty of that swill from the galley in the next few weeks."

He waved to his brother Tommy, who was directing the deckhands. "Going for coffee. Might even find some doughnuts, if you're lucky."

The three of us walked back the way Karen and I had just come. In the few minutes since we'd passed, a couple businesses had their lights on and were getting ready for the day.

At the end of the dock, Barton turned left along the bay

front. "I don't know much," he said as he walked, "but I can tell you, those guys were determined to get a boat, and they didn't much care how they did it."

"So they did try to find another boat," I said. "Did they come in The Tank?"

Barton nodded. "They hung out there a couple nights, and I think they actually got something lined up. Not sure about that, though."

He held open the door of a tiny storefront, gesturing us inside Dockside Donuts. The smell hit me first: strong coffee, sugar, and hot oil in equal measure. Behind the counter, a small man in a white uniform with an apron wrapped around his slender frame slid fresh doughnuts onto trays behind the display-case glass.

Barton closed the door behind us as the aromas began to sort themselves out. Caramel, maple, chocolate, apple, cherry; an elaborate array of flavors tempted my nose and set my stomach grumbling.

We'd left the apartment without breakfast, and the smell of the doughnuts was an exquisite form of torture.

I broke first, beating Barton and Karen to the counter. Unable to make up my mind and unwilling to wait while I debated with myself, I solved the problem by ordering a large coffee, and both a maple bar and an apple fritter. I'd worry about the calories later. Much later.

By the time Karen and Barton had their coffee, I was halfway through the maple bar and had decided the fritter would have to go home with me.

Barton picked out a couple dozen doughnuts for his crew, and I noticed Karen made sure her debit card got to the clerk before Barton could reach for his wallet. It was a tactic I'd seen her use before, one that made the other person feel that they owed her something. In Karen's case, that something was almost always information.

We walked back outside, and Barton gestured to a bench on the sidewalk, overlooking the bay. It was early enough we didn't have to worry about displacing the tourists for another half hour or so.

"So, what can you tell us about the divers?" Karen said as soon as we sat down.

Barton didn't look at her. He stared out at the water, the wake of a single departing sport fisher gently rocking the boats moored at the dock.

"The two of them came out here," he said. "They were looking for a boat. Said they was over from Jacksonville, looking to dive Pensacola Bay, and maybe out into the Gulf.

"I pointed them to a couple of the dive boats, but their story didn't set right with me. Why come up here to hire a boat if they wanted to go all the way out into the Gulf?"

"Two guys?" I said. "There were three when they got picked up. Wasn't the other guy with them?"

Barton shook his head without looking my way. "There was just two of them, and they didn't mention a third. I got the feelin' it was only the two of 'em wanting to dive."

"So where did the third guy come from?" Karen asked.

"Don't rightly know," Barton said. "You might try Tim Carpenter at the Dive Center. I thought they'd worked something out with him." He shrugged. "But it don't look like that happened."

"I've heard some stuff about Tim," Karen said. "Heard he plays fast and loose sometimes. You think he'll talk to us?"

"Tell him I'll vouch for you," Barton offered. "Tim cuts corners now and then, but he's not a bad sort. Just don't go mentioning Riley if you can avoid it. Them two don't always see things the same way, if you know what I mean."

"If you mean Riley's Mr. Straight Arrow," I said, "then, yeah, I know what you mean."

"I wouldn't've put it that way, Glory," Barton said. "But you got my drift, for sure."

"How did he get on with Bobby?" I asked. "If we tell him we're trying to help *Bobby*, would that help?"

"It might," he said. "Him and Bobby was drinking buddies down at The Tank. Hell, everybody was Bobby's drinking buddy. The place isn't the same without him."

I didn't point out it had only been a few days since the last time Bobby had been in The Tank. The truth was, I didn't know how much time he'd really spent there since he'd started running off to Mermaid's Grotto to see Megan. It also made me wonder just who all was hanging around The Tank, and if any of Bobby's drinking buddies might have had a reason to want that diver dead.

Just what I needed: more questions without answers.

Chapter 17

WE LEFT BARTON WITH THE BAGS OF DOUGHNUTS and walked back up the hill to my car. I made a show of checking my watch, but Karen wasn't taking the hint.

"We have time, Glory. A quick stop at the Dive Center, that's all. Find out what Tim knows, then you can get home and open the shop."

Unless, of course, Tim Carpenter actually had something useful to say.

TIM WAS JUST UNLOCKING THE FRONT DOOR OF HIS storefront when we pulled up. The Dive Center had an established customer base, so they kept their expenses down by renting a large space a couple blocks from the waterfront. They contracted with boat owners, arranged charters, and dealt in new and used equipment. They weren't the only dive shop around—there were several in and around Pensacola—but this was where Barton had sent the two strangers.

Karen grabbed the bag with my apple fritter off the seat and jumped out while I was still setting the brake. So much for taking the pastry home.

I caught up with her as she followed Tim through the door into the shop. He switched on the lights and flipped over the "Open" sign on the door before he accepted the offering from Karen.

"I just wanted to ask a couple questions," Karen said in her butter-wouldn't-melt voice. She might be a determined and stubborn newshound, but she knew what worked when she wanted something.

Tim was older than us, closer to our parents' ages. He'd bought the Dive Center about fifteen years ago, after spending many years on an oil rig. A little rough around the edges, he used that lack of polish to project the image of a local "character" for the tourists, and to maintain an iron hand when aboard a charter. But he was still susceptible to flattery, a pretty girl, and bribery by apple fritter.

"Well, thank you, missy. What is it I can do for you?"

"I just wanted to talk about those guys who got themselves busted for smuggling. The two who came looking for a dive charter."

Tim took a bite of the fritter. I could see the apple filling, still warm enough to ooze out the sides of the pastry, and smell the warm cinnamon and sugar glaze. He nodded at Karen to go ahead, and licked a crumb of sugar from his fingers.

"We talked to Captain Grover over on the *Excelsior*. He said he steered the guys your way, and you might be able to tell us what they were looking for." She smiled sweetly, and I swear I expected her to bat her eyelashes.

"They came in here." His voice was wary, as though he suspected she were trying to trap him. "They wanted to hire me for a charter, but they didn't have a boat, and I couldn't find one for them."

He gave her a sharp look, his eyes hard and glittering in the leathery folds of his sun-darkened skin. "Something familiar about you, girl." His brow furrowed. "Are you that news gal, the one on the radio?"

"I'm surprised," Karen said. "Most people don't recognize me."

He grinned and preened a little. "Got me a pretty good ear for voices. So you talked to Grover? What did he tell you?" He took another bite of fritter and waited for Karen to continue.

"Not much," Karen admitted with an oh-so-innocent shrug. "Like I said, he told me they were looking for a dive trip and he gave them your name."

She continued for another couple minutes, giving the old man time to finish my pastry and lick his fingers.

"I'm sorry," she said, interrupting her story. "I should have brought you some coffee with that fritter! Where are my manners?"

I nearly hurt myself trying not to roll my eyes.

"No, no. I should have offered you a cup," he said, heading toward the back of the shop. "Just let me get the pot started."

Karen followed him, protesting that she'd already had quite enough coffee. I trailed along behind, trying not to feel like a third wheel.

The shop itself was spacious, with large front windows

letting in the growing morning light. The aisles were wide, with racks of fins and suits hanging in neat rows. Along one wall, an army of tanks waited for adventurous souls to strap them on and explore the bays, rivers, and ocean. I tried to ignore the price tags as I passed the displays.

I had never tried scuba diving. Although I loved the water, the cost of lessons and gear, and the trips that followed, was out of my budget even in the best of times. Instead I snorkeled when the rare opportunity presented itself and swam in the bay or the Gulf when I got the chance.

At the back of the shop, Tim Carpenter was starting an aged and stained coffeemaker. He dumped coffee from a grocery-chain can into the basket, eyeballed it, and added a bit more before shoving the basket into the machine.

"Just a couple minutes," he assured Karen, as though he hadn't heard a word of her protests.

Karen let it drop and went back to her original questions. "Barton—Captain Grover—thought you might have worked something out with the two guys, but he said he heard it fell through."

"Those two were more trouble than they were worth. They came in acting like they owned the place, and wanted the whole world with a fence around it. I told 'em I could get a boat and I'd captain—but they'd have to follow my directions—and we'd need another hand to watch them all the time they were in the water.

"I don't let anybody dive without somebody watching 'em all the damned time. Can't trust some fool tourist not to do something stupid and get in trouble, and I can't rescue him—it's usually a man—and run the boat at the same time.

"I just won't take any chances when somebody's paying me to keep them safe as houses."

And the tourist foots the bill for a deckhand, with Tim skimming a percentage off the top. *Safety concerns* was a much nicer explanation than padding the bill. I had a hunch this was the kind of thing Barton had been talking about when he said Carpenter "cut corners."

"So did you find them a hand?" I asked.

Tim's face twisted into a disgusted expression. "No. Told them I had a guy lined up, but they kept insisting they wanted to find someone on their own. And they did. Came in a day or so later with a guy they claimed was a local, said he knew all the best spots around. Like he knows this place better'n anyone *I* know!" Indignation rang loudly in his voice.

"I've been diving in these waters my entire life. Spent twenty years in the Gulf on a rig and another five in Pensacola. Dived places most people don't know exist, and I know all the best divers in a hundred-mile radius.

"Sure as hell—beggin' your pardon, ma'am—didn't know this guy. I gotta admit, he talked a good game, and he acted like he'd be okay taking orders, but I wasn't sure. Know what I mean? Seemed like he was more used to giving orders than taking them."

Karen nodded. She took the coffee mug Tim thrust at her and gave me a look that told me I better do the same. She didn't want anything distracting him from his story.

"So, where was I?" he said, putting the stained carafe back on the warming tray.

"He looked like he was used to giving orders?" Karen prompted.

"Yeah, yeah. Anyways, like I said, I wasn't so sure he'd take orders, and I won't even untie a boat if I don't think everybody on board knows who's in charge. So I told them I couldn't get a boat, they were all spoken for, and I couldn't help 'em. Pure broke my heart to turn down their money." He pulled a long face. "But I knew good and well that they were going to be more trouble than they were worth."

"Do you know where they went after you turned them down?"

He shook his head. "They hung around The Tank for a day or so, but word got around and nobody wanted to work for them. Don't know how they got hooked up with Bobby Freed." His eyes narrowed, and he stared at Karen. "You're a Freed, aren't you? You related?"

Karen shrugged. "I was married to his brother once. But everybody makes a mistake now and then." Her casual tone was at odds with what I knew, but she was taking Barton's warning seriously.

"I always liked Bobby"—at least that much was the truth—"and I think he's getting a raw deal. The cops decided he was their guy, and they aren't looking very hard, so somebody has to."

Tim's head bobbed in agreement. "Cops can't see past the end of their noses. They decide a guy's guilty, and that's it.

"Good on you for trying to help Bobby."

"Thanks."

Karen gave him a sly smile, hinting they were on the same side when it came to the police. "Is there anything else you remember about those two, or the hand they picked up here in town? I'm guessing you didn't know the guy?"

"Can't say as I did. He looked a little familiar, like I might have seen him in The Tank or around the docks, so he might've been local. I just never met him." A grin split his weathered face. "And if I never met him, he couldn't have been that good a diver."

Karen forced out a chuckle.

I managed a weak smile, but I didn't think we were going to get much more out of Tim, except possibly another cup of really wretched coffee.

I made a show of checking my watch, and feigning a shocked face. "I have got to get to work!"

"She's my ride," Karen said. She grabbed my coffee cup and dumped it in the tiny sink next to the coffee-maker, along with hers. She swished water around in the two cups, disguising how little we'd actually managed to choke down, and upended them in the drying rack on the other side.

As she did, she looked over her shoulder at Tim. "Is there anything else you remember? Anything else you can tell us before we go?"

"Just tell Bobby to stop around, soon as he's out. I owe him a beer for all the trouble I caused."

"*You* caused?" I blurted out. "Seems to me the two guys and their deckhand caused the trouble."

"I shoulda run 'em off. Instead I just told them to go away, and they went and found Bobby, and now look at the mess he's in. I should've made sure they left town and took their trouble somewhere else."

"Don't blame yourself," Karen said. "You couldn't know."

"I could have guessed. Once I knew they weren't the usual run of tourists, that should have been a clue."

Karen stood completely still. I matched her reaction.

Tim looked from me to Karen and back again. "What?"

"You just said they weren't the usual tourists," Karen said. "What did you mean?"

Tim thought about it for a minute. "Not exactly sure why I said that," he answered finally. "Just little things. Driving a rental car, but they had all their own gear. Now how did they get it here? Most tourists, they either drive their own car, or they rent gear—it's too expensive to ship tanks and weight belts and so on.

"And they didn't need a map, or directions. Didn't have a GPS in the car, either. It was like they'd been here enough to know how to get around.

"I don't know if they said so, but I got the idea they were from east of here, maybe all the way out to the coast. But I don't know for sure what made me think that."

"Well." I laughed nervously. "It doesn't take much to figure out how to get around Keyhole Bay. You take the highway east or west, and you follow the bay down to I-10 and Pensacola."

Tim nodded. "You got me there," he said.

I walked toward the front door, eager to get outside. Karen followed a minute later, after thanking Tim once again for his help. As she joined me on the sidewalk, she leaned in close and whispered, "Thanks for the use of the fritter. I should have thought to bring something with me. I owe you one."

We reached the car and I unlocked the door for Karen. "No." I said it before she could open her mouth. I knew she was going to have some insane idea of what we should do next, but I had a shop to run, and I couldn't waste any more of my Sunday morning.

To be fair, I knew we hadn't wasted our time. And I wanted to clear Bobby, too. I just didn't have anyone to cover for me, and I didn't get paid vacation days. Every minute I was away, I could be losing sales. And sales paid the bills.

"After work," she said, as though that were what she intended to say all along. Which I didn't believe for a minute.

"What after work?"

She wrestled with the balky seat belt, finally settling for holding the latch together for the short drive back to my place. "After work we have to go check out that apartment."

"Apartment?" I was already running down the list of things to be done at the store, and I couldn't remember any apartment being mentioned this morning.

"The local address for Chuck and Freddy. We need to see if we can find out anything from their neighbors or the landlord."

"Are you crazy?!?"

I pulled the Civic into the parking space behind the shop and shut off the engine. "Are you out of your mind? They made bail, Freed. That means they'll be around. Do you really think that's a good idea?"

"We'll be careful," she said.

Like that made it all okay!

She jumped out the passenger door and dug her cell phone out of her purse. She jabbed her finger at the screen, and put the phone to her ear, tuning me out.

I unlocked the back door and went inside. She could say whatever she wanted; I wasn't going to "check out" the apartment of two criminals.

Chapter 18

SO WHY WAS I STANDING OUTSIDE A MASSIVE APART-
ment complex at seven o'clock on a Sunday night? I had an
excuse. I was trying to help keep Karen out of trouble.

But what was her excuse?

Apparently she didn't need one.

We'd turned into the main entrance of the complex and
parked in the area reserved for visitors. Nonresidents were
restricted to the front lot, while each apartment cluster had
its own lot with assigned spaces.

Stern warning signs informed us we could be towed
without notice if our vehicle was in an assigned spot. The
Civic was no prize, but it was better than nothing. I made
sure I was parked in a space clearly marked "Visitor."

Karen had confirmed the building and unit number on the
court records before we left the house. I didn't ask her if it
was a public record. I was pretty sure I didn't want to know.

It took us a few minutes to figure out the arrangement of the blocks of apartments. Each building had a
street number, but the numbers were discreetly hidden behind lush plantings. The streets themselves meandered
through the complex, with plenty of cul-de-sacs and dead
ends.

After a few minutes of walking around pretending
we knew where we were, we realized the street names were
alphabetical. We easily located Keel, one block over from
Jetty, and spied a building number.

The unit we wanted was another block down, but once
we understood the layout it was easy to find.

The building itself was a stacked block of eight apartments, four up and four down. The apartment we wanted
was on the ground floor, its entry door tucked into a semi-
private alcove away from the street.

"Now what?" I asked Karen. "There isn't anything to
see here. Do we go talk to the neighbors? Find the manager
and try to wheedle some information out of him? Knock on
the door and ask why they're trying to frame your brother-
in-law?"

"I'm a reporter," Karen said. "I'm here to ask them some
questions, let them get their side of the story out." She
smiled. It reminded me of a shark. "You'd be amazed what
people will tell me, if they think I'll put their version on
the air."

"And what am I doing here?"

"You're my assistant," she said, as though that explained
everything.

"And you expect them to *believe* that?"

"They will. Trust me."

I wasn't so sure, but I let her confidence carry me along as we walked up the concrete path to the door.

Karen rang the bell. We listened to the chime echo through the apartment, but there were no footsteps, and no one answered the door.

She rang again with the same result, and knocked on the door, calling out, "Mr. Irving? Mr. Davis?"

A young Hispanic woman came down the stairs from one of the second floor units. As she passed us, she nodded. "I don't think they're home," she said. "I haven't heard anything all day." She made a disgusted face. "Usually they're playing their music really loud, while my baby is trying to sleep. I asked them to turn it down, but they're not so nice about it. But today it's quiet all day, and Roberto got a really good nap."

"Thanks," Karen said. "I'll just leave them a note." She made a show of pulling a pad and pen out of her bag as the woman walked away with a wave.

Once we were alone again, Karen tried the bell one more time. When she was sure there was no answer, she jotted her name and number on a sheet of paper.

"It's worth a shot," she said.

She tried to stuff the note into the doorjamb, but the door was loose in the frame and the note wouldn't stay put. Karen jammed it in the space and tried to pull the door tighter.

The knob turned in her hand, and the door swung open.

"Hello?" Karen called softly. "Anyone home?"

No answer.

Karen looked back at me, then pushed the door farther open, and called again.

No answer.

Convinced there was no one in the apartment, she pushed the door wide and stepped inside, motioning me to follow her in.

I shook my head, but she waved insistently. "Hurry up," she hissed, "before someone sees us."

I glared at her, but I followed her in, and she closed and locked the door behind me, stuffing the note back in her bag.

The stink of stale cigarette smoke assaulted my nose, and I stifled a sneeze. *Unpleasant* was an understatement to describe the stink of smoke and fast-food grease mixed with the faint rubbery smell from the dive gear.

"You mean someone like that woman who talked to us?" I asked. "Someone who might, I don't know, *remember* two women at the door of the apartment when no one was home?"

"She doesn't like these two, and she won't be going out of her way to tell them anything. We're fine." Karen dismissed my concerns as she prowled through the living room–kitchen area. "We won't be long," she promised.

Somehow, I wasn't reassured.

"What are we looking for?" I asked, wandering aimlessly through the cluttered space. A sound system with giant speakers dominated one wall of the living room. There wasn't much furniture, just a battered secondhand sofa and a couple rickety-looking stools standing near the kitchen counter, but the space was crammed with diving gear and trash. From the looks of it, the two men lived on fast food and take-out Chinese.

Karen flipped through a stack of papers piled on the kitchen counter, shaking her head. "Junk mail." She put the stack back where she found it.

I looked at the mound of diving gear. It was the only clean, organized thing in the apartment, as far as I could see. Leaning closer, I noticed identification tags on several of the pieces.

"Karen."

She glanced up from where she was rummaging through papers. "What?"

"Come look at this." I waved her over.

She looked at the tags I pointed out, then dug into her bag, coming out with her cell phone. She tapped at the screen, pointed the phone at the tags, and snapped several pictures of each one.

Satisfied, she went back to looking through papers.

My heart pounded so loudly, I was sure the neighbors could hear it. We didn't know how long the two would be gone, and I was sure they wouldn't take kindly to our invasion of their space.

"Can we go?" I whispered. "What if they come back?"

"One minute," Karen said. "I just need to see if there's anything else that might help me figure out what's going on."

I felt like I wanted to throw up. If these two were responsible for what had happened to Bobby, I didn't want to be here when they got back.

Just as the thought entered my mind, I heard a car door slam outside, and voices coming up the walkway from the parking area.

Frantic, I looked for a place to hide, but there was no place in the living room.

I made a hissing sound at Karen and scurried down the hall toward the back of the apartment.

She followed me, and we crouched at the end of the narrow space, next to a closed door that I suspected led to a bedroom. Given the state of the living room, I didn't want to open the door. But there might be a back way out, or even a window, and I would do it if I had to.

The voices came closer, and I held my breath. Beside me I could hear Karen's breathing stop, and I knew she was holding hers, too.

I heard the sound of keys rattling, and then a door opening.

On the other side of the alcove.

A neighbor.

Adrenaline washed through me, leaving me shaky and unable to stand up for a moment.

When I finally got to my feet I turned to Karen. Her eyes were wide, and I knew she had been as scared as I was.

"Can we go *now*?" I asked.

Chapter 19

NOTHING WITH KAREN WAS QUITE THAT EASY.

We waited several minutes while the neighbors came and went, taking things in and out of their apartment. Each passing minute brought us closer to the time when Irving and Davis would return and sent my pulse racing.

Karen, unable to stand still, turned the doorknob and looked into the bedroom. I took a deep breath and looked over her shoulder.

The room was messy, with clothes strewn around, left wherever they had fallen. It smelled of unwashed socks and cheap body spray. A bare mattress filled the center of the room, with two rumpled sleeping bags on top of it.

On the far side of the room, covered by dun-colored drapes, was a set of sliding glass doors. The sun had set, but it was still light out, and a sliver of light shone through the gap where the drapes hadn't been closed tightly.

A closet, its sliding doors shoved to one side, covered another wall. On the floor of the closet, two suitcases stood open, their contents spilling across the carpet as though someone had dug through looking for clean clothes, and just left the unwanted items wherever they landed.

Karen started to back out of the room when we heard a key in the lock of the front door.

I shoved her in front of me and managed to get the bedroom door closed silently before the front door opened.

From the living room, two deep male voices floated down the hallway. They were discussing their dinner, which I gathered from their conversation consisted of burgers and fries from a fast food chain a couple blocks away.

Within seconds their voices were drowned out by the thumping of a bass guitar and the wail of a woman's voice bemoaning the loss of her man.

Fighting the shakes, I shoved Karen toward the sliding glass doors. It was our only way out, unless we wanted to pass the two residents of the apartment on our way to the front door. Not a good idea.

The slider was latched.

Karen ducked inside the drapes.

She managed to throw the latch and shove the door a few inches before it jammed against the broomstick in the track with a loud *clunk*.

I reached down and grabbed the stick, pulling it out of the track.

I wasn't worried about making noise any longer. If the clunking sound hadn't been covered by the heavy thump of the music, they'd heard the door and they would be coming down the hall right this second.

Now all I wanted was to get out of the apartment without getting caught.

I ran out the door after Karen, pulling it shut behind me. It wouldn't slow the two men down much, but it was all I could do.

I turned around and realized we were in a tiny enclosed courtyard, a few square feet of bare concrete and scrub grass surrounded by a six-foot tall wooden fence.

Karen had already made an instant assessment of our predicament and decided on a course of action. She was busy prying back a loose board at one corner of the fence. The opening looked too small for a full-grown woman, but it's amazing what you can accomplish with the proper motivation. Namely, when two men you're sure are criminals—and who have good reason to be angry at you—are chasing you.

Karen and I squeezed through the fence, not caring what or who was on the other side. I pushed the fence board back in place.

From inside the fence I heard a man's voice, one of the two we'd heard inside the apartment. "Chuck, did you leave this slider open again? Dammit, I told you to be more careful!"

The other voice, higher pitched and more nasal, responded, "I swear, Freddy, I latched it, and I put the stick in. No way I left the place open with all our gear inside."

I fought back the urge to laugh out loud. Yes, he had locked the slider to the completely fenced yard, and put the broomstick in the track.

He'd just left the front door unlocked instead.

Karen and I started back toward the car on shaky legs.

My breath came in little panting gasps, and I didn't speak, for fear my voice would come out as a squeak rather than actual words.

The farther we got from the apartment, the more I relaxed. My legs stopped shaking, and my breathing evened out. We had made it out of the apartment without being seen, we were almost back to the car, and Karen had taken several dozen pictures that we could scour for clues later.

"Did you find your friends?"

Karen froze and I nearly ran into her. On the sidewalk just a few yards from our car, a laundry basket propped on one hip, was the woman from the upstairs apartment.

"They didn't get back," I said, shaking my head. "We waited around a few minutes, but I need to get home. We left them a note."

Karen recovered enough to join in. "Maybe when I see them I can mention the thing about the stereo."

The woman's eyes widened, and she looked like she was afraid of the men. "Oh no. You don't need to do that," she said hastily. "I don't want to be a bad neighbor. It's not that big a thing. Really."

She hefted the laundry basket. "My sister gave me some clothes for the baby," she explained, her words running together in a nervous rush. "Her little one outgrew them. I need to go put them away . . ." The rush of words trailed off as she took a wide berth around us and headed back the way we came.

"Really, Freed?" I said, unlocking the doors of the Civic. "Did you have to say that?"

"You saw her," Karen glanced over her shoulder at the retreating back of the small woman. "She won't say a word to those two, for sure."

"Well . . ." I slid into the driver's seat and started the engine. It coughed and sputtered but reluctantly came to life. "You still scared her. It wasn't very nice."

"And if she told those two about us? How nice would that be?"

I backed out of the parking space and looked back at the woman carrying the basket. She was walking away, but she stopped to cast an apprehensive glance over her shoulder before she hurried on.

She was probably memorizing my license plate.

"Tell me again why we had to take my car?"

"Hey, you're the big investigator," Karen said. "I'm just a reporter. Besides, Riley's using my car to take his family to visit Bobby."

"His family has plenty of cars." I turned out of the apartment complex and headed back toward Keyhole Bay. Now that we had some distance between us and Charlie and Freddy, the whole thing began to feel like a foolish juvenile prank.

What did we think we were going to accomplish?

IT WAS GETTING DARK BY THE TIME I PARKED THE Civic behind the shop and unlocked the back door. Karen followed me into the front while I checked on Bluebeard.

He'd been busy while we were gone. A stack of T-shirts had been knocked to the floor, and one was unfolded on top of the mess. On the front of the shirt, a treasure chest spilled its contents across a sandy ocean floor.

"Bluebeard!"

He stuck his colorful head out of his cage and gave me a beady-eyed stare. "Trying to #^*^&$% sleep here!"

I crossed the room to his cage and returned the stare. "Don't give me that baloney, Bluebeard. You tore up the shop while I was gone. Why?"

He refused to look at me, craning his neck to look past me to where Karen was refolding the shirts and putting them back on the shelves in their proper order.

"Sunken treasure!" Bluebeard said, as though that explained everything. "Nasty pirates!"

"Not you, too! I know Jake didn't want the pirate thing in the window, but it's only for a couple weeks. You know that."

"Nasty pirates," he said again, before retreating into his cage. From the dark recess I heard a muttered "Trying to #^*^&$% sleep."

I didn't believe it. Bluebeard wasn't given to commenting on my marketing choices, or my decorating skills. When he chose to leave me a clue, there was usually a more important message than disapproval of a store display.

Besides the shirts, a row of snow globes had been shoved around and one had toppled over into a basket of shell bracelets on the shelf below, and several pockets of postcards had been emptied onto the floor.

I picked up the snow globe and checked the dome for leaks before putting it back on the shelf. It took a minute to re-sort the rows so I could get the tiny scuba diver with a treasure chest back into his proper place.

Now I was certain Bluebeard was trying to tell me something. I just had to figure out what.

"I guess he knew where we'd gone," I said to Karen, showing her the displaced globe. "That's the one he took off the shelf."

She helped me pick up the postcards and sort through

them, looking for an explanation to why Bluebeard had chosen those particular ones.

There were shots of the Gulf, impossibly blue water full of beautiful yachts and tall-masted sailing ships. There was a peg-legged cartoon pirate with a parrot on his shoulder and a treasure chest at his foot. A word balloon warned the recipient to "Keep yer hands off mah treasure!"

Nothing that I hadn't already figured out. Pirates and underwater treasure. The exact thing I'd set up to promote Southern Treasures to the spring break crowd. It felt like there had to be more to Bluebeard's selection, but I was suddenly mentally and physically exhausted from our near miss at the apartment complex.

"Sorry you don't like it," I said as I put the merchandise back in place. "But you like your treats, and there won't be many of them without the tourists, so too bad for you."

I turned out the downstairs lights, leaving the faint night-lights to keep the shop dimly lit.

Upstairs, Karen sat at the kitchen table while I rooted around in the refrigerator for some dinner. I found leftover soup from the previous night that I put on to reheat. There weren't any biscuits left, so I dragged out a frying pan and started water heating for fried cornbread.

Karen spread her gadgets out on the table and started transferring pictures from her phone to her tablet. Occasionally she would go "Hmmm," or "Huh?" but for the most part we were quiet while we worked.

I put shortening in the frying pan to heat and poured boiling water over self-rising cornmeal to make the cornbread. I stirred the cornmeal mixture and set it aside to cool enough to handle while I checked the soup.

The pot was getting warm, but the soup would need a

few more minutes. While I waited for various temperature-related adjustments, I put plates, bowls, and spoons on the table.

As I did, I glanced over Karen's shoulder to see how she was progressing. She had several folders open and was sorting through the pictures she'd taken, putting them into logical groups. At least I assumed they were logical. This was Karen, and she was approaching this the way she would a work project, so I thought it was a safe assumption.

The phone rang, and I picked it up, carrying the handset back into the kitchen with me to keep an eye on the food.

"Hi," Jake's voice was warm and friendly. "I saw the light on a few minutes ago and thought I'd check in and see how you're doing."

"Uh, fine," I answered. After the day I'd had with Karen, I wasn't sure, but it didn't seem like the time to go into it. "Are you still at the store?"

He laughed. "Guilty as charged. Just finished doing the orders for next week and getting ready to head out. Have you had dinner yet?"

The question slipped into the conversation so casually, I didn't think before I responded. "I was just heating up some leftovers, actually. There's a ton of soup left from last night. You want some?"

"Sure."

At the same time I heard Jake's quick response, Karen yelped at me from the table. I shrugged and waved my hand at her in a gesture that said "What was I supposed to do?"

"Karen's here," I said into the phone. "I should have warned you before you said yes." I made a face at her.

"Are you sure it's okay?" Jake asked. "I mean, I don't want to intrude if you two are busy with something."

He had no clue how right he was, but I wasn't about to admit it. "No, nothing important," I lied. "Just come on over when you're through. One of us will come down and let you in."

As soon as I disconnected, Karen pounced. "He's coming for dinner?"

"Yes." I started forming the cornbread dough into flattened balls for frying. "I'm sorry if that bothers you. Really, I am. I just said it without thinking about what we were doing—"

My apology was interrupted by Karen's ringing laughter. "You are so busted! This is, what? Three nights in a row? Let me see." She started counting on her fingers. "There was dinner on Friday, before you met with me and Riley, then he was here with the remodeling crew last night and was the last person to leave, and now again tonight?"

She shook her finger at me. "I'd say that definitely qualifies Jake as being in the boyfriend category."

I turned back to the stove and checked the temperature of the oil in the frying pan. It was hot. I put the first batch of cornbread in the pan, listening to the sizzle as hot oil met wet cornmeal. I watched the edges begin to crisp and turn light gold before I turned the discs over in the oil.

"I don't know what it is," I said. I knew I sounded defensive, but I was still so unsure of where I stood with Jake. It certainly felt like boyfriend territory to me, but what did I have to judge by? Maybe we were just friends with potential.

I had emptied the frying pan and put in another batch of cornbread when the bell rang downstairs. I looked over at Karen, who waved me back to my cooking. "I'll go let your boyfriend in," she said.

"Not my boyfriend," I muttered, turning the second batch of cornbread. But even I wasn't convinced by my argument.

Karen returned in a couple minutes with Jake.

"Bluebeard had to cuss us out." Jake laughed as he came in the kitchen. He slipped his arm around my shoulders and gave me a quick squeeze.

"Anything I can do to help?" He filched a hot piece of cornbread from the plate next to the stove and blew on it before taking a careful bite.

"You could stop stealing the food before I can get it on the table," I answered. I avoided the temptation to rap his knuckles my spatula.

"Yes, ma'am."

Karen, in the meantime, had put another place setting on the table. She slid her work to one end and set three places for us at the other end.

A few minutes later we all sat down with steaming bowls of Ernie's soup and a plate heaped with small golden rounds of fried cornbread.

My stomach growled loudly, and I realized I'd been running all day on the maple bar I'd had at the crack of dawn, a couple pots of black coffee, and an apple I'd shared with Bluebeard early in the afternoon.

"I did interrupt something, didn't I?" Jake said, looking at the stack of Karen's gear. "Sorry."

"Don't worry about it," Karen said. She turned to me. "You might as well tell him, Martine. You will eventually."

I opened my mouth to protest, but she silenced me with a look. "You know you will."

Jake looked at me and back to Karen, a question in his eyes. He knew he'd stepped into the middle of something.

"Are you sure?" I asked Karen.

She shrugged. "He's heard all the rest, hasn't he? And after the message from Bluebeard tonight . . ."

Jake's eyes narrowed. "Message from Bluebeard? What did he say this time?"

"Besides 'Trying to #^*^&$% sleep,' you mean?"

He helped himself to another piece of cornbread and nodded at me to continue.

"Actually, I think it's your fault," I said. "He said something about 'sunken treasure' and 'nasty pirates.' He seemed to be upset about something to do with pirates and treasure. You haven't been talking to him about the front window display, have you?"

"No. I don't make a habit of talking to Bluebeard." He broke the cornbread into small pieces on his plate, avoiding my gaze. "But you don't really believe it's about the window, do you? There's more to this story."

I took a spoonful of soup, stalling my confession. But Jake could outwait me, as I was discovering. I swallowed my soup and started talking.

I told Jake about visiting the docks before daylight, about talking to Barton Grover and Tim Carpenter at the Dive Center. He listened carefully, a quick grin appearing when I confirmed our suspicions that the divers had tried to recruit other boats.

"So they caught up with Bobby at Mermaid's Grotto and roped him in by talking to him in front of a girl he was trying to impress," Jake said when I told him what Carpenter had mentioned about everybody at The Tank turning them down.

"That," Karen said, "and the chance to pocket a wad of cash. And, I have to admit, Bobby likes to feel like he's helping someone out. If he thought he could get all three at once, he was a perfect target."

We ate in silence for a couple minutes as Jake digested what we'd told him. He cleaned his bowl and nibbled at the crumbs of his cornbread. Finally, he looked up at me and caught me watching him.

"So," he said, watching me closely, "what's the rest of the story?"

Chapter 20

I SIGHED AND LOOKED AT KAREN. "CAN I PLEAD THE Fifth on this one?"

"You could," she said. "But I don't think it will do you much good."

"You do know I'm sitting right here?" Jake said. There was a hint of amusement in his voice. "I just want to point out that I can hear every word you say, which has two results: first, it tells me that there *is* something more to this story, and second, it makes me even more curious."

His voice sobered, and he went on. "But if there is seriously something you don't want to tell me, I can respect that. You'll tell me when you're ready."

Karen used one of Bluebeard's favorite words and reached for her tablet. "Just remember we gave you the chance not to know this part," she said. She was only half joking.

She powered up the tablet and started opening folders of photographs.

It was the first time I had seen the pictures. Jake and I both moved around the table and sat on either side of Karen as she slowly displayed each of the shots she had taken.

There were several from our early morning foray to the waterfront, including something I guessed was purely accidental—a view of the docks with *Ocean Breeze*'s empty slip on the right edge of the photo. It was a reminder of why we were doing this.

Karen closed the folder and moved to another one. There were pictures she'd taken in the Dive Center, and I was impressed. She got pictures of the shop without me being aware of what she was doing, and I'd bet Tim Carpenter hadn't noticed either, since he likely would have objected if he had.

There wasn't anything of significance in those photos, and she quickly closed the folder. But they might be useful later.

She had a group of folders for the pictures inside Chuck and Freddy's apartment, but before we started through the photos, we had to explain to Jake how we got them. As Karen and I took turns telling him about our adventures, he went from amused to horrified to disbelieving. "You took a board off the fence?" he asked.

"We didn't take it all the way off," Karen said. "We just pried it up a little more so we could squeeze through the opening."

"We put it back," I added.

Resigned, Jake looked back at the pictures on the screen. "Looks like a lovely place," he said drily. "I can see why you wanted to get in there."

I was tempted to describe the smell, but it wouldn't have helped the situation, so I kept quiet.

"Did you find out anything useful?" he asked. I wasn't sure we were forgiven, but I welcomed the change of topic.

Karen began with the pictures of the scuba gear. The tags on the tanks identified them as rentals belonging to a shop in Jacksonville and listed an address and phone number for their return if found.

She moved on to shots of several pieces of mail forwarded from a Callahan address with a PMB number.

"PMB?" I asked. It was a designation I hadn't seen before.

"Private mailbox," Jake answered. "Not a Post Office Box, but like one of those services where you have your mail sent."

"Why would you do that?" I said. "Why not just get a PO Box?"

"Lots of reasons. There might not be boxes available if the post office is small, or if you travel a lot, the service will forward your mail, or they have better hours, or if you get a lot of packages." He shrugged. "It doesn't necessarily mean anything."

"So their gear was rented," Karen said. "Their mail was being forwarded by a mailbox service. They were living out of suitcases, and they didn't have much furniture. Looks like they weren't intending to stay very long."

"Makes me wonder how long they'd been here," I said. "If they weren't planning to stay, why rent an apartment instead of staying at one of those long-term motels?"

"Might be cheaper over a couple months," Jake suggested. "Or maybe this was a temporary place while they worked out what they were doing. Or, given whatever they were up to, it was so nobody paid much attention to them."

"Good idea," Karen said. "Even at those long-term places, there are housekeepers and clerks and the like who keep track of people coming and going. If they didn't want anyone noticing them, an apartment in a gigantic complex is a lot more anonymous." She beamed at Jake like he was a prize pupil. "I bet you're right about that."

Something was bothering me, niggling at the back of my brain. "There's something else," I said. "I'm not exactly sure what, but there's *something*."

"That's very helpful." Sarcasm tinged Karen's voice.

"No, I know it isn't helpful," I said. "But I feel like there's some connection here that we're missing. Something I heard somewhere in the past few days that relates to what we found in that apartment.

"Besides the trash and the neighbors," I added.

"Neighbors?" Jake said.

I told him about Karen trying to terrify the poor woman who lived upstairs. "I think she was trying to memorize my license plate," I joked. "In case we showed up on one of those 'most wanted' television shows."

"I really think she's afraid of those guys." Karen repeated what she'd said earlier. "I haven't seen them, except when they were marched through the police station the night Bobby was arrested, and I really wasn't paying attention. But I don't seem to remember them as looking very friendly."

"They had just been arrested," I reminded her. "Most people wouldn't look very friendly under those circumstances."

"I suppose," she said.

We looked through the rest of the pictures, but there wasn't anything remarkable.

I kept going back to the nagging thought I was missing something while I cleaned up after dinner. Jake helped with the dishes while Karen fiddled with her techie toys. She made copies of the pictures and dumped them on my laptop while I put away the clean dishes and wiped down the frying spatter on the stove.

I stifled a yawn and realized exhaustion was dragging me down. When I looked over at Karen, I could see she felt the same way.

"Are you going back to work tomorrow, Freed?"

She shook her head. "I had about a month of vacation time built up, and I convinced the station manager this would be a good time for me to take it. And really, it's been less than a week."

I stopped and thought back. It was only Sunday, and Bobby had been arrested on Wednesday. Five days.

"I guess you're right," I said. "Sure seems like a lot longer to me. Probably to you, too."

She nodded.

The evening had reached that awkward moment where someone has to be the first to leave, and no one quite knows what to do next. At least I was sure it wouldn't be me, since it was my house.

Karen broke the impasse by reaching for her bag and starting to stow her gadgets.

"Do you want me to drive you home?" I asked.

She shook her head. "Riley said he'd pick me up. Least he can do, since I let him borrow my car." She opened her cell phone and punched speed dial before Jake or I could offer any alternative. Though, to be honest, I was relieved not to go back out; I was really too tired to be driving anywhere.

When she hung up after telling Riley she was ready to go home, I again asked the question that had never been answered. "Just why did Riley need to borrow your car? The Freeds have several cars of their own."

"You want the truth?" She sounded a little sheepish. "You cannot repeat this to anyone."

"What, did you have a convincing lie ready? Really, Freed, this isn't junior high. Do I need to pinkie swear?"

"Just promise you will keep this to yourself. I told Riley I wouldn't tell anyone, but I'm pretty sure he expected me to tell you."

I heard a decided snort as Jake fought back a chuckle at our exchange.

"Okay. I promise. But this had better be good."

"It's about Riley's folks."

I sobered. The older Freeds were lovely people, and Karen loved them like her own family.

"Riley's dad is so freaked out over this thing with Bobby, Riley doesn't want him driving. Doesn't *trust* him to drive. But he can't say that. He can't drive his dad's car without a fight, and he can't fit everyone in his truck. So he took the SUV. He can take the whole family, and he tells them he has to drive since it's my car. Then he tells his dad that he—his dad, not Riley—needs to concentrate on his mom because she's upset."

I tried to imagine the situation Riley was in, but I didn't have anything to compare it to. I'd only ever known my parents as a child, never as an adult, and the idea of taking care of your parents was completely foreign to me.

We made small talk for another couple minutes until Riley arrived to take Karen home. Wherever home was for her at the moment.

Jake and I walked Karen down to the back door, where Riley waited with Karen's SUV idling next to my battered Civic.

Next to her immaculately maintained new vehicle, the Civic looked even more decrepit. I would have to replace it one of these days, but I kept stalling. I had an aversion to car payments and higher insurance rates.

I watched Karen climb into the passenger seat and strap herself in. Riley leaned toward her, but quickly reversed himself. He put the car in gear and pulled away with a wave.

Jake hesitated at the door, as though he were uncertain about coming back in.

"I'm tired, and I do have to work tomorrow," I told him, "but I could use a glass of wine, and I'd be glad to have some company for a little while."

Jake accepted my invitation and followed me back up the stairs to my apartment.

As though by unspoken agreement, the subject of Bobby—as well as the related subjects of the divers, the dead federal agent, breaking into strangers' apartments, and the Tuesday opening of the commercial fishing season—was dropped. Instead, Jake flipped through my collection of DVDs and found a movie while I poured a couple glasses of wine.

I must have dozed off at some point, because I jolted awake as the credits were rolling. Embarrassed, I tried to apologize, but Jake just waved away my protests.

"I just hope you'd already seen the movie, since you slept through the end," he teased. "But now that you're up, I need to be getting home. Tomorrow's a work day."

I yawned, and this time I didn't even try to hide it. I

looked around for my wineglass, but it was already on the counter, along with Jake's.

I gave him a tired smile and followed him downstairs. He went out the back door, and I locked up and set the alarms before heading back upstairs.

Bluebeard, for once, didn't wake up and yell at me about disturbing his sleep.

Chapter 21

A QUIET MONDAY SEEMED LIKE A SPECIAL TREAT after the hectic activity of the weekend. Bluebeard, uncharacteristically subdued, spent most of the day dozing on his perch. I checked in deliveries and restocked shelves, leaving the occasional customer to Julie.

Between customers, Julie returned again and again to the nursery area in the back. She fussed with the arrangement of diapers and blankets, and folded and refolded the stack of tiny shirts and sleepers that filled the drawers of the changing table.

Late in the afternoon, I passed by the alcove on my way to pull more stock from the storeroom and spotted Julie sitting in the rocking chair. Her head rested against the back of the chair, and her eyes were closed, but a frown wrinkled her forehead and drew faint lines at the corners of her eyes.

I almost let her be, thinking she might actually be asleep, but she shifted in the chair and her frown deepened.

"Are you okay?" I asked, moving to her side. "Is something wrong?"

She shook her head without opening her eyes. "Just tired," she said. "I get tired so easy right now. I swear I must sleep about ten hours every night, and I still want to take a nap in the afternoon."

I propped my shoulder against the wall and leaned back. "Well, from what I hear, you better get all the sleep you can before she gets here. Because once she arrives, you won't sleep again for months."

A dry chuckle escaped her lips. "I've heard all the horror stories from my so-called friends," she said. "And not just about sleeping, either. Some of them just couldn't resist telling me about how terrible their pregnancies were, or how painful labor is, or some other horrible thing that like to scare me half to death."

She opened her eyes and looked up at me. "Why do people have to tell you those things? All they do is make you afraid, and it's not like you can do anything about it, anyway." She leaned her head back against the chair. "Doesn't feel very friendly to me."

"I wish I had an answer for that. Some people just don't think before they open their mouths."

"I did get one good piece of advice, though," she went on. "My friend Penny told me to get rid of Jimmy's big ol' truck. She says it'll be a huge pain getting the baby in and out of that thing. Her husband has one, and she hates to go anywhere in it."

"Truth be told," I answered, "I wondered why you didn't

get rid of that thing a long time ago. Owning it always seemed like it was Jimmy's idea, not yours."

"I thought about it, but every time I did it just seemed like such a hassle, and I didn't really want to go to Fowler's. You know how that is."

I nodded. Her ex-husband had worked for Matthew Fowler, the local car dealer, before his arrest. I could understand why she wouldn't want to go there, but there wasn't another car dealer in town.

Trading in the truck would mean taking it down to Pensacola and finding a dealer there to give her a decent price. It was really only a few miles to Pensacola, but sometimes it felt as though it were a world away.

"Maybe I should just sell it to you," she joked. "You could use a truck, couldn't you?"

The image of Jimmy's extra-tall, tricked-out pickup sprang into my brain. "I'd probably need a stepstool just to get in it," I said.

Make that a ladder. At five-seven, I wasn't a tiny woman, but I recalled the truck towering over me.

Julie winced, and closed her eyes for a second.

"Are you *sure* you're okay?"

She nodded without opening her eyes. "Just an occasional cramp. Mom says it may be a little false labor. Nothing to worry about, she says."

Easy for her to say. She didn't have an employee sitting in her shop who just might decide to have a baby at any moment. And like the character in *Gone with the Wind*, I didn't know nothin' 'bout birthing babies.

"You know, it's almost quitting time, Julie. Why don't we call it a day? You can go home early and I can close up."

She didn't argue. While she gathered up her purse and sweater, I turned the sign in front from "Open" to "Closed."

I locked the door behind her and set the alarm, watching the two green lights come on to indicate it was armed. I turned down the shop lights and made a last check on Bluebeard.

He was already in his cage and settled in for the night. I gave him a pat and he hopped out onto my arm and snuggled against my chest, his head tucked under my chin. It felt like he was ready for an early night, too.

I had almost reached the stairs when the phone rang. I answered reluctantly, really wishing I could just ignore it.

And immediately wished I had.

"Glory?"

"Hello, Peter."

"I've been thinking," he said. That worried me. Every time Peter started thinking, it meant trouble for me.

"Yes?" I said, warily.

"About what we discussed last week?"

I racked my brain. So much had happened in the past few days, I barely remembered last week, much less my conversation with Peter. Of course, I did my best not to remember conversations with Peter. It was better for my blood pressure that way.

"Go on," I said, stalling. I hoped he would say something specific that would tell me what he wanted.

"Well, I was thinking about the website, and how you said you didn't have time to do it."

"That wasn't what I said, Peter. I said I was doing what I knew how to do, and I needed time to learn to do more. Did you even look at the site?"

"Of course!" His indignation came clearly across the phone. "You don't need to take that tone with me."

He sounded so much like Aunt Missy, I expected him to add "young lady," just as his mother had when I was a young girl and she didn't approve of my behavior.

Which was most of the time. I had never been enough of a lady to satisfy her.

I drew a deep breath but didn't reply.

After a few seconds of silence, Peter continued.

"Well, I've been looking into getting some help in that department, and I think I have a solution. There's a guy down in Pensacola. He comes very highly recommended, and his rates are quite reasonable. I've been talking with him, and looking at some of the sites he's done. I'm pretty impressed with his work."

I held my bottom lip between my teeth, biting back the words that threatened to tumble out.

"Anyway, he just e-mailed me to say he has an opening. He can come up one day this week to meet with you and see what you need. It'll only take a couple hours for the assessment, and about ten hours for the basic site."

I couldn't bear to hear any more.

"Who's paying for this?" I asked.

"It's a business expense, Glory. A necessary one. We need to get this done, and it's clear you don't have the time to do it." He left unsaid his obvious judgment that I wasn't managing my workload well, and *should* have time.

"And just how much is his 'reasonable' rate, Peter?"

"It's only a hundred an hour, Glory. And he won't even charge for the travel time to come up and meet with you."

One.

Two.

Three.

"And he'll do the maintenance. Said it would only be a couple hours, twice a month, to update everything."

Four.

Five.

Six.

"Oh, and one other thing!" The joy in Peter's voice was palpable, and I could envision him in his excited mode, practically wiggling in his seat. It wasn't a pretty sight.

Seven.

"He said he'd help you establish a social-media presence. Show you how to do all the networking sites and stuff. All part of the standard contract."

Eight nine ten.

"Peter! Stop it! You're talking about at least a thousand dollars to start, and four or five hundred a month to keep this up. And that's before you even start this whole social-media thing. There is no way we can afford it."

"But Glory"—the whine was back, and growing—"we need to do this. And if you don't have time to do it yourself, you need to pay somebody to do it for you. I just found you somebody who can do that."

I stopped myself from using some of Bluebeard's favorite words. "No, Peter, we *don't*. Not unless you are willing to pay for all this out of your share of the profits. We *can't* afford it, and we *won't* afford it, and if you promised this guy anything, you will have to call him, or e-mail him, or send him a social-media message, or whatever you need to do to tell him there is no job here. I will do the best I can, and if that isn't good enough for you, then you figure out another way.

"Good night, Peter."

I hung up the phone and let fly with a string of profanities. I don't swear in front of other people, but it was just me and Bluebeard, and it felt good to let out the anger that welled inside me.

Bluebeard stuck his head out of the cage at the burst of curses and added a few of his own.

"Idiot!" he said quite plainly before stomping back into his cage.

Apparently, Bluebeard shared my opinion of Peter's business abilities.

And buying him out had just moved up my priority list.

Chapter 22

AT FIRST I THOUGHT IT WAS THE CAR ALARM THAT woke me, but as I struggled to consciousness I realized Bluebeard was making an awful racket downstairs.

Not an angry, making-a-mess kind of racket but a frightened, I-need-to-run-away squawking; a noise I'd heard rarely in the past, and never for more than a few seconds.

I flung a robe over the ratty T-shirt and shorts that served as my pajamas and ran for the stairs, stuffing my phone in my pocket.

I grabbed my home-security system—an old wooden baseball bat—as I sprinted down the stairs.

Halfway down, a sobering thought managed to seep into my still-half-asleep brain: whatever was causing Bluebeard's distress was *downstairs*. And I was about to run straight into who-knew-what.

I slowed my feet, though my heart still galloped at a

frantic pace, and tried to listen for any noise besides the squawking of the parrot.

I heard nothing inside, but outside the car alarm continued blaring. It was a common enough sound; people unfamiliar with their rental cars regularly set them off, but they usually weren't this close.

They usually weren't right outside my back door.

And the inside alarm hadn't gone off.

Forcing myself to ignore Bluebeard's cries of distress, I drew a deep breath and tried to take stock of the situation.

No alarm meant one of two things: there was no one inside, or the alarm wasn't set. I concentrated on remembering what happened before I went to bed, struggling with the remnants of sleep that clogged my brain and the adrenaline rush that demanded immediate action.

I'd been angry when I went upstairs because of my phone conversation with Peter. And before talking to Peter, I'd sent Julie home early. No, before talking to Peter I'd checked the locks and set the alarm. I remembered looking at the two green lights just before the phone rang.

Confident I wouldn't meet anyone at the bottom of the stairs, I ran down the rest of the flight. I glanced in the direction of the alarm control box. Two green lights, exactly as I'd left it. It was set and hadn't been tripped.

That left two problems: a squawking parrot and a screaming car alarm. The car alarm could wait. The few neighbors who could hear it would just have to understand.

Setting the baseball bat on the counter, I flipped on the light switch and ran across the shop to Bluebeard. He huddled in the back of his cage, clearly distressed.

At the sight of me he came to the front of the cage, but didn't come out. There was a flash of recognition in his eyes, and an almost-human intelligence, followed by a single, clear word.

"Fire."

I looked around the shop. I had both smoke and carbon monoxide detectors, and I'd just changed the batteries on both. Just like the alarm controls, unblinking green lights assured me there was no problem in the shop.

"Fire," Bluebeard repeated. His fear and panic receded, but his insistence increased. "Nasty pirates. Fire!"

The car alarm continued its rhythmic blaring, and my brain finally cleared enough to assemble the pieces.

Car. Alarm. Fire.

I ran for the back door. Leaving the baseball bat where I'd set it down, I wrenched a fire extinguisher off the wall of the storage area before I opened the door.

Fire boiled in the interior of the Civic. Glass was gone from the windows on the driver's side. Flames licked the empty window frames and curled around the edges toward the roof.

I pulled the pin on the extinguisher and unhooked the nozzle. I didn't want to get too close, but I needed to aim at the base of the flames, as I'd been taught.

I moved a step closer. Heat pushed at me like a giant hand, holding me back. I heard the windows on the far side shatter from the heat, thankful I was out of the path of the flying glass.

A couple loud pops came from inside the car. Something exploding, but I didn't stop to wonder what.

I squeezed the trigger and tried to direct the cloud of chemicals through the window to the source of the flame.

Black smoke was starting to pour from the broken windows, making it difficult to aim the chemical flow.

Not that it mattered. The extinguisher emptied in a matter of seconds, the contents completely inadequate against the growing flames.

I moved back, driven away by the heat and flames. The phone in my pocket bumped against my leg, reminding me it was there.

I dropped the extinguisher, fished out the phone, hit the emergency call button, and waited for the 911 dispatcher to answer.

"Nine-one-one. What is your emergency?"

"My car's on fire!"

"What is your location?" The dispatcher's voice was calm, as though she got these kinds of calls every day. Which she probably did.

I wasn't quite as calm. "Southern Treasures!" I shouted.

"Do you have the address, ma'am?" the unflappable voice asked.

I babbled for a few seconds, then blurted out the street number.

"I've dispatched the fire department," she replied. "Can you tell me about the fire?"

The sound of breaking glass came from the far side of the car as another window shattered.

"It's inside the car," I said. "In the passenger part. Some of the windows were already broken when I found it, and another one just broke. There's a lot of smoke. Really dark, black smoke."

"All right," she said. "Is there anything close to the fire? Anything it might spread to?"

I whipped my head around, looking to see what was close to the car. The trash cans were a few feet from the front bumper, against the wall of the building, but the heat was too intense. I wouldn't be able to move them.

"It's close to the building, and the trash cans are next to it, but I don't think I can get close enough to move them."

"Don't try to," she said. "I just need to tell the crew what to expect. We don't want you to do anything that might get you hurt. Just wait for the fire crew."

I nodded, then was struck by the futility of the gesture. "I understand. I'll wait."

The dispatcher continued talking, asking me questions that barely registered. I think I answered her, but I had no idea what I said.

The smoke grew darker and denser, billowing out the windows in the glow of the flames and disappearing against the darkness of the night sky. The acrid stench of melting plastic stung my nose and brought tears to my eyes.

After minutes that felt like an eternity, I heard the wail of a siren approaching.

"I hear them," I told the dispatcher.

The fire truck turned the corner two blocks away, its strobing lights bathing the parked cars in flashes of red and blue.

The siren cut off abruptly as the truck slowed in the middle of the street behind the flaming Civic.

I looked back at the car just in time to see the front tire catch fire, the flames circling the wheel and disappearing behind the fender.

Four men in heavy turnouts and helmets bolted from the truck. One of them grabbed the nozzle of a hose, pulling it toward the car. Another one manned a valve on the truck.

The men called back and forth as they maneuvered the hose into place. At the first man's signal, the valve opened and water poured onto the flames through the broken-out passenger window.

I heard the hiss of water hitting the flames. Steam billowed out, mixing with the black smoke.

The firefighter played the stream of water over the side of the car, alternating between the front and back windows. The flames fought back, leaping up again as soon as the water stream moved away.

A third man approached the hood and tried to trigger the release, without success. After several tries he took a pry bar to one side of the hood, levering the edge up so his partner could direct the stream of water under the hood.

Steam rolled out from under the hood. The flames retreated from the tires and pulled back from the window frames.

The firefighter continued pouring water into the car from all angles. In the windows. Under the hood. Into the wheel wells. Underneath the car.

The smoke slowed, and steam continued to boil out of the windows, but not as heavily as before.

After several minutes, the flames died down. The water poured into the car from the hose and leaked back out under the doors without turning into steam.

The men visibly relaxed, a signal the fire was under control. The flow to the hose slowed and then stopped.

And I finally got a good look at the destruction the fire had caused.

There wasn't much left of my Civic.

The tires had melted off the rims. All the windows

were broken. The paint had blackened and bubbled, its original color lost under a layer of ashes and a sheen of oily smoke.

Two of the men began winding up the hose, reeling it back onto the truck, and the other two approached me.

As they drew near, I suddenly became aware I was standing behind my shop barefoot, in my pajamas and robe, with a serious case of bedhead.

I straightened my robe, pulling it close around me and tugging the belt tighter. I ran my fingers through my hair, pulling it back from my face and twisting it into a loose knot at the base of my neck.

The first man wore a helmet that identified him as Clark. I assumed it was his last name. Behind him, the other man's helmet read "Robinson."

It took a moment for the name to register.

Robinson. *Jake* Robinson. My neighbor and maybe-kinda boyfriend. And I was standing here in my pajamas.

It made no sense. What was Jake doing in fireman turn-outs, helping put out the fire in my car? I had to be mistaken; it must be some other Robinson.

"Are you okay, Glory?" he asked, concerned.

No, it was Jake all right.

"Uh, yeah. I think so," I replied, brushing a loose strand of hair away from my face. "I'm not hurt."

"This was your car?" Clark asked.

"Yes, sir."

"Can you tell me what happened?"

"As much as I know," I said. I told him a noise woke me up, I came downstairs and found the burning car. I didn't mention that the noise was Bluebeard, or that he'd blamed it on the "nasty pirates."

One, it wouldn't help figure out why my car caught fire. And two, he wouldn't believe me.

I might tell Jake later, in private, since he already knew Bluebeard's secret. Once he explained what he was doing here. But it wasn't something I wanted to put in the middle of the fire investigation.

Clark asked me a few more questions, but I couldn't give him any useful answers. He told me a police officer would be by in the morning to take a report, in case I remembered anything else. After about five minutes, he abandoned me and went to check on the two firefighters who were stowing the hoses and packing up their gear.

Once we were alone, Jake moved in protectively. "Are you sure you're okay?"

"I said I was," I snapped. "But what are you doing here? And why are you wearing that getup?"

"This?" Jake waved at the bulky turnouts. The heavily insulated jacket and baggy-looking pants disguised his lean, muscular build. His helmet hung low, completely covering his dark hair. Only his deep blue eyes below the flipped-up face shield were visible.

"Uh, yeah. That."

Now that the fire was out, I felt a cold predawn breeze swirl against my legs. I shivered and wrapped my arms around me. I tucked my hands inside my sleeves, trying to fend off the chill that ran up my spine.

"I'm not so sure you're okay," Jake said. "I think we need to get you inside where it's warm."

"It was quite warm out here until just a few minutes ago," I joked, but Jake didn't see the humor.

To tell the truth, neither did I, but I wasn't going to give in to the panic that clawed at my throat and roiled my stomach.

Chapter 23

IT TOOK ANOTHER TWENTY MINUTES FOR THE FIRE-fighters to clean up and repack all their gear.

Jake insisted I go inside and get out of the cold and wet while they worked. It didn't take a lot to persuade me.

I checked on Bluebeard and found him in his cage, refusing to come out, even for his favorite shredded-wheat biscuit. He no longer appeared frightened or agitated, but he did seem withdrawn. I decided to let him have some recovery time and went upstairs.

I took an instant shower, letting the hot water warm me and relax the knots in my shoulders, but I didn't linger. I was back downstairs—this time dressed in jeans and a sweatshirt and wearing shoes—before the firefighters finished their work.

I stepped out into my parking area, trying not to look at the blackened wreck that used to be my poor Civic. I carried a fresh pot of coffee and a stack of disposable cups from the stash in the back of the store.

Clark shook his head, but Jake and the other two—their helmets were labeled "Morris" and "Baker"—gladly accepted the steaming cups.

"I have to ride back to the station and pick up my car," Jake said between sips, "but I'll be back in about fifteen minutes to check on you."

"Really, I'll be fine," I protested.

"I'm sure you will," he answered. "But I'm coming back to check anyway."

I started to protest, but I saw the determination in his eyes. It wouldn't do me any good to continue to argue.

"Besides," he said, sensing my hesitation, "you're already showered and dressed. You're not going to get any more sleep tonight, and I thought you might be glad of some company."

When I didn't argue, he headed for the fire truck. "Fifteen minutes," he called back over his shoulder.

I went back inside, locking the door behind me and resetting the alarms. I flipped on one bank of lights, pushing back the darkness in the shop.

I went to check on Bluebeard again and found him sitting in the back corner of his cage, but this time he let me coax him out.

He hopped onto my arm and leaned against my chest with his head tucked under my chin.

I could feel him relax as I stroked his head and fed him bits of shredded-wheat biscuit. I wished I could calm down as easily.

My heart had slowed its racing as the adrenaline drained from my body, but I was still stressed out. Jake was probably right about me needing company; I was still jumping at every noise, and imagining what might be outside in the dark.

"How did you know about the fire?" I asked Bluebeard, not expecting an answer and not getting one.

Frustration built along with the silence. If he knew something—if Uncle Louis knew something—why didn't he tell me?

Questions about Uncle Louis ran circles in my brain, providing a distraction from the imagined monsters outside.

At first I had thought there was something holding him here and once we could fix whatever it was he could move on. That was the way it worked in the movies and on television, after all. But now I knew, because he'd told me, that he didn't want to move on. He wanted to stay in Southern Treasures with me.

I didn't know why he came back to Keyhole Bay after his stint in the army. Didn't know why he never married. Didn't know why he left Peter and me the shop, or why he left me the larger share. Didn't know why he wanted to hang around.

I wanted to know the whys of Uncle Louis's life, but even though I accepted that he lived in the shop, I couldn't get answers from him.

I couldn't stay still. I started pacing through the shop, Bluebeard riding on my arm as I prowled between the displays. Occasionally I'd spot something out of place and put it back where it belonged. But mostly I paced.

I didn't, however, go anywhere near the storeroom. I couldn't bring myself to face the back door or the destruction that lay beyond it.

I started back down the rabbit hole of terrors coming out

of the dark. The image of the smoking remains of the Civic came back to me with an emotional ferocity that hollowed my stomach and made my breath catch.

It had been a close call. Closer than I had let myself realize. If I hadn't woken up. If Bluebeard hadn't screamed for me. If he hadn't told me there was a fire. If I hadn't caught it when I did and called for help.

A dozen or more *if*s screamed in my brain, telling me I had come close to being trapped in an inferno. Just a few more minutes unchecked and the flames could have leaped to the building.

The thought gave me the shakes. Losing the Civic was a nuisance. Losing my business, or my life, would have been a tragic accident.

"It wasn't," Bluebeard said clearly.

"Wasn't what?"

"An accident."

Ice water coursed through my veins. The last time Bluebeard told me something wasn't an accident, I had landed in the middle of a murder investigation.

This time I was already there. It wasn't a comfortable place to be.

"What? How can you say that? How can you answer a question I didn't even ask?"

Bluebeard looked up at me, a steady gaze with that flash of almost-human intelligence.

My frustration boiled over. "This makes no sense! The things I ask, you don't answer. Then you answer a question I didn't ask. Don't you have some rules about what you can and can't do? There must be limits. You can't just go crawling around in my head, listening to my private thoughts and commenting on them."

Bluebeard cocked his head—a quizzical motion, as if he'd never thought about what the rules were. He ruffled his feathers impatiently, as though trying unsuccessfully to shrug off the question.

He hopped from my arm and made his way across the shop to his cage. Retreating to the darkened interior, he settled on his perch, muttering. I couldn't make out most of what he said, but I did catch what sounded like "stinking rules."

Jake tapped gently on the front door, and I let him in.

"I'm really okay," I said before he could speak. "But you were right, sleep is out of the question."

I turned the lights off and checked the alarms—again—before leading the way upstairs. Jake settled on the sofa, and I dropped into an overstuffed chair. I pulled up my knees and wrapped my arms around a pillow like a comforting teddy bear.

Jake opened his mouth, but I didn't want to talk about what happened. I didn't want to be reminded of what I was going to have to face when daylight came.

"You still haven't answered my question," I said, deflecting his comment. "What were you doing on that truck, wearing a fireman's outfit?"

"Being a volunteer fireman," he answered, as though that explained everything.

A volunteer firefighter? That took months of training and testing. It wasn't something you just decided to do on a random Monday night.

"Since when?" I thought we were getting closer, close enough that I trusted him with the truth about Bluebeard. And he hadn't told me about something as simple as joining the local volunteer department?

"Since just before Christmas. I didn't want to say anything to anybody until I passed my exams."

His voice cracked with emotion, and he stopped to draw a deep breath. I wondered why he reacted so strongly, but before I could ask, he continued.

"I wanted to tell you, really. But I didn't want to look like an idiot if I didn't pass the exams."

I shook my head. "Jake, the department needs every able body they can recruit. They'd make sure you got through the exams."

He sat up straighter, shocked. "I didn't want to pass that way."

"No, no, no. I didn't mean anything underhanded. The good ol' boys might cut corners, but not when it comes to the department. On that score they're as serious as a heart attack. I just meant they'd get someone to coach you, or study with you, or whatever it took to get you ready for the exam."

"Oh," Jake said, mollified. "It's just, you know, you've talked about some of the stuff that goes on around here."

Embarrassed that he'd jumped to a wrong conclusion, he was anxious to move on.

"Anyway, I got my certificate on Saturday, and I was waiting for a chance to tell you."

"But things have been a little hectic," I said, letting him off the hook. For now.

He grinned with relief. "Well, I hadn't planned to tell you by showing up at your place in my turnouts."

A shiver ran through me at the reminder of what had happened.

"You don't look okay," Jake said, getting up from the sofa and moving over to crouch down at my side.

"I'm fine for a while, then it hits me," I confessed. "If I hadn't woken up when I did . . ." I shivered again, and Jake put a protective arm around my shoulders.

It felt strange, letting him comfort me. Strange, and dangerous. I was used to being very independent, to taking care of myself, and I'd learned the hard way how easy it is to lose the people you depend on.

I rested my head against his arm, but I couldn't look at him. Instead, I stared out the window toward the bay, where the first faint light of dawn was turning the black sky to deep gray.

Soon the sun would rise and I would have to face the day. There would be the mess to clean up and the hulk to dispose of. I'd have to call my insurance agent, and think about replacing the Civic.

For now, though, I pushed all that aside and just watched the sky lighten toward morning. The rest would come soon enough.

Chapter 24

"WOULD YOU LIKE SOME BREAKFAST?"

Jake shifted slightly, his arm still around my shoulders. He'd knelt on the floor next to my chair for a long time, long enough for the sky to turn from dark gray to pale gray to mauve with streaks of pink and gold. Sunrise was still nearly an hour away, but the promise of a new day grazed the horizon.

I hadn't thought about food until he mentioned it, but as soon as he did, my stomach growled. Loudly.

"I guess so," I said with an embarrassed laugh.

"Then how about letting Keyhole Bay's newest firefighter take you out?"

He stood up and I marveled at how easily he got back to his feet after so long on his knees on the hard floor. He held out his hand to me, and I took it, letting him pull me out of my chair and into his arms.

He hugged me, whispering close to my ear, "You'll get through this. And I'm here to help."

He released me, but kept hold of my hand. "Let's go eat."

His car was at the curb out front, so I didn't have to look at my poor Civic. That could wait a little longer.

He didn't ask where I wanted to go, just drove to Coast Café, uphill from the docks. It was the only place open this early, catering to the fishermen needing a hot meal before heading out for the day. The place was packed, and I realized with a jolt that the commercial fishing season opened this morning. For everyone except Riley and *Ocean Breeze*.

I spotted Barton Grover at a round table with several other captains, swapping lies and talking trash about the coming season. He caught my eye and waved a greeting.

As we passed their table on the way to the counter—the only empty seats in the tiny place—he raised his chin and said, "Hey."

"Hey," I answered.

"You tell Riley he better get his butt in gear, because I plan to kick it all over the Gulf."

It was as close to concern as I was likely to hear in the testosterone-drenched atmosphere, but I knew what he meant. He was thinking about Riley and hoping for the best, and would I please pass that along?

"I'll do that."

I moved on, sliding onto an empty red-vinyl stool at the scarred linoleum counter. Jake turned just in time to see a skinny young man slide onto the remaining empty stool next to me.

He glared at the kid, who paled beneath his gaze. "Just

getting something to go," he told Jake. "I'll be gone before you know it."

Jake retreated a step, standing behind me with one hand on my shoulder. He leaned down, and said softly, "Too late. I already know he's here."

I looked over my shoulder to find him grinning at me.

A sixtysomething woman with an untidy bun of gray hair and reading glasses on a chain handed me a menu. She raised her eyebrows without speaking, and waved the coffeepot at me.

I nodded.

She switched her gaze to my companion, and I watched the transformation come over her as she got the full impact of Jake's blue eyes and megawatt smile.

"Coffee?" she cooed.

She filled two once-white pottery mugs, their sides stained from countless cups of the strong, black brew. She reached past me to hand a mug to Jake before putting one on the counter in front of me.

"Darren!" she snapped at the young man next to me. "Where are your manners? You get yourself off that stool and let the gentleman sit down, 'fore I have to tell your mama!"

She turned away, muttering about "no respect," much the way Bluebeard muttered about, well, everything. I felt a smile tickle the corners of my mouth, but I had to admit she had a point. The boy, probably still in his teens and working his first season, had been raised to respect his elders, and that included surrendering the last stool at the lunch counter.

No matter that Jake wasn't that old—north of forty I guessed, but not far. Nor did it matter that he was in good shape, a fact I could attest to, having seen him haul heavy boxes of books, wrestle crib parts into submission, and tromp around a fire scene in heavy turnouts.

None of that mattered. Jake was older than Darren, and the waitress knew his mama. He got up and offered the stool to Jake.

Jake started to refuse, gesturing at the boy to sit back down. I tapped on his arm, and when he turned to look at me I shook my head once, back and forth.

He sat.

Once he was at my level, I leaned over and explained the intricacies of southern manners regarding one's elders.

"But I'm not old," Jake argued.

"Maybe I shouldn't expect a Yankee to understand," I said. "But around here we are raised to respect our elders, even when the difference is slight. And from that kid's point of view"—I glanced over to where Darren hovered by the cash register, waiting for his order—"you're ancient."

Jake frowned.

"He's probably eighteen, maybe nineteen. Anyone over thirty has one foot in the grave." I grinned, trying to soften the blow. "Sorry, old man. I feel the same way when Julie calls me 'Miss Glory.'"

A line was forming at the cash register as the fishermen finished a final cup of coffee and headed out to start the day.

I wasn't sure about the details—how early they could cast their lines, or spread their nets, or whatever—and I was sure there were other boats that were already on the water. But the sun would be above the horizon soon, and these boats and crews would head out to find the day's catch.

I ordered eggs and bacon and fried potatoes with gravy. Jake gave me a questioning look, then doubled the order.

"Trust me," I said as the waitress stuck the ticket on a stainless steel spinner and turned it toward the cook on the other side of the pass-through. "You're gonna love it."

After his first few bites, he had to admit I was right.

I felt better after a meal and several cups of coffee. It was hard to stay depressed when I was full of crisp, smoky bacon, and fried potatoes with perfectly seasoned gravy. The attentive company didn't hurt, either.

Once we were back in the car, Jake put the key in the ignition, but he didn't start the engine. Instead, he turned to look at me, his expression serious.

"Before I take you home, there's something you need to know. I didn't want to tell you before, but you'll find out soon enough, anyway."

I didn't like the sound of this. My stomach tightened, and I clenched my hands into fists to control them from shaking.

"The captain, Clark, doesn't think that fire looked accidental. He's going to be out there himself, first thing this morning, with an investigation team."

I couldn't control the hysterical laughter that welled up from inside me.

Jake's stricken look instantly quenched the laughter.

I patted his arm in what I hoped was a reassuring gesture. "Sorry. Didn't mean to scare you."

"I'm not scared, just puzzled. It's not the reaction I expect when I tell someone their car was deliberately torched."

"You were so scared. It was all over your face. You thought you were trapped in a car with a woman who had just gone over the edge. And have you had a lot of experience telling people their cars were 'deliberately torched?'"

"Okay. Maybe I was concerned. But there was nothing to be scared of." He didn't answer my question, an omission I was coming to expect from him where his past was concerned.

Actually, it told me more than he realized. He didn't laugh off the comment or admit it wasn't something he'd done often. He completely avoided the subject.

Which meant I'd hit on something. I would have to come back to the topic of torching cars later.

"All right," I conceded. "I didn't mean to *concern* you. But Bluebeard already told me it wasn't an accident. And when you said the captain didn't think it was accidental, well, I had this mental image of Bluebeard in a fire helmet, saying, 'It wasn't an accident.' And somehow that was the funniest thing I had pictured in ages."

"I can see where that might make you laugh," Jake said, although he didn't sound convinced.

"Maybe you have to have lived with Bluebeard and his antics for a few years." I shrugged. "Anyway, I'm really not surprised. After all, this isn't the first time he's said something like that."

"You mean the time he told you about Kevin."

"Yeah. Except this time I'm already involved with a murder investigation."

Jake started the engine and put the car in gear. Without taking his eyes off the road, he asked, "Do you think a murder investigation is a very smart place to be?"

He turned onto the highway, heading back toward Southern Treasures. "I mean, the captain just thinks the fire was arson. He'll probably ask you about insurance and what was wrong with the car."

"He'll what?" I asked, indignant.

"Lots of car fires are insurance arsons, Glory. It's the first thing they're going to think of. Then they'll ask if you had an argument or a problem with anyone recently. I doubt you're going to tell them about poking your nose into Bobby's problems or breaking into those two guys' apartment. But I know it, and I would bet you a year's worth of lattes one of those things had something to do with the fire."

"We just asked some questions, as Bobby's friends. And we didn't break in," I said. "The door was open. We just walked in and took a look around." Even to me it sounded like a weak defense.

"Doesn't matter, Glory, and you know it. You went in that apartment without permission. And how many other places have you gone poking around? You were all over the docks. You went off for a private meeting with Captain Grover. You questioned the guy at the dive shop.

"Everybody in this town knows you, or Karen, or both. They know where your shop is, and what car you drive, and where it's parked.

"And any one of them could get back in his own bed in ten minutes, hardly long enough to even be missed."

He pulled his car down a side street in back of Beach Books and parked in the tiny municipal lot just off the highway.

"You definitely upset someone, Glory. I just want you to be careful." He shut off the engine and turned toward me, concern digging furrows around his mouth and clouding his blue eyes. "I don't want you to get hurt."

"Well, since I can't go anywhere unless I walk, I don't think I'll be doing too much investigating."

Jake conceded my point.

We crossed the parking lot to the highway, just a few steps from Jake's front door.

"Thanks for keeping me company," I said. "And thanks for breakfast."

He reminded me that the fire crew would be back to look at the fire scene behind the store. "If you want me, I'll be right here all day. And if you need to go somewhere, just give me a shout. I'll be glad to play chauffeur."

"Thanks. I'm sure I'll be fine, but I appreciate the offer."

I checked the traffic, still light this early in the morning, and crossed the street to Southern Treasures, letting myself in the front door.

I checked Bluebeard and started a pot of coffee. Julie was scheduled to arrive in a couple of hours, but for the moment I had the place to myself.

I was deep into catching up on paperwork when Linda burst through the front door.

"Glory! What happened to your car? Have you seen what's out there? There's a whole brigade of firemen out back, crawling all over!"

She reached the counter and pulled me into a big hug, patting my back like I was five years old again. "Are you okay, girl? You didn't get hurt, did you?"

"One question at a time," I said, disentangling myself. "There was a fire, and the firemen are investigating. It started in the middle of the night, I woke up, went out and found it, and called nine-one-one."

"And you?"

"Didn't get close enough to get hurt. I'm just fine, Linda. Really, I am."

Her relieved smile was like the sun coming out from behind a cloud. But it faded quickly, as she scolded me. "You like to scared me to death, Gloryanna Martine! What was I supposed to think when I pull up and there's your sweet little car burned to bits? And you're nowhere to be found!"

"You could have called me."

"I did! About a thousand times. And you didn't answer a single time. Not here and not on your cell phone, either."

She was close to tears, and I realized her anger was just a mask for the fear she'd felt when she couldn't reach me.

I reached for my purse under the counter and dug through it, searching for a cell phone that wasn't there. As if to taunt me, I heard the faint sound of the ringer from my storage area. I must have put it down after calling for help and just left it there.

I followed the ringing and found the phone sitting on a shelf next to a box of T-shirts. I checked the call log on my way back to Linda, and saw the evidence of what she'd said. There must have been a dozen or more missed calls, some just a few minutes apart, over the past couple of hours.

"You weren't here that early, were you?" The first call had come in about the time Jake and I had gone to breakfast.

"Early delivery. The distributors are swamped with orders; everybody's stocking up for spring break. Guy took the crack-of-dawn shift last time, so this was my turn."

I apologized probably a hundred times as I told her the story of the fire and Jake coming back to check on me and taking me to breakfast.

"Coast Café?" she guessed.

"Is there anywhere else at zero-dark-thirty?"

She shrugged. "I suppose you could have gone down to Pensacola, to one of those twenty-four-hour places."

"I don't think either one of us wanted to go very far away."

I poured a couple cups of coffee, thinking I'd already had enough to last me the rest of the week, and Linda kept me company while I waited for Julie.

We were discussing the coming spring break crowds when the phone rang.

It was Anita Nelson. Julie's labor pains were no longer false; she and Stan were taking Julie to the hospital.

I hung up and looked at Linda. "Looks like we're having a baby today."

Chapter 25

I LEARNED ONE THING ABOUT BABIES THAT DAY:
they will do things on their own schedule, and all you can
do is go along with the program.

It was the middle of the afternoon when I checked in
with Anita. Julie was fine, but her daughter was taking her
time.

"It's really only been five hours," Anita said. "It'll be a
while yet. But I promise to call as soon as she's here."

"Thanks. Tell Julie I'm thinking of her."

In the few months Julie had been working for me, she'd
become like family. A little cousin, perhaps, whose company I enjoyed and who I admired.

She had taken some pretty hard knocks last fall, but she
refused to let them keep her down. She picked herself up
and kept going, making the best of a bad situation.

I liked to think we were a lot alike.

I called Jake and gave him the news. Which was that there was no news.

"Did you get ahold of your insurance agent?"

"Yeah. He says I'm covered, as soon as the fire department files their report of the cause of the fire."

"That might take a few days," Jake said. "Do you have loss-of-use coverage?"

That sounded familiar, but I didn't know for sure.

"Check on it, Glory. It'll pay for a rental car while you're waiting for everything to work out."

"I will."

"In the meantime, why don't you let me drive you over to Fowler's? You can get a look at what's on the lot. It'll be easier to get away now than it will on the weekend—or next week, in the middle of spring break."

I hesitated for a microsecond before agreeing to his plan. I'd answered Clark's questions, done a pile of paperwork, and cleaned Bluebeard's cage. And the sooner I started the process of buying a new car, the sooner I wouldn't have to rely on other people to get around.

I hadn't heard from Karen all day. I'd tried to call her earlier, but her number just went to voice mail, and I didn't want to tell her about the car in a message. It would have to wait until she called back.

I left another message for her before I locked up the shop.

I stepped outside, stopping to examine the window displays. In spite of Jake's kidding, they had come out well. The fake jewels and bits of costume jewelry glittered against the dark blue fabric I'd used to line the space, and the candlesticks with their drizzles of wax dripping down their sides were the right finishing touch. Sometimes I actually looked like I knew what I was doing.

I ducked into The Lighthouse and waved a greeting to Chloe behind the counter. I ordered two lattes to go and a couple scones. On impulse, I had her bag a few of Pansy's muffins. I'd take them to Sly. Even if I didn't have much time to visit, the muffins should keep me out of trouble. I made sure there was a doggy treat for Bobo, too.

Each time I walked into Beach Books, I was struck by how warm and welcoming it had become. Jake had added chairs in many of the corners, encouraging visitors to linger and explore the books before making their choices.

He explained that he thought it actually helped sales. The longer a customer spent in the store, the more they bought. It made sense, but privately I thought the increased sales might have a lot to do with the knowledgeable and gracious owner. And a killer smile didn't hurt, either.

That smile was on display when I came in the store, directed at a teenage girl with an armload of paperbacks. "There's no school next week," she said as she stacked the books on the counter, "so I need something to read."

Jake eyed the stack as he began scanning the prices. "This ought to keep you busy for a while."

"Only a few days," she said with a touch of pride. "If I don't have homework, I can read a book a day, sometimes more."

"Well then, let's hope for no homework." He took the plastic card she offered and swiped it through the machine.

The girl entered her code, then flashed him an impish smile. "Oh, there is," she said. "But *I'm* already done."

Jake locked the door behind her, still smiling. He turned

to me and cocked his head toward the departing teen. "Now there is a girl after my own heart. An avid reader, and not afraid to admit she's smart. I like smart women."

"How about women who bring coffee?" I teased, handing him a cup, "and scones?" I waved the bag, letting the sweet smell of the cranberry scones tempt him.

"That always gets my attention."

He reached for the bag, but I kept it out of reach. "We have to save some of these for Sly."

Jake groaned with comic exaggeration. "Well, let's get going, then, so I can have at least one of those. The smell is killing me!"

On the short drive to Fowler's, Jake asked me if I had any idea what kind of car I was looking for. I had to admit, I didn't have a clue.

"I've thought about a truck, for the store," I told him. "But I always figured if I had a truck I would still want something small for running around town. Like Ernie's Miata, and Felipe's scooter: something that worked for running errands but didn't use a lot of gas or eat up my tiny parking space.

"Julie even joked that she should sell me Jimmy's truck, but that thing is a monster. Besides, she'll get more for it if she sells it to someone who wants all the tricked-out gear Jimmy put in it."

"I'm amazed she didn't get rid of it immediately."

I explained to him what Julie had said about selling Jimmy's big ol' pickup with all the bells and whistles. As we pulled into the lot at the back of Fowler's Auto, I shared some of her trepidation.

I hadn't been inside the shop since the day I'd discovered who killed Kevin Stanley. I'd gone around the back, to the old junkyard where Sly lives, but I hadn't ventured into the sales area or the repair shop, and I'd have been glad to avoid it for a while longer.

My heart sank when I saw the giant price numbers on the windshields. I had deliberately avoided looking at the price of cars for a long time, and I definitely had a case of sticker shock. A little mental arithmetic told me the payment on one of the cars on the front line would be a budget-buster.

"Ouch!" I said softly to Jake. "Now I remember why I didn't want to buy another car."

"I'm sure we can find something," he answered. "We just need to keep looking."

My unease wasn't helped by the appearance of Joe Fowler, the owner's son.

Matt Fowler was a walking definition of good ol' boy. He, and the men like him, were the primary reason I would never be a member of the Merchants' Association. Although he was only a few years older than Karen and me, we had never moved in the same circles.

His son was trying hard to be just like his father, and it appeared to be working. It wasn't a pretty picture.

Joe stuck out his hand to Jake. "Hi, folks. Joe Fowler, sales manager. How can I help you today?" The question was clearly directed at Jake. As a female, I was just an ornament, and his disinterested glance told me I wasn't doing a very good job of it.

It told me something else about Joe Fowler: he wasn't a very good salesman. A good salesman remembers names and faces, he has a mental contacts file that tells him instantly who someone is and what they need. If you've met a really good salesman, he'll recognize you instantly years later.

Joe didn't recognize me. In spite of spending a lot of time last fall trying to convince me to pour a ton of money into repairing the Civic, he didn't remember me.

"I'm looking for a car," I said, stepping in front of Jake. "Something cheap, that gets decent mileage."

Joe chuckled. "Isn't that what we all want?" He gestured to a back row of the sales lot. "We have a few low-cost vehicles, but we don't keep many of them on our lot. Frankly, most of them wouldn't be worth your hard-earned dollars, and we take them to the auction. But we do have some excellent options that are just a few dollars more. Let me show you."

He spent an annoying half hour trying to convince me I should buy several cars, a two-year-old pickup, and an SUV I knew wouldn't get anywhere near the mileage he claimed.

A pair of young men walked on the lot, and I was finally able to shoo Joe away. Frustrated and miserable, I was ready to go home, crawl in bed, and pull the covers over my head.

"We can go down to Pensacola," Jake offered as we headed back to his car. He glanced at his watch. "I think some of the bigger dealerships will be open late."

I shook my head. Looking at the prices of the cars on Fowler's lot depressed me. Comparing the stickers to the meager balance in my savings account had pointed out just how tenuous my financial situation remained.

Sure, there was my "secret" account, the one I tried not to think about. I'd started tucking away a few bucks from my small salary every payday. It wasn't a rainy-day fund or an emergency account; that was what my regular savings account was for.

This was my Buy-Out-Peter Fund. And I wasn't going to

raid it for something like a car. I'd wait to see how much the insurance paid; I'd get a bicycle or a skateboard before I'd touch that account.

It wasn't money. It was my future. A future without Peter hanging over my shoulder, offering his unwanted and unnecessary advice.

I opened the door to Jake's car and spotted the white-paper bakery bag on my seat. The treats for Sly and Bobo. I'd forgotten them in the misery of looking at cars.

"I'll move the car over there," Jake said, climbing in behind the wheel. "Bobo will cheer you up. Especially if you brought anything he can have."

"I did. How could I come with a bag of goodies and not bring something for Bobo?"

Jake parked next to the chain-link fence at the back of Fowler's service area.

The junkyard, which I had initially thought belonged to Fowler, butted against the parking lot. Just inside the fence was an area the local police used for a secure impound lot. A row of mostly intact cars and small trucks faced the parking lot, grease-pencil markings telling the time and date they had been impounded. Behind them was a row of larger pickups and big trucks parked parallel to the fence, effectively creating a barrier between the vehicles and the actual junkyard.

We got out and walked around to the gate, which was chained but not locked. The padlock that would secure the chain hung open, allowing us to swing the big gate open.

At the sound of the squeaky hinges, Bobo came bounding toward us at a run. When he spotted who we were, he slowed slightly, wiggling in doggy greeting, his tail wagging.

I handed the pastry bag to Jake and crouched down to greet Bobo. I petted his broad head and scratched behind his ears. He was a mutt of the junkyard variety, but I could see clearly the influence of Rottweiler ancestors in his dark coat and large head full of sharp teeth. If you didn't know him, he would look menacing.

We followed Bobo around the row of trucks and past the metal racks of car parts that held Sly's extensive inventory. The shelves, reaching higher than my head, held large pieces of metal, engine blocks, cylinder heads, manifolds, and dozens of smaller parts I couldn't identify. They crowded together in a mystifying jumble that only Sly seemed able to understand.

A small forklift, used to reach the top shelves, blocked our path, and we detoured around it.

That's when I saw the Civic.

I gasped. My knees buckled momentarily, and I grabbed Jake's hand to steady myself.

I knew it was being towed, but I hadn't thought about to where. It made sense it would be here until the insurance company and fire department were through with it.

I just hadn't been prepared to confront it.

"Miss Glory!"

Sly had come out of the cinder-block building where he lived. He caught sight of me and hurried over, trying to put himself between me and the Civic.

I gave him a hug.

Jake wandered over, peering closely at the Civic. It was the first look we'd had in the daylight. The damage was worse than I had imagined, and the stench of burned plastic clung to the wreckage like a heavy blanket.

The tires had melted, leaving the car sitting on the rims.

There was no paint left, just a layer of crumbling black residue. All the windows stood empty, even though I had closed them tightly when I parked it. Headlights and taillights had broken or melted, leaving behind gaping holes.

The interior was worse. Exposed springs showed where the seats had been, stinky black puddles all that remained of the worn vinyl upholstery.

I watched as Jake walked around the car, occasionally poking at a piece of debris with the point of a pencil. He craned his neck through one of the windows, examining the back seat without touching anything.

The hood was buckled where the firefighters had pried it open to reach the fire in the engine compartment. Broken wires jutted from unrecognizable chunks of metal, their insulation melted in the heat of the flames.

It made some kind of sense to Jake, who nodded and made little humming noises every couple minutes. I guessed he'd had a class in fire investigation as part of his training, and he was getting a chance to try out what he'd learned.

At his side, Bobo's attention was riveted on the bakery bag, his sensitive nose quivering in response to the tempting smells coming from the bag.

I took the bag from Jake, digging out one of the doggy-safe treats. "May I?" I asked Sly. He nodded, and I let Bobo see what I had.

"Sit!" I commanded. Sly insisted that Bobo mind his manners, and he'd taught me how to make the big dog behave.

Bobo immediately plopped his hindquarters down in the dust, waiting with high-voltage anticipation for the hard baked, bone-shaped treat. Pansy couldn't let dogs in The

Lighthouse, but she provided water dishes on the sidewalk and canine-friendly items alongside her chocolate muffins and lemon scones.

Like Jake's chairs and my parrot, it was one of the things that made our little downtown shopping strip a friendly place to visit.

"Good boy." I tossed the treat, and he leaped into the air, catching it on the fly. His massive jaws crushed the faux bone, and the pieces quickly disappeared. It was an impressive display and one that made me glad I was a friend. I wouldn't want to be on Bobo's bad side.

I handed the bag to Sly. "There's a couple more Bobo treats, and some of Miss Pansy's muffins for you."

"That's mighty nice of you, Miss Glory. No man in his right mind would turn down anything that came out of Miss Pansy's oven." He peeked in the bag, inhaled deeply, and sighed. "I do believe I could use a muffin this afternoon."

He looked back at me. "But don't think this gets you out of telling me about that parrot. You promised me a story."

"You'll get it," I answered. "But first you need to answer a question for me: just how well *did* you know my Uncle Louis?"

Sly stood motionless for a full minute. He drew a deep breath and looked over at Jake, then back at me. "Y'all better come inside where we can get comfortable."

Chapter 26

THE INSIDE OF SLY'S SMALL HOME WAS NOTHING like I'd expected. That he was close to seventy and a lifelong bachelor created an expectation of dark, mismatched furniture, selected for comfort and functionality rather than decorative potential.

Instead, I found myself in a spacious room that felt like something out of a Caribbean vacation brochure. The rattan settee was covered with cream-colored cushions and littered with pillows in bright hues. Sparkling glass topped the bent-wood tables, and several large plants softened the whitewashed cement block walls.

The layout was a lot like my apartment: The kitchen opened into the living area, with a small dining table in the space between. There were two doors on the far wall, and I was willing to bet they led to a bedroom and bathroom.

A huge grin split Sly's dark face, exposing the gaps where he'd lost teeth. "Not what you were expecting, was it, girl?"

At a loss for answers, I shook my head.

"My daddy was from around here, but my mama came from the Dominican Republic. She worked for a very wealthy American family and came here with them when she was still a young girl. She married my daddy and stayed here the rest of her life, but she always talked about her home." He gestured at the vibrant colors and the lush greenery. "I know this isn't how it really was, not for a poor family. But it still reminds me of my mama."

It was the longest speech I'd ever heard him make. A wave of understanding and regret washed over me.

I had gone in the opposite direction, divesting myself and my home of everything that reminded me of my parents, shunning reminders of my loss. But Sly had embraced his mementos and honored his mama and daddy.

Maybe it was time for me to do the same. I filed that question away for later examination. Frankly, it scared the hell out of me.

"It's a lovely home," I said. "You must be very comfortable here."

Sly went into the kitchen. He took cobalt blue mugs from a lemon yellow cupboard and put them on the counter. "I put the coffee on when Bobo said there was company," he explained as he filled the mugs. "Didn't know I'd have muffins to go with it, though," he added as he emptied the bakery bag.

I took a mug of coffee but waved away his offer of a muffin. "I just had a scone. I brought those for you."

Sly nodded and put the plate on one of the glass-top tables. "In case you change your mind."

Sly gestured to the settee. Jake and I took the invitation and sat down. Sly took a chair across from me.

"I'll tell you about your uncle," he said. "But first I want to hear about what happened to your car. And then you owe me an explanation 'bout that parrot."

I gave Sly a rundown on the fire, leaving out the most incriminating parts. When I finished, he gave me a stern look. "So you two girls are out digging around in this bad business, and suddenly your car catches fire? Sounds pretty suspicious to me. Maybe you ought to take it easy for a few days."

"Does to me, too," Jake agreed. "But in case you hadn't noticed, it's pretty hard to tell this lady what to do."

"But we have to do something! They arrested Bobby, and they think he killed that agent."

"And you're chasing around looking for the guys who did," Jake said. "It appears someone is objecting to your poking around." He turned to Sly. "You try to talk some sense into her."

"It doesn't matter," I said. "Since whoever it is is already mad at me, it won't matter if I keep looking. So there isn't anything to talk about."

I turned back to Sly. "You promised to tell me about Uncle Louis, and how you knew him."

"He was a good man," Sly said. "Treated me like a real person, even when most of the white folks 'round here didn't agree with him."

He got a faraway look in his eyes, as though watching the past play out on a distant movie screen. "I was just a baby when Mister Louis came back to Keyhole Bay. It was right after the war, the big one. I was one of those baby boomers they talk about, 'cept mostly they're talking about white folks. But there were black baby boomers, too.

"Anyway, I grew up right here in this house. Went to what they called the 'colored school' back then, out in Piney Ridge. Didn't have buses back then, but my daddy fixed up an old bike for me, and most days I rode my bike to school, right up to the time I graduated high school."

I tried to imagine what Sly had gone through to get an education. Piney Ridge was five miles outside Keyhole Bay. The roads hadn't been much more than gravel and mud when I was growing up. How much worse they must have been decades before.

"My daddy taught me mechanicin' when I was in high school. Learned to take care of cars for our friends and neighbors."

I must have looked startled, because he nodded in my direction. "Yep. There was a neighborhood here. Long time ago. Mostly rented houses that got bought up and bulldozed to build businesses. My daddy owned this land, and he refused to sell, so here I sit."

"Go on," I said.

"Well, like I said, I got to be a pretty fair mechanic. Could take apart an engine, figure out what was wrong with her, and put her back together, good as new, by the time I was in tenth grade. Mister Louis heard about me, and he came out here, looking for somebody to take care of his old truck."

"Why you?" I asked. "I don't mean to be rude or insensitive, but you're telling me about segregated schools and so on. Why wouldn't he have gone to another mechanic?"

Sly's grin matched his name. "Don't rightly know, Miss Glory. But I heard rumors he got into a tussle with the one other mechanic in town, and refused to let the man touch his truck. Something about Louis calling him a 'low-life cheat,' or some such."

The story explained a lot of things about Uncle Louis. I remembered him as a loner, a man who kept his own counsel and followed his own path.

Jake nudged Sly to continue. "So he brought you his truck?"

"Sure did." Sly got up and refilled out cups, talking over his shoulder as he walked into the kitchen. "I did right by him, and he did right by me. Paid me what the work was worth and kept coming back."

He turned off the coffeepot and settled back in his chair.

"We got to talking one day, right before I graduated. I was trying to figure out what to do with myself, and your uncle was good enough to listen to a scared kid. The Vietnam War was heating up, and I knew I wasn't going to college. I knew the draft board would be coming for me."

"What did he say?"

"Told me I'd get a better assignment if I enlisted, and with my skills I could get assigned to a motor pool. Might even get to stay stateside."

He shook his head. "I listened to part of his advice. I enlisted, and I did get into the motor pool, but I volunteered to go to Vietnam. I came back just before my daddy passed, and I've been here ever since."

"Did you see Uncle Louis after you came back?" I asked. There were a lot of years between 1966 and Uncle Louis's death in 1987.

"From time to time."

Sly got up again, going to the kitchen for another doggy treat. Without saying so, he made it clear the subject was closed.

I let it go. For now. I knew there was more to the story, but he'd already given me a lot to think about.

Sly had kept his part of the bargain. Now it was my turn.

Chapter 27

"YOUR TURN," SLY SAID, GIVING VOICE TO MY thoughts. "You promised me the story of that parrot."

I stalled. "Bluebeard? I inherited him from Uncle Louis, along with the shop. Didn't you already know that?" Giving up my secret, adding another person to the circle, was difficult.

Jake reached over and patted my hand where it rested on my knee. He knew what was coming, what I had to confess, and he was trying to let me know it was all right.

Not that it was. There was nothing all right about telling someone my shop was haunted by the ghost of my dead uncle.

"I knew that, Miss Glory. But what I don't know is how that parrot knew my name."

"I assume because he heard Uncle Louis call you by name." It was the obvious explanation. If you didn't count the possibility that it *was* Uncle Louis.

Sly shook his head. "Makes sense," he said. "Except I never was in that shop while Louis was alive. There's no way Bluebeard ever heard him talk to me."

That stopped me cold. Jake squeezed my hand, but I couldn't tell if he meant to be supportive or if the news had startled him as much as it had me.

There was no other explanation. No excuse I could use.

It had been Uncle Louis talking. Greeting his friend, and calling him by his given name, the way one would a youngster.

"I, uh, I didn't know that, Sly. I just assumed you'd been in the shop, and that's how Bluebeard knew you."

Sly held my gaze for a moment, and I had to look away. I had never been a very good liar, and I couldn't stand up under his scrutiny.

"Did you?"

I felt like I couldn't breathe.

Bobo got up from his place on the floor and padded over to me. He laid his head against my knee as though he sensed my distress and wanted to offer his support.

Sly continued to look at me, his face a study in patience, as I struggled to adjust. I knew about Uncle Louis, I accepted his presence. I'd told Karen, and Linda. Felipe and Ernie. Jake. This list grew longer as time went by. Even Riley knew.

So why was it so hard to tell Sly?

Because everyone else, everyone who knew so far was an old friend, with the exception of Jake. And each of them was someone I felt close to, including Jake, even with all his secrets.

Sly was a different story. Listening to him talk about his life, about how he'd come to know Uncle Louis, was like a living, breathing history lesson. It was a direct link to Uncle Louis, the times he lived in, and the life he'd led.

Somehow, telling Sly would open a door I would never be able to close, and it scared me.

I drew myself up and swallowed the fear. If I could face down a killer, this shouldn't be that hard.

Even if it was.

I didn't know where to start. There wasn't any easy way.

"I hoped so," I admitted. "It would have explained things. But I knew better. It was Uncle Louis, Sly. He was talking to you."

"Hot damn!"

It wasn't the response I was expecting.

"Beggin' your pardon, Miss Glory," Sly continued before I could respond. "Excuse my French, but I shoulda known. If anybody was going to hang around, I would've bet it would be Louis Georges."

"What do you mean?" I was still too stunned by his reaction to figure out what he was saying.

"Mister Louis had a bit of a reputation, you might say. He didn't shy away from stirrin' things up a bit, as it were. Sometimes I think he tried to provoke people, just to see what they'd do. But he stood up for what he thought was right, too. Like I said, stirrin' things up."

"Uncle Louis?"

"Yep." Sly gave me one of his gap-tooth grins. "The very one. Glad to hear he's still around."

I was struggling with the concept of Uncle Louis as a pot-stirrer when my cell phone rang. I glanced at the display and apologized to my companions.

"I have to take this."

"Glory." The exhausted voice on the other end was Anita Nelson. "Julie wanted me to call you first thing."

Her voice cracked with emotion. "Rose Ann Nelson arrived about twenty minutes ago, and she's the most beautiful baby in the world. Mother and daughter are both doing just fine."

"Congratulations!" I said. "And tell Julie I send my love. When can she have visitors?"

"Most any time, the doctor says. They're going to keep her here tonight, let her get some rest before she takes the baby home. But she said she'd love to see you, if you have time."

I realized that neither Julie nor her mother knew about my car, and this certainly wasn't the time to tell them.

"I think I can come by in a little bit. I just have a couple things to take care of first."

"Of course."

There was an unfinished feeling to the conversation, and I asked Anita if there was anything else.

"Yeah," she said, "there is. I just want to thank you for this. If it hadn't been for you, I don't think Julie would have ever gotten away from that horrible man. And I wouldn't have my beautiful granddaughter. You don't know how much this means to me."

She broke the connection, but I couldn't have said anything anyway. Not with that giant lump in my throat.

Sly raised his eyebrows in question, and Jake asked, "Baby?"

I nodded mutely.

"When?" Sly asked, and I remembered the conversation at my place on Saturday.

"When can we see her?" Jake asked.

I finally managed to regain the ability to speak. "The baby arrived about twenty minutes ago, according to Julie's mom. And she can have visitors most any time. She asked me to come by, but I didn't promise, since I don't have a car?" I said, letting my voice rise into a question at the end.

"On the way home," Jake answered. "If you don't mind my tagging along."

"Seeing as how you're my transportation for the foreseeable future, I really can't object, can I?"

I looked back at Sly. "You missed by a few hours. Still, that's pretty close."

"Thanks. Did I hear you right? You don't have any car now?"

I gestured toward the door. "Just the one sitting out there," I said. "I don't think I'll be driving it again, and looking at cars this afternoon just depressed me. Anything I like is way more than I want to pay, and anything in my price range looks like a rolling death trap."

"So I'm her wheels," Jake said lightly. "At least until the insurance company decides what they're doing."

Sly shook his head as he stood up. "Mr. Big-Shot Fowler won't have a decent deal on that lot, but I might have a couple ideas where to find you something. Just let me give this some thought."

He made a shooing motion with his hands. "Go on now. Miss Julie will be wanting to show off that new little baby. 'Sides, it's time for me to be makin' supper, 'fore I eat another one of those muffins."

THE HOSPITAL, LIKE EVERYTHING IN KEYHOLE BAY, was only a few minutes' drive. In a town only five miles in any direction, nothing was very far from anything. Except in the summer, when tourist vehicles packed the main drag, slowing traffic to a crawl during the day. We would get a preview next week, but for now the streets were clear.

We found Julie's room crowded with her family and friends. Anita hovered at her bedside, patting her daughter's arm and beaming at the bundle resting in the crook of Julie's elbow, oblivious to anything else.

Stan, Julie's dad, stood awkwardly against the window on the far side of the room, as three young women crowded around the bed, cooing at Julie and the baby. It sounded sort of like a flock of doves.

The women looked familiar, but I wasn't sure if I knew them or just recognized the type. They were near Julie's age, all wearing engagement or wedding rings. One of the rings, larger and flashier than the rest, caught the light and sparkled dramatically.

That triggered a memory, and I realized who they were: Julie's high school crew, the other cheerleaders on her squad. They had come to Southern Treasures in a group last fall to buy memorial T-shirts and gossip about Julie. I hoped they were past that now.

From the door, all I could see in Julie's arms was a roll of blankets and a teeny stocking cap. I assumed there was a baby in the middle of the roll, based on the crowd around the new mother, but I couldn't really tell from where I stood.

Jake hesitated at the doorway, taking stock of the situation. He headed straight for Stan Nelson, the two exchanging a greeting in low voices. Stan nodded, and walked toward me with Jake.

As they reached the door, Stan looked over at his wife. He said "Anita" twice without a reaction.

"Grandma."

Anita's head shot up, and Stan laughed. "You've been waiting for that forever, haven't you? I'm going down to the cafeteria with Jake here to get some coffee. Can I bring you anything?"

"I'd love a cup of tea," she said. "But take your time."

He turned to me, including me in the offer. I shook my head.

Anita finally caught sight of me hovering in the doorway and waved me into the room. "I'm so glad to see you, Glory." She enveloped me in an awkward hug.

She released me and went back to her post at the head of Julie's bed, pulling me with her. "Isn't she beautiful?"

I wanted to ask whether she meant Julie or the baby, but I was certain I knew the answer. Julie looked exhausted, her hair damp and stringy despite being freshly combed into a tidy ponytail. Her normally pale face was nearly as white as the sheets, faint blue veins visible beneath her porcelain skin, and her eyes drooped with fatigue.

Somehow, even with fatigue pulling her down into the bed, there was a light that glowed in her shadowed eyes when she looked at the baby in her arms.

Close up, Rose Ann looked like every other baby, in my limited experience. Impossibly tiny, her blotchy skin wrinkled like an old woman's, a scowl scrunching up her face like one of those dried-apple dolls.

Beautiful was not a word that came instantly to mind.

Unless you were her grandmother. Or her mother.

Julie smiled up at me when I moved closer. "She's perfect," she whispered. "Absolutely perfect."

Chapter 28

AFTER THE TURMOIL OF THE PAST WEEK, A QUIET
Wednesday was a much-needed break. The early birds
of the spring break crowd had arrived, and a steady flow
of customers came through the shop, looking for their
treasure.

As an added enticement, I'd added a miniature chest on
the counter, filled with inexpensive trinkets. Every youngster took home a memento of Southern Treasures, courtesy
of my treasure grab bags.

Between Bluebeard and the treasures, I had plenty of
customers through the door. Sales were slow, but more than
adequate for this early in the holiday season. Or they would
have been, if I wasn't looking at the necessity of buying
another car.

By the end of day, I hadn't heard from Karen in nearly
two days, an unheard-of gap in our usual twice-a-day

phone calls. She finally called just before I closed up for the day.

"Sorry I've been out of touch," she said. "Riley and I were down in Pensacola all day, talking to lawyers."

"Ugh. Sounds miserable. Although," I said, "it could be worse."

"How?" Karen's usual upbeat, energetic tone was gone, replaced with weary skepticism.

I told her exactly how much worse it could be.

"Are you okay?" she asked, shocked, when I told her about the fire. "You didn't get hurt, did you?"

"I'm fine. But the Civic is a loss. I'm waiting to hear from the insurance company about what they're going to do. The last thing I heard was that they have to wait for the fire investigators to determine the source of the fire. Which is a polite way, according to Jake, of saying they want to be sure I didn't torch it myself before they pay off."

"Jake?"

I realized how much Karen had missed in a single day. "Hang on," I said. "I'm going to close up, then I'll fill you in on everything."

I set the phone down long enough to turn over the "Open" sign and lock the doors.

I was on the phone nearly an hour, bringing Karen up to speed on all that had gone on the previous day. I told her what I'd learned about Sly and Uncle Louis, and ended with the news about Rose Ann.

"At least there was some good news to end the day," she said, and I agreed.

Karen promised to pick me up for dinner the next night. It was Ernie's turn to cook, and the boys would want a full report on everything that had happened since Karen had raced out of the house to rescue Bobby.

And there would be a lot to tell.

I trudged upstairs and dug through the refrigerator, looking for something to cook for dinner. I hadn't been to the grocery store in several days, and my choices were limited. I could either make ramen noodles, or I could walk over to Frank's Foods.

I was tempted to settle for the noodles, but I didn't have any fresh fruit or vegetables for Bluebeard. I dragged a shopping bag out of the closet, stuck my wallet in the back pocket of my jeans, and went downstairs.

As I crossed the shop, Bluebeard whistled to get my attention. He'd been busy all day, entertaining customers with his squawks and whistles. He called everyone a "pretty girl" or "pretty boy," and occasionally made wisecracks from the safety of his perch, which allowed him to stay out of reach of small hands.

I walked over and gave him a pet. "Yes, you were the star attraction today, weren't you?"

He preened, arching his neck and looking down at me from his perch. No false modesty there.

I gave him a biscuit. "I'll have something more in a little bit," I promised. "But I have to go to the store. You take care of things here, okay?"

"Sylvester."

The single word stopped me in my tracks. I turned back around and looked at Bluebeard.

"Sylvester?" This time it was a question, though I wasn't entirely sure what he wanted to know.

"I saw Sylvester yesterday," I answered. "He was very happy to see you, Uncle Louis."

"Good boy."

"Yes, he was a good boy. He's not a boy anymore, he's a grown man who's had an amazing life, but he sure remembers you. Says you helped him out a lot when he was younger."

"Good boy," he repeated softly.

I petted him again. "I think you were a pretty good boy yourself."

The late afternoon sun was still warm, and I broke a sweat halfway to Frank's.

Cheryl waved at me when I came in the door, and I waved back as I grabbed a basket and headed for the produce section. Bluebeard could eat most any kind of fruit or vegetable, and fortunately we shared many favorites. Carrots and apples were high on his list, along with bananas, and I put a few of each in my basket, along with salad greens and a bell pepper.

Cruising the meat case, I spotted a small package of chicken legs. Oven fried with a green salad, they'd make dinner with enough left over for lunch the next day.

No need to worry about dinner tomorrow, that was Ernie's job. All I had to provide was conversation, and I had plenty of that to share.

Chapter 29

AS IT TURNED OUT, KAREN DIDN'T NEED TO PICK ME
up for dinner on Thursday. Late that morning I got a call
from Jake. "Ernie just called and invited me to join you for
dinner tonight," he said. "So you can ride with me, if you'd
like."

I accepted his offer, and called Karen to alert her to the
change of plans. "Great!" she said. "Felipe called to invite Riley, too. So we'll see you there about six thirty?"

I agreed and hung up, wondering what Ernie and Felipe
were up to. They had never tried to meddle in Karen's personal life or mine, at least not like this. Then again, maybe
they were just trying to recognize the fact that we were
moving toward being couples.

Were we really? Was I that close to Jake, or was it just a
casual thing? Sure, he'd helped me through the fire, and
we'd kissed a few times, but what did that mean?

I had no idea, and I felt as though I were back in junior high, trying to guess whether he liked me as a friend or *really* liked me. I found him attractive, and I was pretty sure I wanted whatever this was to continue, but I had questions, and the fire department was one of them. Why hadn't he told me about volunteering? Or anything about his life before Keyhole Bay?

Maybe, if I could get some answers, I'd feel better.

The short drive to Felipe and Ernie's house, though, wasn't long enough to even ask.

When we parked at the curb, Karen's SUV wasn't anywhere to be seen. But before we got to the front door of the simple cottage, it rounded the corner and parked behind Jake's car.

Riley hopped out of the driver's side, and ran around to open Karen's door, a move I hadn't seen from him since high school. I tried not to stare.

Karen handed her ex a bottle bag and a six-pack, then climbed out of the SUV. With Riley's hands full, she took a key from her giant bag and locked the doors. Apparently, Riley now had his own key, too.

Felipe met us at the door. "Ernie's been cooking all day," he said, taking the bottle bag from Riley.

"Yum," Karen said, as our noses caught the rich odor of baking ham wafting from the kitchen.

"Smells wonderful in here," Jake agreed.

Felipe led us into the dining room, which opened into the kitchen. Ernie stood at the stove, a white chef's apron double-wrapped around his slender waist and tied at the front.

Two covered pots sat on the back burners, their mysterious contents leaking wisps of steam into the kitchen. On the front burner, a skillet held melting shortening next to a tray of cornbread discs ready for frying.

The counter that ran along the adjacent wall was cleared of clutter, a testament to Ernie's intense organization. The only thing that remained was an electric deep fryer, unplugged and cooling.

Ernie greeted us all warmly, with hugs for Karen and me, and back-slapping handshakes for our dates. He gratefully accepted a cold longneck from Riley, twisting off the cap and taking a long pull.

Riley distributed bottles to the rest of us, taking the last one for himself. With the addition of Riley and Jake, we had the correct number for a single six-pack. I took it as a good omen.

Ernie began frying the cornbread, sliding the discs of dough into the hot grease and waiting patiently as they turned a faint gold around the edges before turning them over.

Felipe took a bowl from the refrigerator, placing it on the sleekly modern teak sideboard next to a tray of crackers.

While their antique shop tended toward the ornate and Victorian, at home Felipe and Ernie were definitely midcentury modern, given to teak in the minimalist lines of Danish modern.

I investigated the appetizers, delighted to find a bowl of Ernie's homemade pimento cheese. Growing up, pimento cheese was a lunchroom staple. Ernie served it with buttery crackers, a traditional childhood sandwich filling transformed into a savory predinner snack.

Conversation flowed as Ernie finished cooking, though we avoided any serious discussion. That would wait until we were all seated and could pay attention to the conversation.

They had all heard about Julie and Rose Ann and quizzed me and Jake about our visit to the hospital.

"How's the baby look?" Felipe asked. I think he was the only one of us with any maternal instinct.

"Like a baby," I shrugged. "Red and wrinkled. And tiny."

My answer was greeted with a round of laughter.

We each offered our help, but Ernie insisted he had everything under control, and he did. Even his apron remained spotless as he lifted the cornbread patties from the frying pan to a paper-towel-lined cookie sheet to cool.

He took a ham from the oven, pecan pieces scattered across its top, and a tray of golden-fried okra, which accounted for the cooling deep fryer. In a few minutes he turned off the back burners and uncovered their contents. One pot held dirty rice, which he heaped into a serving bowl, and the other contained stewed tomatoes that went in another bowl. He covered a serving plate with perfect pieces of fried cornbread from the cookie sheet.

While Ernie sliced the ham, we carried the bowls and platters to the table. With the table already loaded with amazing food, Ernie brought out a platter of ham, and took his place at the end nearest the kitchen.

As always, the first few minutes were taken up with passing bowls and plates and questioning the cook about the various dishes. We had established the routine when we decided to turn our regular Thursday night dinner into an exploration of traditional southern cooking. As we took turns, each cook shared their recipes, and we all learned about new dishes.

Jake had been invited to dinner a time or two, but this was a new experience for Riley. Several times I saw him looking around the table as though he were seeing us all for the first time. Which, in a way, I guess he was.

We settled in, savoring the saltiness of the ham, the bite of the stewed tomatoes, and the moist goodness of the fried cornbread. Ernie was an accomplished cook, and his food was always the best.

The conversation eventually turned from the cooking to what had happened since we'd last been together, and that night we had a *lot* to talk about.

Karen and Riley knew about the Civic, of course. Felipe and Ernie had heard via the gossip tree that was the Merchants' Association, since several of the members were also on the volunteer fire crew.

"I heard at yesterday's breakfast," Ernie said. "Clark had just come off his shift, and he was telling us about someone's car burning up. I believe his exact words were 'Someone torched a car.' But I had no idea it was yours, Glory. How bad is it?"

"It's a total loss," Jake said.

The three men turned to look at him, startled that he had answered the question. Karen looked at me, her glance asking why Jake was answering for me.

"Jake was there," I said. "But maybe I better let him tell you about that."

All eyes turned expectantly to Jake.

"I joined the volunteer department," he said. "A few months back. I didn't want to say anything until after I passed the exams, which I did last week. With all that was going on"—he nodded at Riley and Karen—"I just hadn't found the right time to tell you all. And then on my very first shift I got called out on a car fire, and it turned out to be Glory's car."

He accepted the congratulations of the group with grace, but Felipe asked the question we were all thinking: "How could you have had any question about passing the exams? You're a smart guy, and the department tries to help all they can."

Jake's chuckle was self-depreciating. "I spent the last few years in a desk job," he explained. "The physical is demanding; you have to perform a lot of tasks while wearing full turnout gear. I wasn't sure if I could do everything they required in order to get my certification."

Riley cast a critical eye over Jake. "You look pretty fit to me, and I have to be able to judge whether a guy can make it on a fishing boat. I'd hire you."

"I'll keep that in mind if this bookstore thing doesn't work out."

A cloud passed over Riley's face. "Assuming I can ever get my boat back."

That turned the conversation from Jake's firefighting to the state of the murder investigation. It was the first Felipe and Ernie had heard about our excursion to the apartment in Pensacola, and they agreed with Jake and Riley that we had taken a foolish chance.

"There's still something about it," I said. "Something that keeps trying to make a connection in my head. It's like when you see something out of the corner of your eye, but when you turn around and look, there's nothing there."

Karen nodded. "I know what you mean. We saw something in there that's important, but I just can't put my finger on it."

I helped Ernie clear the table, and we sat back down for another glass of wine before he started dessert.

"You'll see," was all he would tell us when we asked what he was serving.

At Riley's suggestion, Karen got her tablet from her magic bag, and she brought up the pictures from our little trip to Pensacola. At this point, there was no sense in hiding what we'd found.

The tablet was passed from hand to hand, as each of us looked at the pictures. Jake and I had already seen them, but Riley hadn't, and of course Ernie and Felipe hadn't, either.

"These are their dive tanks?" Ernie asked, pointing to one of the photos.

"Yeah. Rented from some dive shop over in Jacksonville, so they must have brought them with them."

"Jacksonville?" Riley suddenly sat up straight. He was staring intently at Karen. "They were from Jacksonville?"

"Callahan, actually. But close enough."

Riley shook his head. "There's something about Jacksonville, something I heard just in the last week or so."

A gasp escaped from my lips as I made the connection. I knew what Riley had heard. Someone else had come from Jacksonville recently.

"Megan Moretti," I blurted out.

Chapter 30

"IT COULD JUST BE A COINCIDENCE," ERNIE CAUtioned. "She might not have anything to do with them."

"True enough," Riley said. "Or they might have gone in Mermaid's Grotto because they knew she was there and they thought she could introduce them to somebody."

"Small towns have a reputation," Jake added. "When they couldn't find anyone to charter for them, maybe they thought a girl with local connections could help."

"Or maybe she's in cahoots with those two." Now that the connection, however tenuous, had been made, Karen was ready to run with it.

Ernie wasn't convinced. "She grew up around here, right? And she went over to Jacksonville a couple years ago?"

"Closer to five," Karen shot back. "Long enough," she added darkly.

"Long enough for what?" Riley asked. "Long enough to

get homesick? Long enough to lose her job and come back home?"

"I don't know," Karen replied. "But I know how to find out."

Uh-oh. When Karen talked like that, things happened. And they weren't always good. It was the same kind of impatience that had gotten us into that apartment in the first place.

"I don't like the sound of this," Ernie said. "You always talk like this just before you go and do something crazy."

"It's not crazy. I have friends in Jacksonville, people who have connections. If there's something to find out about Megan Moretti, or about our pals Chuck and Freddy, they'll know where to find it.

"If I leave first thing in the morning, I can be there and back in one day."

"I'll go with you," Riley offered. "I can keep you company and help with the driving. That's a lot of miles for one person in a single day."

"I can manage," Karen replied. "It's a long drive, but I've done longer. I'll just take an audiobook, and it'll pass the time."

"I might be able to help out, though." Riley wasn't getting brushed off that easily.

"No, really. I'll be fine. You should be here with your family. They need you right now."

"It might be nice to get away for a day," Riley answered. "I can't fish, and all I do is sit around the house trying to get my mom to eat something." He looked around the table. "I don't think she's eaten an actual meal since Bobby was arrested."

"All the more reason you need to be there," Karen said.

"You're the only one who's been able to get her to eat anything."

"I am trying to tell you I could use a break!"

Riley was practically shouting, and I could see the stress building. He'd been under a lot of pressure in the past week, and at first he'd caved. But now he was itching for a fight, looking for an outlet.

And Karen gave him one.

"And *I* am trying to tell *you* I need to do this by myself. I'm going to see some old friends who are working for news stations in Jacksonville. They have sources, like all good reporters, and I am going to have to ask them to try and tap those sources for information.

"It's something I need to do face-to-face," she said in an overly patient voice that bordered on condescension. "And it's something that will be better done alone."

Riley's face turned red, a sign he was getting ready to blow. "I don't suppose," he said, sarcasm dripping off every word, "that these are male friends, are they?"

"For heaven's sake!" Exasperation sharpened Karen's voice, and she turned a withering gaze on Riley. "I have some old college classmates over there. A couple of them are guys. *Married* guys. You know, the kind with wives and kids?"

"Oh," he said, not backing down. "*College* friends."

I'd expected Karen and Riley to find a way to blow their budding reconciliation to hell. I just hadn't expected them to be able to do it so soon. And so publicly.

It appeared that Karen's education, and Riley's lack of same, had become one of the landmines in their relationship. And they had stepped squarely on the detonator right here in front of us.

"They're just friends," Karen said, her voice growing chilly. "The kind of people you help out when they need you."

Riley's pride couldn't stand the jab. "You don't need to do me any favors!"

He shoved his hand in his pocket and pulled out her car key. Slamming it on the table in front of her, he shoved his chair back and stood up.

He stopped and turned to the rest of us, struggling to control the temper that raged in him. "Thank you all for inviting me to dinner. Ernie, the food was wonderful. I'm sorry, but I have to go now."

With that, he stormed through the house and out the door.

An uncomfortable silence followed his abrupt departure.

"I guess he's walking home," Karen said finally, picking up the car key and stuffing it in her pocket.

We tried to resume the conversation, but Riley's exit left us all tiptoeing around the topic of Bobby and his problems.

"Stop it," Karen said. "That was embarrassing, sure. But you all know Riley and I couldn't stay married. It shouldn't come as any surprise that our conversations can get a little, um, intense.

"I'm still going to Jacksonville in the morning, and I'm still going to try and learn if there is a connection between Megan Moretti and our two friends from Callahan."

"And if there isn't?" I voiced the question that was in all our minds.

"Then I'll know. And Megan Moretti can have *both* the Freed brothers if she wants them. But I need to find out. Because if it exists, that connection might be the one thing that can get Riley back on his damned boat, and out of my hair.

"Now what's for dessert?"

I didn't believe for a minute that she wanted Riley out of her hair. I had seen her put up a brave front before, and she wasn't fooling me. There would be tears later, but for now she had to pretend that everything was fine.

Ernie rose gracefully from his seat, grateful for a safe topic. "Bananas Foster," he announced. "If you'll just give me a few minutes."

He retreated into the kitchen.

"And I thought Ernie's dessert was going to be the biggest fireworks display tonight," Felipe muttered.

I couldn't help giggling.

Karen gave me a dirty look, but it was her own fault. She knew, better than any of us, how much she and Riley made each other crazy, and she'd been an active part of their reconciliation, from what I'd seen. The fireworks had been inevitable.

As Ernie started cooking, we all drifted toward the stove, eager to watch what he was doing. None of us had ever actually tried making the dessert, though we'd all eaten it.

It was always fun to watch Ernie. Of all of us, he was the most practiced in the kitchen. Though he denied it, Felipe claimed Ernie had worked in some of the best-known kitchens in New Orleans, and had had the opportunity to observe some of the masters up close. Whether he actually had or not, he was an entertaining—and accomplished— cook.

Like a chef on television, he had his ingredients laid out ahead of time. He carried a tray from the walk-in pantry with several small bowls of ingredients and a bunch of pale yellow bananas.

He put a heavy skillet on the burner, turned the flame on low, and put in most of a stick of butter. While the butter melted, he peeled the bananas and split them lengthwise, laying them gently on a plate.

He was enjoying himself—not just the cooking, but performing for an admiring audience—as he added brown sugar and spices to the melted butter. He stirred in the sugar and spice, and poured in a bright yellow, syrupy liquid.

"Banana liqueur," Felipe offered, acting as commentator to Ernie's performance. "Don't worry, the alcohol will cook off."

"Not entirely," Jake said. "But some of it will."

Ignoring the conversation, Ernie stirred until the sauce began to simmer. Working carefully, he laid the bananas in the gently bubbling sauce, and spooned the hot liquid over them before turning them over.

While he worked, Felipe took a carton of French vanilla ice cream from the freezer, and carried in a second tray from the pantry. On the second tray, each of a set of six dessert plates held a small waffle.

Ernie placed two banana halves over each waffle, then turned back to his sauce. I could see a smile playing around the corners of his mouth, and I knew something special was coming.

He took the next-to-last bowl from his ingredient tray, full of a dark, aromatic liquid. As he started to pour, I identified the smell of dark rum.

The rum hit the hot syrup, igniting into blue flames. Ernie stirred carefully as the rum burned for a minute or two. When the flames died out, he tossed in the contents of the remaining bowl, finely grated orange zest, and ladled syrup over each banana-covered waffle.

As soon as Ernie ladled on the syrup, Felipe added a scoop of ice cream and handed each of us a plate. We put the plates on the table and broke into a spontaneous round of applause.

Ernie flashed us a brilliant smile and took a bow.

Somehow, while we were all watching Ernie, Felipe had managed to make a fresh pot of coffee. We settled back at the table to try Ernie's creation.

The aroma was heavenly, but the flavor was out of this world. Spicy-sweet syrup contrasted with the mellow flavor of the sautéed bananas, and each bite was a combination of textures: crunchy waffle, firm banana, and the smooth creaminess of the ice cream.

"Ernie," I said between bites, "you have outdone yourself this time."

Next to me, Jake groaned. He swallowed a bite and rolled his eyes. "I wondered why you didn't eat very much dinner."

"I should have warned you. Ernie really likes to make desserts. I mean, he's good at everything, but he goes all out on dessert. I've learned to save room."

"I wish I had," Jake said. "I'm stuffed, but this stuff is so good, I can't stop eating." As if to prove his point, he lifted another forkful to his mouth.

I started to say that Riley didn't know what he was missing, but thought better of it. Because Riley was missing a lot more than dessert tonight.

Karen ate quietly, caught up in her own thoughts. She had always been decisive, willing to trust her own judgment. But this time she was facing a cost she hadn't expected.

She turned down a cup of coffee, saying she had to get home and get some sleep so she could make the drive to Jacksonville in the morning.

I walked to the door with her, while the three men remained discreetly at the table. I was Karen's oldest and closest friend, and they chose to give us a few private moments.

"Don't you dare say 'I told you so,'" she said the minute we were out of earshot. "Do not say it."

"I wasn't going to. In fact, I was going to ask if you needed some company. I rode with Jake, and I can go with you if you want."

She shook her head. "I knew better than to get involved with him again. I *knew* better. But I thought—I hoped—things had changed." She put her arm around my shoulders and squeezed. "Thanks for the offer, but I'm going home to go to sleep, and I'm driving to Jacksonville at first light. By this time tomorrow I expect we'll have our answer."

Chapter 31

JAKE AND I LINGERED A FEW MINUTES LONGER, helping Felipe and Ernie clear the table and get the dishwasher loaded. Given the feast Ernie had prepared, it seemed fair.

Ernie took advantage of the traffic in the kitchen and dining room to draw me aside for a moment. "Felipe and I have been talking," he said softly, "and we were thinking about asking you and Karen if you wanted to expand our dinners to six.

"Of course, after tonight that doesn't seem likely," he cut his eyes toward the front door, where Riley and then Karen had already departed. "And it seems insensitive to suggest it right now. But give it some thought, and we'll bring it up after things have settled down."

It looked like Jake had passed muster. Felipe and Ernie had not only accepted him, they wanted to reach out and include him in our circle. It was as if they were giving their blessing to our budding relationship.

"Thanks, Ernie. And tell Felipe thanks, too. I'll give it some thought."

I had two concerns about his suggestion. First, I still had some unanswered questions about Jake, questions I would need to settle somehow before he became a permanent—or even semipermanent—part of my life.

And second, how would his inclusion change the group dynamic if Karen was the only unattached person? Like I said, she was my oldest and closest friend, and I wouldn't hurt her for the world.

A few minutes later, the kitchen once again spotless and the dishwasher humming quietly, Jake and I thanked our hosts again and headed out to the car.

As we pulled away from the curb, Jake spoke up. "If you don't mind, I think maybe we ought to take a little spin past the Mermaid's Grotto. We could have a little nightcap in the bar, have another look around . . ." His voice trailed off, as though it had just been a random thought.

I knew better. Jake thought Karen was right, that there was a connection between Megan Moretti and the two men from Callahan, and he wanted to take another look at her with that thought in mind.

"I suppose we could," I said, matching his casual tone. "I don't know where I'd *put* a nightcap, but I like the idea."

So instead of turning toward home, Jake turned toward the docks. Mermaid's Grotto was one of the few places open after dark, and there was plenty of parking in the public lot.

I was just about to get out of the car when I spotted something that made my heart stop.

Riley Freed's truck, parked next to Mermaid's Grotto. Where Megan Moretti was working.

I didn't for a second believe he was involved in anything underhanded, but Karen's remark came back to me with the force of a blow to the midsection.

"Megan Moretti can have *both* the Freed brothers if she wants them."

Megan had always wanted Riley, and maybe Bobby, too. Now it looked like she just might get her wish.

"Are you going to get out?" Jake was standing by the car, holding my door open.

I shook my head, still staring at the truck. Jake followed my gaze, but he didn't know Riley's truck, and he turned back, a questioning frown on his face.

"Is there a problem?"

I nodded. "Get back in the car. Please. Hurry!"

Jake didn't stop to ask questions. He closed the door and walked back around, sliding in behind the steering wheel.

"You okay? You're acting really strange."

"We can't stay here," I said. I pointed to the well-worn pickup parked on the far side of the lot. "Riley's here."

"Riley?"

"That's his truck."

"Do you think he's involved in this?" Jake was incredulous. "I would never have guessed."

"No, no, no. I can't imagine a world where Riley Freed would be involved in anything shady. But he just broke up with his ex-wife—*again*—and there's a hot babe in there who's been after him since she was thirteen.

"What do you think?"

"I think," he said, starting the car and pulling out of the

parking space, "that it may just be a guy drowning his sorrows. Or it may be a guy looking for a sympathetic shoulder. Either way, it's none of our business."

As we drove away, I sighed deeply. "I wish you were right," I said. "But two of my best friends just broke each other's hearts for the second time. At some point it will end up being my business."

We drove the few blocks home without speaking. Jake walked me to the door of Southern Treasures and waited, as had become his habit, while I checked the alarms and the doors. Then he kissed me good night and lingered on the sidewalk until I locked the door behind him and reset the alarm.

Bluebeard's wolf whistle cut through the shop as soon as Jake's back was turned.

"Is that necessary?"

The only answer I got was a cackle. It was as close as he could come to a laugh. Apparently it amused him to harass me.

"Just for that, no banana."

"Banana?"

It was a hollow threat, and we both knew it.

Bluebeard didn't have anything else to say while I gave him his treat and checked his water. But just before I went upstairs, he said clearly, "People don't come back for no reason."

I had a hunch Megan Moretti's reason just might be Riley Freed. And the thought saddened me as I climbed the stairs to bed.

Things didn't look any better in the morning. Karen texted me from Tallahassee at about nine thirty. She was making good time, and had a lunch date with someone she called "an old friend" when she got to Jacksonville. She said she'd call as soon as she knew anything.

I managed to last another hour before I was pacing the floor. I had to know why Megan had come back. Did she have her sights set on one of the Freed brothers? And if so, which one?

She had seemed sincerely glad to see me the night Jake and I had been in the Grotto, and I thought we'd had a connection. Maybe I could at least talk to her.

And if she thought she was serious about Riley, maybe I could convince her it wasn't a good idea.

I made up my mind. Mermaid's Grotto would be closed for another half hour, but the crew should be there, getting ready for lunch. Maybe I could get a few minutes with Megan before she started her shift.

I knew I shouldn't meddle, but I just felt like I had to do something before I exploded. It gave me a lot of sympathy for Riley.

I stopped at The Lighthouse for a latte-flavored bribe. If I was going to make a quick trip to Mermaid's Grotto, I was going to need a car, and I didn't have one of my own.

Jake didn't like the idea, even with the lagniappe of a free latte. Maybe I should have brought a scone, too.

"All I want to do is borrow your car for half an hour," I said. "Maybe if I can talk to Megan I can find out if she's really after Riley. And if she is, maybe I can talk her out of it."

"That's nuts!"

"Maybe so, but I have to try. Now, can I borrow your car, or do I have to walk?"

Jake shook his head. "You are one of the most stubborn women I have ever met." He walked over to the front door, flipped the lock, and hung up the sign with a clock face that said he'd be back at eleven fifteen.

"Half an hour," he said. "And I'm going with you."

I knew it wouldn't do any good to argue.

The parking lot at Mermaid's Grotto was empty except for a few employee cars ranged along the back fence. I showed Jake the path around the building to the back door, where a bored-looking dishwasher lounged against the wall, smoking a cigarette.

"Is Megan working?" I asked in my sweetest voice.

The guy shrugged. Did that mean yes or no?

"Is she here?"

Another shrug.

"*Habla ingles*?" Jake asked.

He shook his head, and dropped the cigarette in the gravel, grinding it beneath his heavy rubber boot. Then, without speaking, he opened the back door and went inside.

From inside the kitchen he looked back at us and motioned for us to follow him.

I looked at Jake, who imitated the guy's shrug.

We followed him into the kitchen.

A restaurant kitchen just shortly before opening is a study in controlled chaos. Everyone was focused on what they were doing, and no one paid any attention to us.

The dishwasher pointed around a service area, and went back to his dish bay.

We went around the service area and spotted a door leading into the bar. But when we went through, there was no sign of Megan. The only person in the place was a guy

with a toolbox and a shirt that proclaimed him an employee
of Big Al's Aquarium Service. "Robert" was embroidered
over his pocket, if it could be trusted.

"Robert?" I asked.

"That's me. Something I can do for you?"

"We were just looking for Megan, the bartender."

"Sorry, nobody's here yet. They don't come in until
after I finish servicing the tank." He nodded at the back
bar space. "Gets a little cramped back there when I'm
working."

Curiosity got the better of me, and I moved closer, trying
to see what he was doing. "I remember when there were
mermaids in that tank," I said, "but just barely."

"Me, too." He stuck out his hand. "Bob Bailey. I've been
taking care of this tank for a long time. But not back to
when there were mermaids," he added hastily.

I chuckled. "Not unless you started when you were in
preschool."

"Feels like it sometimes, but no."

Jake moved up next to me, his curiosity piqued. "How
does this work?" he asked.

Our original objective abandoned, we peppered Bob
with questions. Delighted with such an attentive audience,
he answered our questions, even volunteering a little bit of
history.

"When the mermaids were here, part of the pool was
open, like the one at Weeki Wachee Springs. But when they
converted to a reef tank, they had to completely close it in,
because the fish need a constant temperature. Too hot, or
too cold, and they can't survive."

"Is that what you're checking?" I asked.

"Oh no. That's monitored automatically. There's sensors

in the tank, connected by cables to a controller that keeps the temperature in the proper range. If it goes too high or too low it triggers an alarm, and I come running, sort of like when a burglar alarm goes off."

"But what if a sensor fails?"

"There's enough of them that one won't matter. It would take a bunch of them to trigger the alarm. Never had that happen in any of the tanks we service." There was a distinct note of pride in his voice. He took his work seriously.

We watched him fiddle with an electronic box tucked inside a control panel behind the bar while he talked. It turned out Big Al, the owner of Big Al's Aquarium Service, was his dad, and he'd been servicing the pool since the mermaid days. "There isn't an inch of this tank I don't know. Been coming in here with my dad since I was a kid."

I wondered aloud why I had never crossed paths with Bob, as small as Keyhole Bay was. I guessed we were near the same age.

"Oh, we lived over in Pensacola when I was growing up. Dad was a Navy diver before he started the aquarium service. I moved over here a couple years ago, when I got tired of living in the city."

I could have stayed and asked questions for a while longer, and I suspect Bob would have happily answered, but I had promised Jake I would keep my visit to half an hour. Even though he hadn't said a word—and in fact seemed as fascinated as I was with the things Bob was telling and showing us—I knew we had to get back to our shops.

I got Bob's business card, telling him I'd love the chance to talk to his dad about the mermaid shows. "I was obsessed with them when I was a kid," I explained. "I told my father I wanted to grow up to be a mermaid."

Bob nodded. "I was jealous of the girls," he admitted. "There weren't any boys in the show back then, and I was bummed out that I couldn't be a performer."

"Thanks," I said, sticking the card in my pocket. "See ya around."

By then the front door was open, and we didn't have to go back through the kitchen. I hadn't seen Megan come in, but it would be too late to talk to her, anyway. I would have to catch her later.

Chapter 32

JAKE DROVE BACK TO BEACH BOOKS, DETOURING past Curly's drive-through window to pick up lunch. I offered to buy his burger as a thank-you, but he declined. "I don't want you to get the idea you can rope me into these things with a cheeseburger," he said. "Or a latte."

"Darn, you figured out my evil plan."

"Sure did." He handed me a paper bag with my lunch and pulled back into traffic. Two minutes later, we parked behind Beach Books. When Jake unlocked his front door, it was sixteen minutes after eleven.

I'd kept to the schedule I'd promised.

As I crossed the street, I noticed a truck parked in front of my store. The lines of the rounded hood and tall cab were from an era before tail fins and protruding headlights. Old enough to be an antique, it looked both original and pristine.

The forest green paint gleamed, the chrome twinkled, and the glass was perfect. It looked like it must have the day it rolled off the showroom floor.

As I approached, I recognized the driver.

Sly was sitting behind the wheel.

He hopped out when I reached the truck, bouncing the key in his hand as though he were gauging the weight.

"What brings you here?" I asked, opening the door and turning the sign over.

Sly followed me inside. "Your truck."

"My truck?"

"My truck!" Bluebeard said.

"It's gorgeous, Sly. But I can't afford that."

"My truck!" Bluebeard insisted.

"You got that right, Mr. Louis," Sly said.

"My truck." Bluebeard was practically cooing, looking out the window at the truck sitting at the curb.

Sly took my hand, turned it palm up, and placed the key there. "It was Mr. Louis's truck before it was mine. Seems only right that it come back here."

"How am I going to pay for that? It's got to be worth a fortune! Sly, you know I can't afford this. Besides, what are you going to drive?"

"You looked around my place, girl? I got prolly three thousand vehicles out there. Most of 'em's just parts, but I've tinkered with a few over the years. Got a garage out back with a couple dozen in running order. Some of them older'n that one." He waved at the truck.

"My truck," Bluebeard repeated.

"I tell you what. You can buy the truck back for what I paid for it, plus the parts I put in it. Won't take any more than that. I did the work myself—for fun, not for profit—so that don't count.

"That's the deal."

I stared at the truck. It was beautiful, and I was already in love with it. I could imagine myself driving it around town and out on the back roads, searching for merchandise for the shop.

"Are you sure? You might have to take it in payments." I was hesitant to commit to the deal, not knowing how much he'd put into the thing. I was sure some of the parts were rare, and he might have had to pay dearly for them.

"Whatever you need to do, girl. I think you need to have this truck." He cocked his head in Bluebeard's direction. "And I think your uncle agrees."

Bluebeard bobbed his head up and down, an emphatic signal of his approval.

"All right," I said slowly. My stomach clenched in anticipation of the answer to my next question. "How much?"

"Well, seeing as most of the parts came off things that got towed to the yard for scrap, I figure there's about seventy-five dollars in parts. Throw in fifty for the paint— built me a paint booth back when I was doing a lot of repairin'—that's hundred and a quarter. And then there's what I paid Louis for it."

He turned and looked at Bluebeard. "You remember our deal, old man? Course you do." He turned back to me, a nostalgic smile on his face. "Your uncle sold me that truck when I turned sixteen, rather than let the dealer take it as a trade. Told me it was wore out and I'd need to fix it up, but he knew I could do it.

"He charged me twenty bucks, and let me work it off by

taking care of his new truck. So I never really paid him anything. Then there was, lessee . . ."

He paused and counted on his fingers, deliberately dragging out the time, making me wait.

I tried not to fidget.

Finally he shook his head. "Nope, can't think of nothin' else. I guess you owe me 'bout a hundred twenty-five. You need to make payments on that?"

I think my bursting into tears was answer enough.

I tried to talk him out of it, tried to tell him the offer was much too generous, but he wasn't having any of it.

"What goes around comes around. Your uncle did me a big favor sellin' me that truck when I needed it. Now I can return the favor by selling it back to you and getting it out of my garage."

He patted my shoulder. "I'm gonna go over and get me some of Miss Pansy's baking," he said. "Then maybe you could do an old man a favor and give me a lift home."

I could hardly believe my good fortune. The truck was perfect, and Sly's sincerity convinced me to accept his offer. He gave me the title and a bill of sale in exchange for a handful of bills from the register, and I had a new/old truck.

While he went next door to The Lighthouse for pastries, I called my insurance agent and arranged coverage for my new ride. They still didn't have the final report on the Civic, but with a replacement vehicle I wasn't nearly as distressed by the delay.

I tried to call and share my news with Karen, but my call went directly to voice mail. I hoped that meant she was busy talking to her friends in Jacksonville and would have some answers soon.

I was still on the phone when I saw Jake cross the street. I didn't leave a message, figuring Karen would call when she could. But instead of coming into Southern Treasures, Jake disappeared through the door of The Lighthouse.

A few minutes later, he emerged with Sly. Jake had a coffee in each hand, and Sly had his own cup and a bulging white paper bag. It looked like he'd spent the entire payment for the truck on Miss Pansy's baking.

They stopped on the sidewalk next to the truck, sipping their coffee and talking. Jake caught my eye through the window and motioned me to join them, hoisting one coffee cup to indicate it was for me.

There are some definite advantages to living next door to the best coffee in town.

I walked outside, and Jake handed me a coffee cup. "Vanilla latte," he said, "to celebrate your new truck."

I ran my hand along the curve of the back fender, feeling the smooth paint beneath my fingertips. "She's a beauty, isn't she?" I looked over at Sly, who beamed behind his coffee cup. "I still can't believe she's mine."

"All yours," Sly said. "I signed that paper, and now she's your responsibility. There is one thing, though."

"Anything," I replied instantly. Whatever it was, I owed Sly more than I could ever repay.

"If she needs anything, you bring her to me, you hear? Don't let any of those boys over at Fowler's get anywhere near her. You let *me* take care of her."

I agreed immediately. Given the age of the truck—the registration said it was a 1949—I'd been a little worried about finding someone I could trust if she needed work.

Now I knew where to go if I needed help.

We stood on the sidewalk for several minutes, sipping

coffee and admiring the truck, until Guy Miller stuck his head out the door of his shop.

"Cool truck," he said, walking over and taking a closer look. "Whose is it?"

"Mine."

He looked at me, eyes wide. "Are you kidding? That's an amazing truck! Where did you get it?"

"I just bought it from Sly, to replace the Civic."

"Yeah, Linda told me about the fire. But this"—he waved an arm at the truck—"this is great."

"I think," Jake said, "she should have the name of the store painted on the side. In old-fashioned script letters."

"Absolutely," Guy agreed. "Gold lettering on that dark green. Great idea."

I wasn't sure how Sly would feel, but when I turned to ask him, his grin gave me the answer before he said a word. "I was hopin' somebody would think of that. Mr. Louis had the store name painted on there when he owned it. But I didn't want to be telling Miss Glory what to do with her truck."

My inner twelve-year-old couldn't contain herself any longer. "That," I said, "would be made of awesome."

A few minutes later, Linda came out of The Grog Shop, looking for Guy. The minute she spotted the truck, she rolled her eyes and shook her head. "I should have known that was where my husband disappeared to," she said. "He can't resist."

Eventually the impromptu block party broke up. Jake, Guy, and Linda all had to get back to their stores, and I needed to get Sly home. He said Bobo was waiting for his treats from Pansy's bakery case.

I told my neighbors I was closing up, but I'd be back in

half an hour or so. I knew I wouldn't be able to just drop Sly at the junkyard and come right back. I had to drive my new truck, even if it was only a ten-minute cruise through town.

For one crazy minute I considered taking Bluebeard with me. But I didn't want to take him without a carrier, there wasn't room for both him and Sly in the cab, and I wasn't going to let him ride in the back. He'd have to wait for his ride.

I stuffed my driver's license in my pocket with my shop keys, grabbed my cell phone, promised Bluebeard I'd be home soon, and went off to drive my new truck.

Chapter 33

THE DRIVE FROM SOUTHERN TREASURES TO SLY'S junkyard was way too short. After I left Sly at his gate, thanking him again and again, I drove through town.

The engine purred like it was brand new, the clutch was like silk, and everything felt solid and stable. It was like the answer to a prayer.

I turned off the highway, using the side streets to make a blocks-wide U-turn. On impulse, I took a detour past the docks. I suppose I wanted to run into someone I knew to get a chance to show off my new acquisition.

As I cruised past Mermaid's Grotto, I remembered Bob telling me that Megan would be in for the lunch shift. The parking lot was nearly as empty as it had been that morning, the lunch rush having come and gone.

I pulled in, tires crunching in the gravel, and parked.

This wouldn't take long, if Megan was even here. And if she wasn't, I'd go on home and try again later. Or tomorrow.

I left my cell phone in the spotless glove box and locked the truck, stuffing the key in my pocket. As I did I felt the stiff cardboard of Bob's business card. I was looking forward to talking to his dad and hearing stories of the mermaids. Especially since I'd never gotten to be one.

The front door was unlocked, but no one was in sight when I walked in. I went through to the bar, pausing to let my eyes adjust to the dark interior from the bright sunshine outside.

Behind the bar, Megan moved bottles as she polished the glass shelves, setting up for the evening crowd.

Now that I was here, I had no idea what I was going to say. Jake was right; this was nuts. Still, I'd come this far.

I crossed the deserted room, detouring around thickets of tiny cocktail tables and scattered chairs.

Stepping up to the bar, I caught Megan's reflection in the glass of the fish tank. I realized the tank lights were off, creating an impenetrable gloom where you normally saw schools of brightly colored tropical fish.

Megan saw me at about the same time I saw her. She tilted her head in greeting, but didn't turn around.

"Hey, Glory. How you doing?" She continued her polishing, finally turning around when she reached the end of the shelf.

"Kitchen's closed," she said, "but there might still be somebody back there. Can I get you something?"

"Just a few minutes of your time, if you can spare it. I was hoping we could talk."

"I suppose," she said warily. "Let's go upstairs. Sounds like maybe this should be a private conversation."

I followed her up the stairs to the break room where I'd had to tell her Bobby was charged with murder. We sat on one of the old mermaid's changing benches, Megan straddling the bench facing me.

"Is it—" She swallowed hard and tried again. "Is it Bobby? I can't get in, they won't let me see him. Have you seen him? How is he?"

Her lips quivered with emotion, and tears pooled in her eyes. How could anyone think she was involved with anything that might hurt Bobby? Her obvious anguish over him convinced me she'd had nothing to do with his trouble.

I shook my head. "I haven't seen him. Some of the family has, but I'm more concerned about some other things. Like why you came back to Keyhole Bay."

She stood up from the bench and paced across the room to a hatch on the far side. She opened a cupboard and took out a small canister. "Fish food," she said, stalling.

She opened a hatch in the floor.

"Why did you come back, Megan? You were glad to get out of here when Riley and Karen got married. Riley said you told him you never wanted to see this place again.

"So now Riley's divorced, and you show up again, and hook up with Bobby again.

"Why, Megan?"

She didn't answer at first. She fiddled with the canister, scooping out a measure of food and putting it in a capsule. She filled three capsules while I waited, afraid to breathe, for her answer.

"I heard about Riley, sure. But I was afraid to come back right away. I knew if it was a rebound thing it wouldn't work. I had to wait, to let him get back to bein' himself."

She took another canister from the cupboard, filling another dispenser. She kept her face turned away, as though it were easier to confess if she wasn't looking at me.

"Then Bobby walked in here one night, and it was like the first time I saw Riley, back when we were just kids. And then I didn't much care what Riley was up to, if Bobby was willing to consider getting back together after I treated him so bad."

I got up from the bench and walked over to where she stood with her head down.

"It's okay, Megan. We've all had a crush on the wrong guy now and then. But you recognized your mistake, and you're trying to make it right."

I put my arm over her shoulders. "Thanks for telling me. Karen and Riley, well, they can't seem to stay together, but they can't stay away, either. They'll have to work it out."

I breathed a sigh of relief. "It was just that, well, you came back, and Bobby got in all this trouble, and I just wanted to be sure . . ."

My voice trailed off in embarrassment. Megan had confessed her motives, but I couldn't quite match her candor, though I wanted to. I wanted to try to be her friend.

"Do you think I had something to do with Bobby's trouble? 'Cause I wouldn't want any of Bobby's friends feelin' that way." Her accent thickened as it had the other night, emotion eroding her control.

"I . . . well, no, not really," I lied. I *had* suspected her. Trying to impress her was what had gotten Bobby in trouble. Because he didn't believe she really cared for him.

I followed her gaze to the open hatch. A tube about four feet across. I could hear water sloshing a few feet below us.

The old mermaid access hatch.

The realization came a second too late.

Megan's head came up, her face suffused with anger.

With an unexpected lunge, she grabbed me and pushed me toward the hatch.

I tried to fight back, but she had the advantage of surprise and a strength born of desperation.

I struggled to gain traction on the concrete, but the moccasins that were comfortable in the shop were too slick.

"You're not going to mess this up," she said through gritted teeth. "No more than you already done."

"What? Mess what up?" I asked. If I could keep her talking, maybe I could find a way to escape.

Her grip tightened. "You know what. You can pretend you don't, but I know better. Me and Freddy and Chuck, we're getting out of here. Coulda had a good score, if you hadn't started snooping."

She shoved again, and I felt one foot slip over the edge of the tunnel.

I lurched to one side, trying to avoid the open air below.

"I made Chuck use the gaff hook, with Bobby's fingerprints on it. That should've been enough. Until you stuck your nose in."

Shove.

"Then Freddy said you'd back off if we torched your car. But no! You come sniffin' around here, playing innocent."

Shove.

"Well, Miss Innocent, let's see how well you swim."

Shove.

My foot slipped, and I was airborne, dropping through the hatch into the cool water below.

Above me the hatch slammed shut, cutting off the light from the break room.

I was alone in the tank, and no one would notice me until they turned on the tank lights for the dinner crowd.

If I lasted that long.

Chapter 34

I COULD FLOAT.

I could swim.

I could tread water.

I could hold my breath.

What I couldn't do was fight the cold.

According to Bob, the tank was kept slightly below eighty degrees. It wasn't unpleasant, but it was cool, and it didn't take long before I felt chilled.

I'd heard Megan dog the hatch after she slammed it shut, but I climbed the rungs on the side of the tube and tried anyway. It wasn't designed to be opened from the inside; the mermaids had always had open water as an emergency escape route, and the fish didn't care.

I pounded on the heavy cover, but it didn't budge. All I succeeded in doing was battering my hands.

My moccasins had disappeared when I hit the water, and

standing on the narrow metal rungs cut into the soles of my feet. Clinging to the rough metal, pitted from years of salt-water exposure, scraped my hands.

I abandoned my perch and dropped back into the water.

Salt water stung my eyes as I laid my head back and tried to stay calm.

There were several inches of headspace between the water and the tank cover, as well as a couple feet at the top of the tunnel. I had enough air.

For now. But I had no idea how long it would last.

The first shiver passed through me, a warning. I couldn't lay back and wait for rescue that might not come for hours. I had to do *something*.

I touched my pockets, searching for a tool. I had no idea what I needed, or how I would use it, but I took inventory.

Driver's license.

Car key and shop keys.

I remembered my cell phone, sitting in the glove box of the locked truck. I told myself that, even if it survived the dunking, there wouldn't be a signal in the tank. It wouldn't have made any difference.

A few crumpled dollar bills, and a couple quarters.

A soggy business card.

Bob's business card.

Bob, who had patiently answered my questions about how the tank worked.

Cold seeped through me, and I fought against panic. I had to think clearly, to remember anything that might help me escape from the tank, or at least bring help sooner.

Growing up near the water, basic safety had been drilled into us from early childhood: stay calm, don't waste energy thrashing around; most of all, stop and think before you act.

Thinking, however, wasn't that easy.

I tried to concentrate, to remember my conversation with Bob, but my mind kept skittering off on other things.

Megan knew Freddy and Chuck. They were in this together, and she knew about my car.

Anger gripped me, and I slammed my fist against the surface of the water. Curses rained from my mouth, a shower of invective that would have made Bluebeard proud.

Bluebeard. He'd tried to warn me, told me people didn't come back for no reason. Sly had come back for his mama and daddy. Why had Megan come back?

For a good score, whatever that was.

I forced myself to abandon that line of thought and go back to my conversation with Bob. *Our* conversation. Jake had asked questions, too.

He'd asked Bob about the sensors failing.

With an effort, I teased the answer out of my weary brain.

There were a lot of sensors. One failure wasn't a problem.

But several failures would trigger the alarm. And Bob would come running.

All I had to do was disable several sensors.

One problem: I didn't know where they were.

No, two problems: it was dark.

So, if I were a sensor, where would I be?

Underwater? Well, duh. That didn't exactly narrow down the options. But they would be hidden from sight.

So eliminate anywhere in front of a window. That helped.

I paddled along one wall, feeling for the change from glass to concrete that would signal one of the pillars between the windows.

Sure enough, I could feel a cable running along the wall. Fastened to the wall every few inches with straps drilled into the concrete.

I tried to pry the cable up, using my keys. It only moved a fraction of an inch, not far enough for me to get a grip or pull it loose. I felt along the wall underwater, reaching for the sensor at the end of the cable.

I reached as far as I could, feeling only cable. I rested at the surface for a moment, my face turned up to the few inches of airspace. I drew a couple deep breaths, then one final breath, held it, and dived down along the wall.

I felt my way along, keeping one hand on the cable as I went deeper.

From the outside, I had guessed the tank at eight or ten feet deep. But as I moved down the wall I knew that was wrong. From the outside, the top several feet of the tank weren't visible, hidden behind panels to create the illusion of a solid wall of water.

I let out a tiny stream of air bubbles and dived deeper, searching for the end of the cable. I finally found it near the sandy bottom.

A sensor probe had been fitted to the end of the cable. I grabbed the probe and tried to twist it. It didn't move. I felt carefully around the edges, straining to feel how the probe attached to the cable.

My lungs clenched, and I clamped my lips together to combat the impulse to breathe. I'd only gained a few seconds, but I hoped it was enough.

I pulled at the connection with all my strength. It moved slightly, but I couldn't stay down any longer.

I shot up the tank, one hand stretched above me to keep me from hitting my head on the top of the tank. My fingers touched the cover, and I braced my arm, bringing my body to a sudden stop. My face broke the surface of the water, and I knew I had avoided a collision by only an inch or two.

I thought about what I'd felt at the end of the cable: heavy rubber insulation with a metal band crimped around the end. Pulling had yielded a tiny movement, but it had moved.

I just had to find a way to do more.

Repeating my breathing, I dived back down. This time I could move down swiftly, knowing where I was going.

I touched bottom and reached out for the cable, locating it almost immediately. I took my key ring from my pocket. With the cut side of one key, I sawed at the insulation. After a few strokes, I felt one of the cuts snag on the rubber, tearing away a chunk of insulation and exposing bare wire.

Weakened by the loss of insulation, the wires succumbed to a rapid series of bends and tugs. The probe came away in my hand, and I shot for the surface, my lungs burning with the need for oxygen.

One. I had disabled one sensor. I had no idea how many more I needed to disable, or how long I could continue exerting myself before exhaustion forced me to quit.

I just knew I had to keep going.

I rested at the surface, breathing slowly, feeling my heart return to a more normal rhythm.

Then I went looking for another sensor.

There was at least one sensor on each concrete pillar.

When I found the next one, I headed for the bottom, but there was no probe anywhere I could find. I came back to the top and started down again, feeling my way along the cable. The sensor was down about ten feet, still several feet above the bottom of the tank.

Two dives later I had disabled the second sensor.

When I returned to the surface this time, the air felt thicker, as though it didn't contain as much oxygen. I told myself it was my imagination, fear and cold playing tricks on my mind.

I moved along the wall, past another expanse of glass. I dropped beneath the surface, straining to see into the restaurant, hoping someone would appear and I could get their attention.

The salt water stung my eyes, and I couldn't see anything in the dark beyond the glass. There was no one to rescue me.

Another pillar. Another cable. I felt my way along the wall to the end of the cable and tugged at the sensor. Rose up to get a breath and dived back down.

Three down. More to go.

By the fifth sensor, I could hardly move. Fatigue made me clumsy, and I had to keep returning to the surface more often, but the air didn't revitalize me.

I need to rest. To recover, just for a few minutes.

I stroked my way across the tank, heading in the direction where I thought the hatch was. I ran into a wall. Disoriented, I took another breath of the stale air and crossed another part of the tank.

Another wall.

Exhaustion dragged me down, and I struggled to keep my head above water. If I could find the hatch, I could try to hang on to the metal rungs until my strength returned.

I hoped.

Think. Stop and think. The warning came back to me. I tried to brace myself against the wall, to hold myself up, while I figured out what to do next.

Follow the wall. If I just moved along the wall, I would have to come to the hatch at some point. It was so simple.

Why hadn't I thought of it before?

I started inching along the wall, struggling to control my arms and legs. I felt like each limb weighed a thousand pounds, and my muscles were made of spaghetti. Each movement took an incredible amount of concentration.

My eyes closed against the assault of the salt water, I inched along. At some point I started talking softly, telling myself to keep moving, to go just one more foot.

The airspace over my head opened up, the cover no longer inches from my face. I had found the hatch.

I dragged myself to the first rung above the water and draped my arm over it, hanging by the crook of my elbow. My feet bounced against a lower rung, but I didn't have the strength to stand on it.

All I could do was hold on.

And hope.

Chapter 35

LIGHT BLASTED AGAINST MY EYELIDS. I WINCED and ducked my head to get away from the assault. Water covered my face and I jerked up, prying my eyes open.

Above me, a tube stretched up several feet to a dark circle. Loops of metal jutted from the wall, my arm locked over one of them so tightly it had cut off most of the circulation to my hand. My fingers felt numb, and when I moved my arm, sharp needles of pain stabbed at the flaccid extremities.

As I watched through swollen eyes, the dark circle floated away from the top of my tube. It was replaced by a round face, pinched into a worried frown. The owner of the face seemed surprised to see me.

"What are *you* doing down there?" he said, jumping back in shock.

I didn't quite know how to answer. I searched my brain, but everything was fuzzy. I didn't know.

"Just hanging around, I guess." I shook my head, trying to clear away the cobwebs. "Where am I?" I looked around, then back up at the round face. "And who are you?"

"I'm Bob, the aquarium guy. And you're in one of my aquariums." His frown deepened. "Are you okay down there?"

"I don't know." That much I did know. "My arm is asleep, I'm really, really cold, and I don't know how I got here."

I looked up at him again. "What are you doing up there?" It seemed like a fair question.

"Aquarium alarm went off. I came to check, and when I opened the hatch, there you were. Can you climb up the ladder?"

I considered the question for what seemed like a very long time. While I thought, I saw Bob pull out a cell phone and make a call. I didn't listen to what he said. It was rude to listen to other people's conversations.

"Can you climb up?" he asked again.

I shook my head. At least I think I shook my head. I moved my head, but I wasn't sure it actually went the direction I intended.

"I don't think so. I can't feel my feet, and this one arm hurts like hell—pardon my French—from hanging over this wire thingie." I shifted slightly, and pain shot through my arm. "I don't think this arm is working right, either."

"I called for help," Bob said. He started stripping off his uniform, but it was okay because he had a bathing suit underneath. "In the meantime, I'm coming down to help you. Is that okay with you?"

"Come on in," I said. "The water's fine." Somehow the

old joke was incredibly funny, and I started to laugh. It quickly turned into a cough that shook my whole body.

My arm slipped off the metal loop, and I drifted under the surface of the water.

Not that I cared a whole lot. It was too much effort to fight, and I felt myself sliding down the wall, deeper into the soft folds of the water.

Something grabbed the back of my shirt and yanked. My peaceful slide was interrupted, and I was dragged back to the surface.

Bob shook me. "Wake up!"

I flailed weakly, but he held on.

Shouts floated in from outside.

"Up here!" Bob answered.

I winced. He didn't need to yell in my ear.

Feet pounded along a floor somewhere, and the shouting men came to the top of my tube.

I looked up. Three shocked faces topped with helmets looked back.

"I found her locked in the tank," Bob said. "She's pretty weak, couldn't climb out on her own. Started to slip under, so I came down and pulled her back up, but I can't climb the ladder and carry her at the same time."

The shocked faces talked to Bob, but I was too tired to pay attention. I closed my eyes and tried to shut them all out. I could yell at them to shut up, but that would be rude.

"Glory!"

The sound of my name brought me back to attention. I looked up, trying to find whoever was talking to me. A new face was at the top of the tube.

Jake. I felt a smile pull at the corners of my mouth. "Hi," I said. "Did you come to take me home?"

Chapter 36

HE DIDN'T TAKE ME HOME, OF COURSE. BUT HE DID ride in the ambulance with me. Riley followed in Jake's car.

The doctor insisted I stay overnight, even though I tried to tell him I needed to get home, that Bluebeard needed me.

"He'll be fine," Jake said, standing next to the bed in the emergency room while I argued with the doctor. "Give me your keys, and I'll stop by and make sure he's okay."

After the doctor left to arrange for my admission, Jake leaned over and whispered in my ear, "And I'll make sure he knows you're okay."

I'd tried to answer the firemen's questions, but my brain refused to work at first.

Once I warmed up a bit, I started to remember how I'd landed in the fish tank. By the time the doctor allowed Boomer to talk to me, I was able to explain what happened.

He excused himself and went out into the hall to make a

call. It wasn't polite to eavesdrop, but I figured I'd earned the right to know what was going on. I strained to hear, and he didn't try very hard to keep the conversation private.

"Put out an APB for Megan Moretti, and check on those two lowlifes from Callahan. I got a hunch they're gonna try to jump bail. I'd hate to see Jimmy lose a bond over those two."

He sure would. Jimmy, the bail bondsman, was his wife's brother-in-law, and the two sisters were close. If Boomer let those two slip away, there'd be trouble at home, for sure.

Boomer returned and resumed his questioning.

"She said they were going to have 'a good score,' but I have no idea what that meant. Sorry."

"That's okay. The federal guys said it was all part of a big scam, something about recovering some kind of price-less historical stuff off a wreck. Big international brou-haha, and we don't need to worry our little local heads about it."

I nodded my head and winced at the pain it caused. "Bet you loved that."

"I don't know why I'm tellin' you this," he said, "and I will deny I ever said it, but this thing was a mess from the beginning.

"The guy was too green, they let him go undercover, and they didn't tell us were running an operation in our backyard. He completely missed the connection to Moretti, and wasn't reporting in like he was supposed to. He messed up, and one of those guys killed him."

"Chuck," I said softly. "Megan said it was Chuck."

"Thanks. I'll pass that along." Boomer looked like there was a lot more to the story, but he wasn't going to share it with me. Instead, he asked a couple more questions, jotting my answers in his notebook.

"I'll probably have some more questions," he said, "but there are some people who are waiting for you to get settled in your room so's they can talk to you." He stuck his pen and notebook in his shirt pocket and tipped his Smokey Bear hat. "You take care, Miss Glory."

It took another three-quarters of an hour before an orderly came and wheeled me down the hall to a room. It looked pretty much like every other hospital room I'd ever seen, although this was the first time I'd seen it from quite this angle.

As soon as I was tucked in, Guy and Linda rushed in, Linda gathering me into a bear hug that scrunched up the carefully arranged blankets.

I returned the hug, and repeated the process with Guy. Others pressed in behind them, and Linda said they weren't going to stay, but was there anything they could do to help?

One thing came to mind. I rummaged in the plastic bag at my bedside that held my meager personal belongings, the tiny collection taken from the pockets of my soggy clothes.

I put the truck key in Guy's hand. "Would you mind," I said, "going over to Mermaid's Grotto and driving my truck home?"

Guy's answering grin was as wide as any I had ever seen. "There's an empty stall in our garage," he said. "I'll park it there for you. And you're welcome to use it anytime. A truck like that should have a real garage."

I had a hunch I'd take him up on that. The garage was only a block over. I could deal with having my beauty living a block away.

Linda delivered several messages before she left.

Sly said he'd come by and see me when I got home, and he was glad I was safe.

Julie and Anita would open the shop in the morning, so I wouldn't miss the first full day of spring break. Julie was already anxious to come back to work, especially since we had the nursery ready for Rose Ann.

Linda's eyes twinkled at the thought of a new baby next door, even though she'd made Julie promise to take Rose Ann home as soon as Anita was settled in.

Felipe and Ernie had stopped by the shop already, and Linda had let them in. They'd loaded the freezer with several days' worth of Ernie's cooking, and would be by to see me as soon as they closed Carousel Antiques.

"I'm probably forgetting someone," she said. "But you need to get better. I know you'll have a ton of company, but don't let them pester you so much you don't rest."

I promised, got another hug, and waved good-bye. As they walked out, I saw Guy fingering the truck key like it was a religious artifact. I could see that he and Sly were going to be great friends.

Jake had waited on the far side of the room while I talked to Guy and Linda. After they left, he came and stood by my bedside, looking down at me and patting my hand.

"How did you manage to show up at Mermaid's Grotto?" I asked. It was only one of a million questions that filled my brain.

"Karen. She called from Jacksonville and said she had everything she needed to get Bobby off the hook. Told us to stay away from Megan, and she'd explain everything when she got home." He glanced at the clock. "Which should be most anytime. Anyway, when you didn't come back when you said, I tried to call you. I figured you were out joyriding in the new truck, but I just wanted to be sure. When you didn't answer, I called Riley, and we both started driving around town looking for you."

"Lucky for me you did."

"Naw." He sounded kind of like Jimmy Stewart at his aw-shucks best. "You saved yourself. Bob says you broke enough of the sensors to set off the alarm, and you were hanging on to the ladder in the tank when he got there."

"I had to do something," I said. "But I don't know how much longer I'd have lasted. Thank you for coming to look for me." To my dismay, tears filled my eyes and rolled down my cheeks.

Jake leaned over and brushed them away and kissed my forehead. "Anytime."

He sat in the chair by my bed and I slept, knowing he was there watching over me.

Until Karen arrived, with Felipe and Ernie close behind. The three of them had to have a blow-by-blow report of my adventure, and Karen refused to fill us in on her trip until I had finished.

But before she could launch into her tale, one more visitor came in the door.

Riley.

I tensed, squeezing Jake's hand, waiting for the explosion that was the follow-up to last night's fireworks. But tonight's fireworks were of an entirely different kind.

Karen and Riley were in each other's arms while I was still ducking. Some kind of reconciliation had taken place while I was busy playing mermaid. They finally disengaged, but Riley kept his arm around Karen's waist.

"Bobby wanted to come over and thank you all personally," he said. "But my mom won't let him out of her sight.

"Take it from me, he's beyond grateful. We all are. What you did, the chances you took," he shook his head, struggling with his emotions. "You're the best friends a guy could have."

"I don't know how," he said, looking at me, "but I'll figure out a way to make up for your car. I am so sorry about what—well, I won't tell you what Bobby's calling her, not in mixed company—that woman did to you, all because of us . . ." His voice trailed off, and I saw his Adam's apple bob as he swallowed.

"No need," I said.

"But your car—"

"Really," I interrupted. "It's been taken care of."

I told them about Sly and about Uncle Louis's truck and the deal he'd offered me. "It really was an offer I couldn't refuse, and it drives like a dream."

Jake nodded from my bedside. "I haven't driven it, but I can tell you, it's got to be the best-looking truck in town. Maybe in the state."

We finally got Karen to tell us about her trip to Jacksonville.

She'd driven over and met several old friends for lunch. I noticed Riley seemed mollified when she said there had been a crowd. I think he'd been imagining a private rendezvous.

She'd asked if any of them had contacts in Callahan, and one of them was friends with the chief of the state police barracks responsible for the area.

Her friend—she never did say whether it was a man or

woman, and no one asked—called the state officer and got a rundown on Chuck and Freddy.

It wasn't good. Small-time crooks, they had a string of arrests for petty theft, simple assault, drunk and disorderly. It was a long list.

The officer couldn't say for sure, but there were rumors that the two had started working with Freddy's brother, and the threesome had become involved in bigger things, including smuggling.

Another friend had tapped his sources at the Jacksonville PD and found the connection to Megan Moretti. She was Freddy's sister-in-law and, according to some accounts, the brains of the entire operation.

The source referred to Freddy's brother as Mac, but Karen said she wasn't sure that was his real name, because no one would actually name a kid Mac Davis, would they?

Mac got arrested, and was serving time in the state penitentiary in Raiford. Shortly after he was sentenced, his wife and brother and their pal Chuck dropped out of sight. There were rumors. One snitch said they claimed to have a big job on the horizon, but he didn't know where they'd gone.

"Apparently," Karen said, "the deal was somewhere near Pensacola, so Megan decided to come back to Keyhole Bay. She didn't bother to tell anyone she was married. Or that her husband was doing time."

"So does anyone know what they were after?" Felipe asked. "What was worth killing someone for?"

"I heard a little bit," I offered. "It was some kind of recovery. Historic artifacts on a wreck, and the potential for an international incident, or something."

Karen shook her head. "And Bobby walked into the middle of it without even knowing."

My eyelids were drooping, and Karen and Riley looked like they needed to spend some time talking over the events of the past few days.

Felipe and Ernie exchanged a glance, and Ernie nodded. Felipe came close to the bedside, and gave me a careful hug. "You need to sleep," he said. He looked over at Jake. "Give me the keys," he said. "We'll go check on Bluebeard."

"You sure?"

Felipe nodded. "Somebody's got to stay and watch over our girl. And I think you're probably her first choice."

I think I stayed awake long enough to agree.

But I'm not sure.

Karen's Down-Home Dinner Menus and Recipes

CHICKEN AND DUMPLINGS

Chicken and dumplings comes in a variety of styles: with or without vegetables; with simple broth or rich, gravy-like liquid; with doughy drop dumplings or the fluffier rolled-biscuit type. Each one has its adherents, and different factions will claim their style is the most authentic. Presented here is Karen's choice.

Bouquet garni*
¼ cup unsalted butter
1 medium onion, chopped
3 cloves garlic, chopped
1 whole chicken (5 to 6 pounds), skin on, cut into 8 pieces, including neck
6 cups water
6 cups low-sodium chicken stock
1 teaspoon whole black peppercorns

1 stalk celery, trimmed and halved crosswise
2 to 3 cups all-purpose flour
1 tablespoon kosher salt, plus more for seasoning
1 tablespoon unsalted butter, if needed
1 tablespoon flour, if needed

Cut chicken as for frying or (like Karen) buy a cut-up chicken.

In a large stew pot, melt ¼ cup butter. Sauté onion and garlic in melted butter over medium-high heat. Put chicken pieces in pot, add broth and enough water to completely cover chicken. Add bouquet garni, peppercorns, and celery. Bring to a rolling boil, lower heat, and simmer until chicken is very tender. Remove chicken and allow to cool. Strain bouquet garni, celery, and peppercorns from broth and discard. Return stock to pot, reserving 1 cup, and keep hot.

When chicken is cool enough to handle, remove skin and bones and shred meat.

To make dumplings, mix 2 cups flour with 1 tablespoon salt. Make a well in the middle of the flour, and slowly add reserved chicken stock, a little at a time, stirring with a fork just until a soft, doughy consistency is reached. Add additional flour or stock, a tablespoon at a time, if necessary to reach desired consistency. On a floured surface, knead dough a few times and pat out to ¼-inch thickness. Cut with a knife or pizza cutter into 1-1½ inch squares. Slowly add dumplings to simmering stock, being careful not to let dumplings clump together. When dumplings float to the top, they are done.

If the broth is not thickened to your liking, mix the 1 tablespoon of butter with the 1 tablespoon of flour and add slowly to the broth to thicken.

Put shredded chicken meat in bowls, ladle broth and dumplings over it, and serve.

*To make bouquet garni, bundle the following herbs, and tie with string or place in a small net or cheesecloth bag:

> 5 to 6 fresh thyme sprigs
> Small bunch parsley stems
> 2 fresh sage sprigs

A traditional southern meal always includes several vegetables. Glazed carrots are a southern favorite, and will definitely complement chicken and dumplings.

GLAZED CARROTS

> 1 pound carrots, cut on the bias into ¼-inch slices
> 2 tablespoons butter
> 3 tablespoons brown sugar
> 1 pinch salt
> ¼ cup orange juice

Put sliced carrots in a shallow pan, add water just to cover, and simmer until tender, about 8 minutes. Drain. In the same pan, melt the butter, add the brown sugar, salt, and orange juice, and stir over medium-low heat until sugar is melted and glaze thickens.

Beans of all sorts are a mainstay of southern cooking.
Boiled, baked, or in soups and stews and gumbos, a lot of
southern meals include some sort of beans. Simple, fresh
green beans, when available, can be a great addition to
your meal.

GREEN BEANS

1 pound fresh green beans, trimmed and cut into 1½-inch pieces
1 quart water
1 ham hock, diced
¼ teaspoon salt
dash sugar

Place diced salt pork and water in saucepan, cover, and
cook over medium heat for 5 minutes. Add beans, salt, and
sugar, and simmer for approximately 30 minutes, or until
beans are tender.

A southern meal, even one that includes dumplings,
should have some kind of bread for sopping purposes.
After all, you don't want to waste any of the tasty sauce,
broth, or gravy that accompanies your main dish.

BISCUITS

2 cups all-purpose flour
1 tablespoon baking powder
1 teaspoon salt
1 tablespoon white sugar
⅓ cup shortening
1 cup milk

Preheat oven to 425 degrees. Combine dry ingredients in a bowl. Pinch in shortening with fingers until mixture resembles coarse meal. Stir in milk gradually, just until dough pulls away from sides of bowl. Turn out onto floured surface and knead 15 to 20 times. Roll out about 1-inch thick and cut with a floured cutter. Place on ungreased baking sheet and bake 13 to 15 minutes until edges brown.

The standard southern beverage, sweet tea, appears at every meal. Southerners like their sweet tea, and most traditional homes will have a pitcher or two in the refrigerator.

SWEET TEA

6 cups water
6 tea bags (traditionally, plain black tea)
1 cup sugar

Bring the water to a boil, add the sugar, and stir to dissolve. Steep the tea bags in the sweetened water to the desired strength, and serve in tall glasses of ice. Garnish with mint sprigs or lemon slices, if desired.

The deep color and distinctive flavor of red velvet cake make the perfect finish for a southern meal. Topped with cream cheese frosting and decorated with pecan halves, it looks as good as it tastes.

RED VELVET CAKE

12 tablespoons (1½ sticks) unsalted butter, softened
3 cups sifted cake flour
3 tablespoons unsweetened Dutch-process cocoa powder
1 teaspoon baking soda
½ teaspoon salt
1¾ cups sugar
⅓ cup vegetable oil
3 large eggs, at room temperature
1 tablespoon red food coloring
2 teaspoons apple cider vinegar
1 teaspoon vanilla extract
1 cup buttermilk

Preheat oven to 350 degrees. Line two greased 9-inch cake pans with greased parchment paper. In a bowl combine flour, cocoa powder, baking soda, and salt.

Using a mixer, cream together butter, sugar, and vegetable oil until fluffy, about 4 minutes. Add eggs one at a time, then beat in food coloring, vinegar, and vanilla.

Turn mixer to low speed, then add buttermilk and flour mixture alternately, starting and ending with flour, until just combined. Divide the batter between the pans and bake 35 to 40 minutes, until a toothpick inserted in the center comes out clean. Turn pans about halfway through.

Cool layers in pans on cake racks for about 10 minutes before turning out to cool completely. (Refrigerating or freezing the cooled layers will make them easier to frost.) With a long serrated knife, split the layers horizontally to make 4 thin layers.

32 ounces cream cheese, softened

2 sticks butter, softened

2 pounds confectioners' sugar

1 tablespoon lemon juice

½ teaspoon vanilla extract

⅛ teaspoon salt

Using a mixer, beat cream cheese and butter together until fluffy. Add sugar, lemon juice, vanilla, and salt, and continue beating until smooth.

To assemble the cake, place one layer on a cake plate, top with about 1-1½ cups of frosting and smooth. Continue adding layers, ending with cake. Cover entire cake with a thin layer of frosting as a crumb coat—it doesn't need to be perfect. Chill the cake for 15 or 20 minutes to set the crumb coat, then frost with remaining frosting.

Garnish finished cake with a ring of toasted pecan halves and dust sides with crushed pecans.

Ernie's Exquisite Elegance

If your only experience with pimento cheese is the mass-produced version packed in tiny glass tumblers, this savory spread will be a real eye-opener. This version calls for all extra-sharp cheddar, but experiment with different cheeses and combinations, such as Monterey Jack, pepper Jack, or white cheddar.

PIMENTO CHEESE WITH CRACKERS

2 cups shredded extra-sharp cheddar cheese

8 ounces cream cheese, softened

½ cup mayonnaise

¼ teaspoon garlic powder

¼ teaspoon smoked paprika

¼ teaspoon onion powder

1 4-ounce jar diced pimento, drained

salt and black pepper to taste

Combine all ingredients except salt and pepper in a large bowl. Mix thoroughly with a hand mixer or wooden spoon. Season with salt and pepper to taste.

Serve this creamy spread with your favorite crackers, as a vegetable dip, stuffed in celery, or made into sandwiches.

Making fried cornbread is easy and quick. Just be patient letting the dough cool, and watch carefully while it's frying.

FRIED CORNBREAD

1½ cups self-rising cornmeal
½ teaspoon salt
2 cups boiling water

Mix cornmeal and salt in a large bowl. Stir well and pour boiling water over dry ingredients. Stir to mix well. Dough will be slightly runny, but will thicken as it cools. When dough is cool enough to handle, shape into balls about the size of a golf ball. Wetting your hands will help to prevent sticking as you shape. Flatten the balls with your fingers to about ½ inch thick.

Place the shaped pieces on plastic wrap or waxed paper until all pieces are shaped.

Heat about ½ inch of oil or shortening in a large frying pan. When the oil is hot, place a few pieces of cornbread in the hot oil. Cook until the bottoms are golden and the edges begin to brown. Turn and continue frying until the second sides are also golden.

Drain on paper towels and serve with your favorite southern main dish!

Dirty rice gets its name from the chicken livers and ground meat that colors the rice. Cooked with meat, herbs, and spices, dirty rice can be as mild or spicy as you like.

DIRTY RICE

¼ pound chicken gizzards, finely chopped

½ pound chicken livers, finely chopped

1 tablespoon vegetable oil

1 onion, finely chopped

3 cloves garlic, minced

2 cups uncooked white rice

4 cups chicken broth

salt to taste

½ teaspoon ground black pepper

¼ teaspoon cayenne pepper

1 cup thinly sliced green onions, for garnish

Heat oil in large saucepan, over medium heat. Sauté gizzards and onion. When meat begins to brown, about 5 minutes, add liver and garlic. Continue cooking, stirring constantly, until brown.

Add rice, stir well, and add broth and seasonings. Cover and simmer until liquid is absorbed, about 20 minutes. Sprinkle with green onions before serving.

Okra is a staple among southern vegetables. A standard ingredient in soups, stews, and gumbos, it also makes a great fried side dish.

FRIED OKRA

1 pound fresh okra
1 cup buttermilk
1 large egg
2 cups cornmeal
1 teaspoon salt
Vegetable oil for frying
1 tablespoon salt
1 tablespoon smoked paprika

Mix cornmeal and 1 teaspoon salt in a bowl and set aside. In another bowl, mix 1 tablespoon paprika and 1 tablespoon salt and set aside.

Trim stems and tips from okra and cut into ½-inch slices. In a bowl, mix egg and buttermilk. Marinate okra slices in buttermilk mixture at room temperature for 15 minutes.

In a medium frying pan, heat ½ inch of oil to 375 degrees on frying thermometer. Remove okra from buttermilk marinade, let excess liquid drip off, then dredge in cornmeal mixture. Fry in small batches in hot oil, 3 to 4 minutes on each side, until golden brown. Drain on paper towels, sprinkle with paprika mixture, and serve.

Tomatoes show up in lots of southern dishes. They can be baked, broiled, fried, sliced, diced, made into sauce—or stewed. This basic recipe can be enhanced with herbs or spices such as garlic or pepper flakes, depending on your personal preferences.

STEWED TOMATOES

4 large tomatoes
¼ cup chopped onion
¼ cup chopped green pepper
¼ cup chopped celery
2 cups water
1 teaspoon sugar
Salt and pepper to taste

Peel tomatoes by plunging them in boiling water for about 1 minute, then cooling enough to handle. Pierce skin with a sharp knife, and remove skin.

Cut tomatoes into large pieces, put in a saucepan with water, chopped vegetables, sugar, salt, and pepper. Simmer for about 15 minutes, until tomatoes are tender.

Ham. The word evokes the smoky, salty goodness of seasoned and aged pork. Ham hocks flavor beans; fried ham slices accompany eggs; and thin, cold slices make an excellent sandwich. But nothing compares to the pleasure of a perfectly baked and glazed ham, hot from the oven.

BAKED HAM

1 tablespoon spice rub*
1 cup brown sugar
2 tablespoons butter, softened
¼ cup chopped pecans
1 5-pound high-quality fully cooked ham

Combine spice rub, brown sugar, butter, and chopped pecans, mixing until crumbly. Pat the mixture over the surface of the ham, using it all.

Place the ham in a heavy roasting pan, add 1 cup of water, and roast at 350 degrees for 1½ to 2 hours, until internal temperature reaches 140 degrees. Check occasionally and add more water if needed. Let ham rest a few minutes before slicing, and serve with pan juices. If the juices are not thick enough for your taste, pour them into a saucepan and reduce over medium-high heat until thickened.

*To make spice rub, combine equal parts of the following spices:

Anise seed
Fennel seed
Whole cloves
Whole peppercorns
Ground cinnamon
In a spice grinder, blend until ingredients become a fine powder.

Alternatively, use equal parts ground spices,
plus an additional ½ teaspoon cinnamon.

Bananas Foster is more than a dessert—it's performance art you can eat. While the traditional service (from Brennan's in New Orleans) is over ice cream, bananas Foster can also be served over waffles or crepes. And if you believe that more is always better, you can garnish the dish with sweetened whipped cream.

BANANAS FOSTER

¼ cup butter
1 cup brown sugar
½ teaspoon cinnamon
¼ cup banana liqueur
4 bananas, cut in half lengthwise, then halved
¼ cup dark rum
½ teaspoon orange zest
4 scoops vanilla ice cream

In a sauté pan or heavy frying pan, melt the butter over low heat. Add cinnamon and sugar, stirring until sugar dissolves, then stir in banana liqueur.

Place cut bananas in hot syrup and simmer, spooning sauce over bananas. When the bananas begin to brown, carefully add the rum. If the sauce is very hot, the rum will flame on its own. If not, *carefully* ignite the rum with a stick lighter. Cook until the flame subsides, 1 or 2 minutes.

Remove bananas and place four pieces over each scoop of ice cream.

Add orange zest to syrup, stir, spoon generously over each plate of bananas and ice cream, and serve immediately.

Bonus!
Quick and Easy
Hamburger Soup

This soup is not a traditional southern recipe, but it is one that makes good use of staples that are easily found in most kitchens. Easy to make, ready to eat in 30 minutes, and the recipe scales up if you find yourself feeding a crowd. With a plate of biscuits and some butter, it's a hearty meal.

1 pound ground beef
1 cup frozen diced potatoes
2-3 cups frozen vegetables of your choice
1 46-ounce can vegetable juice cocktail
1 tablespoon dried minced onion or ¼ cup frozen chopped onion
½ teaspoon granulated garlic
1 teaspoon parsley flakes
Salt and pepper to taste

In a large stockpot, brown ground beef. Drain off excess fat and add vegetable juice cocktail, plus 2-3 cups water. Bring broth to a boil, add frozen potatoes and vegetables along with herbs and spices.

Simmer over medium heat for 20-30 minutes, until vegetables are heated through.

This soup can lend itself to endless variations. Add a can of kidney beans or black beans; use different varieties of frozen vegetables; make it with leftover roast beef, chicken, or ham—you get the idea. Use your imagination—and your family's favorite foods—to create a quick, one-pot meal.